CAPTIVATED BY HER

CEDAR HILL DUET BOOK ONE

VM RHEAULT

ABOUT THE BOOK

Trapped with her during a blizzard, I didn't stand a snowball's chance in hell of not falling in love.

Rick

The last thing I need is a reporter at my doorstep, and not just any reporter: the infamous Devyn Scott.

Since the construction accident that killed two of my men and turned me into a wounded beast, I've avoided people, but when a blizzard blows in, I can't force her to leave, no matter how much I want to.

I have enough blood on my hands.

Trapped with her for days, she slowly tears down my defenses.

When she starts investigating the accident against my orders, she steps into the line of fire, and she proves what I've always known. I'll never be strong enough to keep her safe.

———

Devyn

I'll get fired if billionaire Rickard Mercer won't give me an interview, but by the time the snow clears, I don't want it.

I want more.

I want to clear Rick's name, and I start looking into the accident that will force him to live in pain for the rest of his life.

Someone caused that accident, and I'm going to find out who.

Because only then will he know he's good enough to take what I want to give him.

My heart.

CHAPTER ONE

Devyn

I know the minute he calls my name that I'm in trouble. I tense, feeling my boss's stare drilling into my back.

"Girl, what did you do *now?*" Alesha, the woman who uses the desk in front of me, asks, shaking her head.

"Breathe," I mutter. I put up with the way Walt treats me because I need this job. I don't let anyone know how much I need this job.

Pasting a smile on my face, I turn and say, "Just a second."

Walt nods once, sharply, and steps into his office.

"Good luck, hon," Alesha says. "With that glower, you're gonna need it."

"Thanks a lot." I try to keep the sarcasm out of my voice. It's not her fault Walt doesn't like me. Well, it's not that he doesn't like me. He likes me fine or he wouldn't have gone up to bat for me when I applied for this job. It's that ever since then, the owners of the *Portland Pioneer* have been breathing down his neck. *They* don't like me, and in two and a half seconds I'm going to find out just how much they don't like me.

Again.

"What's up?" I ask, tentatively stepping into his office.

"Have a seat, Devyn. We need to talk."

I push a piece of hair behind my ear, perch on the edge of the chair in front of his desk, and tuck my hands between my knees to keep them from shaking.

"What do I need to do to prove my worth this time?" I ask, not a little bitter. I draw the shittiest assignments because they want me to quit. And even crappier, I don't know who *they* are. I have no idea who owns this fucking paper and pulls on Walt's puppet strings. I never dared to find out or else I think I'd kill them.

Walt leans back in his squeaky chair and sighs. "You know it's not like that."

"Yeah, it is." Tears want to fill my eyes, but I won't let them. I'm a damned good reporter. I tangled with the wrong person and I *get* that, but I shouldn't have to suffer for it for the rest of my life. Except, that's not how it works.

"I tried, I really did, and they're setting you up to fail with this one. Devyn, ever since you walked into this newsroom, I've done my best by you. I really have."

"It's that impossible, huh?" I give up and rub a tear off my cheek. I don't know what I'm going to tell Talia, my sister. She's depended on me for the past couple of years. Hell, we moved here because of this job, and to get her as far away from Cedar Hill as possible.

He tosses a file across his desk and I open the front flap. A headshot of Rickard Mercer glares at me. God, the man's intimidating. Sexy, hot, and intimidating.

"They want you to interview him," he says, his voice flat.

My answer's immediate. "He doesn't give interviews."

"They . . . don't care. I'm supposed to send you up there with two hundred bucks for expenses and tell you to stay there for as long as it takes."

I close the file and cover Rickard Mercer's vicious frown. "I might as well just quit then. You know how impossible that will be. He hasn't spoken to the press since he was discharged from the hospital." And the words he said to the reporters waiting outside were, "Fuck you."

They'd run the sound bite over and over again. Memes flew around the internet, and Rickard Mercer, the fifth richest man in the United States, turned into a laughingstock in two seconds.

Walt blows out a breath.

"And that was two years ago," I add for nobody's benefit.

"I can't force you," he says, "but if you can't, don't, whatever, then I'm supposed to send you packing. I hate it, but I don't make the rules."

Incredulous, I laugh. I can't help it. "And they think if I'm able to land the interview of the fu—" I stop myself from swearing. Walt hates it— "the year, I'd hand it over to the *Pioneer?* I'd sell that sh—" God, I need to wash my potty mouth— "Well, you know what I'm getting at."

He scoffs. "Maybe they didn't consider it, but if you went up there on their dime and you sold that interview to the highest bidder, I think you'd have a lawsuit on your hands. You're still trying to wade out of the shit Stevie Johansson flung at you. I'd watch it. Don't get any bright ideas."

He's right. Not the part about the lawsuit, but Stevie Johansson is the reason why I'm in Portland, Minnesota, population 15,333, instead of working at the *Cedar Hill Times* on my way to a Pulitzer. I was *thisclose,* and it went up in a ball of flames.

That's why I need this job.

"What am I supposed to do about my sister? I don't like leaving her alone for so long, and Old Harbor's five hours from here."

"I'll check on her."

Hell of a lot of good that will do, but it's all I got. "When do you want me to go?"

"Now. As soon as you can. Go home, pack a suitcase, tell your sister goodbye, and get going. It's supposed to snow up there tonight and the roads can get slick by the water."

I stand and head for the door. "You're going to find me a new job while I'm gone, right?"

"You never know. You could luck out."

I don't bother to respond. My luck ran out a long time ago.

———

"He wants you to do what?"

I fling my hands up in the air and try to be flippant or I'm going to burst into tears. "That's what I said!" I drop on my bed and my small suitcase bumps against my hip.

Talia sits next to me, her expression a mixture of fear and curiosity.

I hate it when she's scared, but the reality is, I'm not getting that interview. I'll drive up to Old Harbor, a medium-sized city that sits on Harbor Lake, ask Rick Mercer to talk to me, and get told off for the trouble. I'll end up spending the night in some crap little motel and driving back the next morning with less than what I went up there with.

"What are we going to do, Devyn?"

Squeezing her hand, I say, "I'll do my best, but we're going to have to move. There's nothing for us here. The *Pioneer* barely pays me enough anyway. Maybe I can find something better in Illinois or Ohio. Someplace where they haven't heard of me. Otherwise, I'm going to have to do something else, but that doesn't matter. The most important thing is paying the bills and getting you through school. Your credits will transfer." I hope.

"I really messed up," she whispers, resting her head on my shoulder.

"No more than I have. Stay out of trouble while I'm gone. Walt said he'd stop by and check that you're doing okay. Do your homework. Keep the house clean. Go to your support meetings. One day I won't be around and you have to keep it together."

She nods. She tries harder than anyone I have ever met, and as the months have passed, things have settled into a quiet normalcy we've both enjoyed.

In somber silence, I finish packing, putting in a few changes of clothes. Sweaters, jeans, thick leggings, pajamas. I'll wear my parka, hat, mittens, and winter boots. Rickard Mercer will kick me off his property in two seconds flat, but at least I'll be warm while he does.

Talia kisses my cheek goodbye, and fiercely, I hug her. I'm thirteen years older than she is, and in more ways than one, I feel like her mother. Our mother's lying in an alley some-where, high off her ass and spreading her legs to pay for the privilege. It's not too far from where I found Talia when we both lived in Cedar Hill. Getting out of that godforsaken city was a miracle, and I'm always waiting for the other shoe to drop.

With her promises and reassurances echoing in my ears, I drive to the closest gas station and fill up my car. I have five hours on the road ahead of me, and I buy a few bags of chips and fill up the largest cup of coffee they have. I let the sugar and caffeine soothe me. It'll be pitch black in a couple of hours and I'll need to stay alert. We've already had a few inches of snow and the road, as I get closer to Old Harbor, will be full of twists and turns.

The silence on the drive is welcome, and it *is* a pretty scenic route. I don't have time to joyride, but I appreciate the pine trees covered in snow and glimpses of the smaller lakes, ice crusted on their surfaces.

Talia and I have lived in Minnesota all our lives, and the thought of leaving the state is both scary and exhilarating. We could do with something new and there's nothing to stay for. I'll never expose Stevie Johansson for the slimeball she is. There's a reason she's never been charged. She can cover her tracks too well, and I was arrogant enough to believe I'd be the one to uncover them. It cost me my job, my reputation, and it put Talia in danger.

Now I'm on this fool's mission.

Rickard Mercer.

Christ.

The second I step foot on his property he'll call the cops or kick me off his land himself. All six-foot-three, two hundred and ten pounds of him.

I stop once at a rundown gas station between Portland and Old Harbor to use the bathroom and throw away my trash. Walt wasn't wrong, and big puffs of snow drift from the sky. It's blacker than pitch by the time the sign for Old Harbor welcomes me to the city limits, population 85,168, but it's easy to see where I need to go.

The lighthouse's beam shines over Harbor Lake, keeping little fishing boats, barges, and everything in between from drifting too close to the rocky shore.

Stiff and tired, I drive around the outskirts of the city and up the narrow two-lane highway where the lighthouse looks over the water.

He's going to throw me off the cliff, and I'll deserve it for being so stupid.

CHAPTER TWO

Rick

The car's headlights cut between the trees and through the dark. There's no one up here on the cliffs except me, no reason for anyone to be up here except me, and I know when anyone tries to bother me to talk me into spilling my guts. The beams aren't the same color as the headlights of Pete's old truck. No, these are weaker, lower to the ground.

How can I tell? You can see everything from two hundred feet up in the air.

I could stay here and wait for whoever it is to leave, but curiosity gets the better of me. Besides my business partner, I haven't spoken to anyone in six days.

I need longer than I should to get to the bottom of the concrete staircase. I'm thirty-nine years old, but I feel like I'm a hundred. The colder months are the worst, my body stiffening up as the temperatures drop below what any normal human being would consider habitable. But I have a fire, I have books, and I have as much whiskey and coffee as I need. I made it through last winter, and I'll survive this one, and the one after that, and the one after that.

The snow isn't thick enough to stop anyone from getting up close and personal, and this car is parked right next to the lighthouse's only door.

The driver's a woman, and her dim headlights bounce against the lighthouse's white paint and back into the car's interior. Her hair is honey blonde and wavy, and she's resting her forehead against the steering wheel.

I pull the hood of my parka up and slightly turn my head, hiding the right side of my face behind the thick fabric. I want her to leave, not give her a heart attack. I step out from the doorway and stand in the pathetic glare, my hands shoved into my jacket pockets. She can feel me and lifts her head. Our eyes meet through the windshield that's dotted with snowflakes, and she swallows and opens the door, a loud squeal echoing over the sound of the water beating against the shore. A storm's coming. She better get her ass out of here or she'll be stuck in Old Harbor for the next little while.

"Mr. Mercer?" she asks, reaching out her mittened hand.

"Who wants to know?"

"My name is Devyn Scott. I'm a reporter for the—"

Her voice is thick and rich, like melting caramel, but raspy too, like someone threw a sprinkle of salt in it.

"I don't talk to reporters. You need to go."

The callers and trespassers have tapered off since the accident, but I still get a few. Over the summer when the second anniversary of the accident came and went, requests for interviews spiked, but I spent a lot of time on the boat without my cell and managed to avoid most of it. Not that anyone *really* cared what I had to say. They wrote their articles and repeated the ugly facts without my help.

She tries to smile, but it doesn't reach her tired eyes. It

barely touches her mouth. "I thought you'd say that, but if I could just have a few minutes—"

"I said no. Storm's coming. You need to get out of here while the weather's clear. You got about an hour, maybe two if you drive fast."

I turn to go back inside, but I pause. There's something about her . . . I brush it off. It's all an act, a way to trick me into opening my mouth. I know very well what a few minutes of my time will pay her and what it will cost me.

I look over my shoulder, expecting her to be scrambling into her car, but she's standing there, covering her mouth, her eyes wide.

Fuck.

When I twisted, I gave her a full view of the right side of my face. If that won't scoot her cute little ass out of here, nothing will.

I point toward the highway. "Go."

I don't wait to watch her drive away. Instead, I slam into the lighthouse and take off my boots and jacket. I drop another log in the fire, pour a cup of coffee, and add a generous splash of whiskey.

For a quiet and private place to recover and recuperate, I bought the Old Harbor Lighthouse and spent close to a million dollars renovating it into comfortable living space. When it was originally built, they hooked up water and electricity which was fortunate for me. I have running water, electricity, and steady internet.

There were a few stipulations before the population of Old Harbor allowed the sale to go through, all of them fine with me. I can't ever tear it down, but I would never want to do that. The light is functional, and still to this day, captains depend on it to keep from drifting too close to the shore. The Old Harbor Historical Society approved the changes I wanted, and I need their permission to do anything more. They also consider me the lightkeeper, and when I bought the lighthouse, I adopted the cost and responsibility of keeping the light in working order. That too, is something I don't mind doing, and the people of Old Harbor, the Historical Society, and I found a solid compromise.

I've been happy here.

They leave me alone, and I leave them alone.

I finish my coffee, letting the whiskey chase away some of the stiffness. My doc warned me about using alcohol to numb the pain, thinking, perhaps, I wasn't too far off from becoming an alcoholic. Better Glenlivet than hydrocodone, I said, and he didn't argue.

I'm low on firewood, and I rinse out my coffee mug and put my jacket on. The first two floors of the lighthouse are heated, but a fire's comforting, and sometimes, if the storms are bad, the electricity goes out. I have a generator, but I like a fire burning too. It took me all summer to chop wood on my good days. It kept my strength up and gave me something to do.

One of the worst things about moving to Old Harbor is the free time I suddenly had. I was married and running a billion-dollar development company, and all of it disappeared in the blink of an eye. I hadn't known what free time was or how punishing it would be to have time to think.

Pushing against the wind, I open the door. It's going to be a bad blizzard, and I'm thankful Pete insisted on delivering an extra load of groceries from the small mom and pop grocery store he owns with his wife in Old Harbor. I'll have enough to get me through.

I step into the snow and swear under my breath first before the words fly out of my mouth.

"What the fuck do you think you're doing? You need to get out of here!" Rage burns swift and hot, and I stomp through the snow to the reporter's car. She's standing there, *fucking standing there,* staring across to where the churning water would be if the darkness and blowing snow didn't hide even the lighthouse's beam, snow crusted in the fake fur of her hood and her hands tucked into her pockets like it's a sunny afternoon and she's enjoying the day. "What the fuck is wrong with you?"

She turns toward me, hearing the words the wind didn't whip away.

Snowflakes are frozen to her eyelashes, and tears cover her bright pink cheeks. Her lips are chapped.

Her headlights give her a clear view of my scar, and she staggers backward against her car that's still running.

This is just what I need.

I grab her shoulder and bark, "Drive to town and get out of the storm!"

Even as I say the words, I know how useless they are. The visibility is worsening by the second. She'll never make it to town in this. One wrong turn would send her skidding into the guardrail, and possibly over the side if she was going fast enough. At the very least, she'd slide into a ditch, but she'd still die of hypothermia before anyone would find her.

"Fuck!" There's nothing I can do except bring her inside.

"I'm sorry," she cries, wiping her nose with a mitten. "I don't have anywhere to go."

"Not now, you sure as hell don't. I should leave you out here to freeze to death."

She straightens. A hard look comes into her eyes, and she blinks away the snowflakes that are still attached to her eyelashes. "Then do it."

"I've got enough blood on my hands. I don't need to add to it. Do you have a bag?"

She nods, her teeth chattering.

"Then grab the goddamned thing and come on."

I turn my back against the wind and wait for her to kill the engine and take a small suitcase out of the backseat.

Letting her deal with her own luggage, I jerk my head toward the door, the violent wind whistling past me, stinging my ears.

I open the door for her, and she pauses, leaving my ass outside. Impatiently, I push her with a hand between her shoulder blades, and she stumbles into the dark foyer.

It's a small space, hooks on the walls for jackets and a storage bench to sit on when I need to tie my shoes and boots. I slam the door shut behind us and the howling stops. The lighthouse was built to withstand gales of up to eighty miles per hour, though weather like that rarely happens in Minnesota.

She can't see anything, and trying to get her bearings, she brushes against me.

Her breath hitches.

"Despite what you may have heard about me, I won't hurt you." My voice comes out in more of a snarl than anything, but her fear reminds me of the last time I saw my wife. The look in her eyes. I don't think I'll ever forget it.

"I'm not scared."

"Yeah, you are, but it's your own fault you're in this situation."

She sniffles. "You're not kidding."

I scoff. "Take your jacket off and hang it on a hook. Leave your boots and make sure you push them out of the way. I'm not very formal around here, but I like to keep it clean. They call me a beast, but I don't live like one, and contrary to popular belief, I don't have magical maid service."

"But you do live in a castle," she says, bumping against me again.

I open the door to the kitchen to let in some light, and I prop it open with a doorstop the shape of a fat cat. "I'm far from a prince. Leave your suitcase. When you can feel your fingers again, I'll show you the guest room."

"Do you have . . . Can I . . . Do you have a bathroom?"

I nod as she slips off her cream-colored parka revealing jeans and a lilac sweater. She tucks her hat and mittens into the hood and kicks off her wet boots. I gave her shit, but I have to give her credit—she dressed warmly. "Yes, but only one, so we'll have to share. The lighthouse is hooked up to Old Harbor's water and sewer. Sometimes the pipes freeze, but it's not that cold out so we don't have to worry about it. Come on."

She follows me through the kitchen to the bathroom near my bedroom. Almost everything I need is on the first floor. The second, and only other inhabitable floor, is where the spare bedroom, my library, and a sitting room are located. When I drew up the plans, I wanted space to move around. I didn't want to feel closed in.

"Everything you need should be in here," I say, pointing to the bathroom. "I'll be in the kitchen."

Her deep green eyes can't leave my face. She's the first stranger in a long time to be this close, and her gaze is uncomfortable. I've met enough of the people in Old Harbor that their stares don't bother me anymore. If we're going to wait out the storm together, I better get used to her gawking at me. I'm not going to hide in my own home.

I return her stare. "Done?"

"I'm sorry." She looks away and shuts the bathroom door behind her.

I put on a fresh pot of coffee, and while she's cleaning up, bring in the logs I'd gone out for in the first place. She's in there for so long I think about checking on her, but she finally steps tentatively into the kitchen.

She looks better. Her face is dry and her hair is free of snarls. She used some of the lotion I have sitting on the vanity, and the light scent drifts to me over the coffee as it drips into the carafe.

"Thank you. For not making me fend for myself out there. It's more than I deserve."

"I don't disagree. Sit. The coffee will be done in a few minutes. What did you say your name was again?"

"Devyn Scott. I work for the *Portland Pioneer*. It's a small town about five hours west of here." She sits on one of the benches that came with the kitchen table instead of chairs. I hired an interior designer to help me outfit the place, and she suggested the set. I like how it fits in with the Old World décor of the lighthouse.

I busy myself with mugs, cream, and sugar. "I know it," I say, looking at her out of the corners of my eyes. She checked me out—I can do the same. "Your name sounds familiar."

"I used to work for the *Cedar Hill Times*."

Something tugs, but then I lose it. My life hasn't exactly been a picnic the last two years, and I can't be bothered trying to remember the name of a reporter who worked for a newspaper that I didn't give a shit about. And still don't.

"Here. Warm your hands with this." I pour coffee into a mug and slide it to her.

She wraps her hands around the large mug and inhales deeply, letting it out in a sigh that does funny things to my insides.

The whole situation pisses me off.

I'm pissed that I think she's beautiful. I'm pissed she's stuck here for the next few days until the storm passes and the plows clear the roads well enough for her to at least drive into Old Harbor. I'm pissed that out of anyone who could be trapped here, it's a reporter who only wants to use me.

I'm so fucking tired of the world.

I've already had coffee, but I pour more into my mug and add my usual splash of whiskey.

Devyn watches me. "Are you in pain?"

"Always." I know what will make me furious. "Aren't you?"

Her answer.

"Always."

I lift the bottle of Glenlivet, offering to pour some into her coffee.

She raises her mug in acceptance, and I add a half an inch of whiskey.

After she sips, her sigh is even more appreciative.

Fuck this. I need to go to bed.

"So, while we're trapped here, you could let me interview you."

I sip my coffee, wishing it was plain old whiskey. I told my doc I'd be careful, and I wasn't fucking around. I've never experienced days so dark, and they weren't over.

She looks at me hopefully, expectantly, a reporter used to getting what she wants. She had to have been good to work at the *Times,* and I wouldn't need to do much digging to find out what caused her fall from grace. There's more to her than blood-thirsty motivation to reach the top. Maybe there hadn't been, but there is now. I can see it in the shadows of her eyes.

"What's in it for me besides attention I don't want?"

"Your say. Your side of the story. The truth. What happened on that construction site? Apologize to the families who lost men that day. Change the narrative. Take control of the conversation for once."

It all sounds like reporter bullshit. Change the narrative. What the fuck for? Nothing anyone has printed since the accident has been wrong.

"You're a real piece of work, you know that?"

"I want to help you."

"I didn't ask for help."

"No, you didn't. What can I give you for half an hour of your time?"

I full-on meet her gaze. Let her rake her eyes over my face. Did she understand what that sounded like? What she was offering?

What she suggested in exchange isn't new. I've heard it all. More than one woman who couldn't look at me without flinching still wanted to trade sex for words. It used to be my money. Now it's for my side of the story.

The fucking joke's on them because there is no side. What happened was my fault. I'd taken responsibility for it a long time ago.

I step over to the table and trail my finger along her jaw and down her neck to the V of her sweater. Tracing my fingertip over the smooth skin of her collarbone, I ask, "What if I want this?"

"Sex won't make you feel better."

"Says you."

She grabs my hand, but surprisingly, she doesn't fling it away or bat at me like my touch disgusts her. "Says me. Tell me what you really want, Rick."

The demand leaves my mouth before I can stop it. "You'll stay here until I feel like talking."

CHAPTER THREE

Devyn

I swallow hard.

I can see it in his eyes that he's lonely, but the request, no, the order, was the last thing I expected him to say after the hissy fit he threw when he saw I hadn't driven into town. I should have. I really should have. I should have checked into a motel the second I drove past Old Harbor's city limits and tried to talk to Rick in the morning, but I wanted to get it over with because I knew he was going to say no. I've always been a good reporter, and still am, no matter what anyone says, but I knew I couldn't convince him to talk.

There's a reason he's a recluse, and it doesn't all have to do with his injuries.

Even with Walt checking on her, I can't leave Talia alone for too long. She's on a slippery slope and unsupervised time could land her in a world of trouble.

"I can give you a few days."

Rick scoffs. "Then you better hope it's enough."

"I have a life, you know. People I care about who need me."

"Then consider yourself lucky. Are you done? I'll show you the bedroom. Yours, not mine." He moves his hand away from my throat, leaving my skin cold where his fingers lingered. "You don't have to worry about me like that. I'm not interested if it's not given freely."

Standing from the bench, I say, "That hasn't been lately."

He glares, and I want to laugh. Maybe I'm just tired or my wires are strung too tightly, but I don't think Rickard Mercer is a bad guy. He didn't leave me outside to freeze to death or force me to try to drive into town. He knew I wouldn't have made it, but it would have been his right to get rid of me.

"What do you know about it?" He steps into the entryway for a second and comes out carrying my suitcase.

I know plenty about it. When his wife left him, it was all anyone could talk about. It's obvious he's not over her, and for once I keep my mouth shut. Slow learner. That's me. "Nothing."

"I didn't think so."

Rick jerks his head, and I follow him out of the spacious kitchen. I've never been inside a lighthouse before, functional or otherwise, and I look around with interest. It feels like a normal house, and it looks like a normal house. Paintings on the walls, cozy furniture, rugs scattered over the hardwood floors. The bathroom has a gloriously large clawfoot tub, and I bet because of his injuries, he soaks a lot. I would too, if I could in a tub like that.

I follow him up a flight of concrete stairs, and at the landing, he opens a wooden door. "This is the second floor. Like I said, there's not a bathroom up here, so if you have to go in the middle of the night, be careful. Ambulances have a tough time getting up the road in the snow, and in a blizzard like this, there's a good chance you'd die while you wait."

"Okay."

The walls are lined with books. More books than I have ever seen in my life, and Cedar Hill's public library is enormous. I hadn't thought of what I'd do to pass the time while I waited for Rick to talk to me, and now I don't have to. I can read my days away. I brought my laptop, but social media never interested me and I'll be happier reading through everything Rick has on his shelves. "Who's your favorite author?" I ask curiously.

"I have too many to name just one." He opens another door revealing another set of stairs. "These go up to the top. Please keep this door closed. I'm not paying to heat the whole neighborhood."

I peer over his arm, cold, dank air meeting my nose, but it's too dark to see anything. "Can I go up? How many steps are there?"

"Two hundred and sixty-five. You can go up, but I would prefer it if I went with you the first time." He meets my eyes as he shuts the door. "Please."

"All right."

He drops my suitcase in front of a door but keeps walking and flips on a light switch. Pale light glows from fixtures mounted along the ceiling. Two large couches sit against opposite walls, and a coffee table that has magazines on it is positioned in front of one. Gorgeous wooden shelves hold more books, some knickknacks, and framed photos of people I can't see from this far away. No plants.

"This is a sitting room of sorts. When I remodeled, I wanted a different place to read besides my bedroom. I don't have a TV. The internet is usually strong enough if you want to stream something. I assume since you're a reporter that you have a laptop with you."

"Yeah, I do."

"That will have to be enough if the internet holds out during the storm. I lost my taste for TV when the news stations couldn't stop talking about me."

"I know how that is." I lost my taste for TV too, when the news stations couldn't stop talking about me pointing my finger at Stevie Johansson. I'd become a laughingstock just as quickly as Rick when he told the press to fuck off. I wish I'd had the balls to do the same. If I had, I wouldn't be working at the *Pioneer,* I can tell you that.

He steps around my suitcase, pushes the door open, and shows me a plain bedroom. "I didn't want to add a second bedroom but the interior designer said I'd regret it if I didn't. Don't know what for, maybe she thought I'd have a wife and kids or something someday, but so far, you're my first guest and probably my last. The lamp by the bed works. The power comes from a co-op and I have a generator if it goes out."

I look around the room I'll be sleeping in for the next two or three nights. A queen-sized bed and nightstand sit against one wall, and a dresser with a small matching bookshelf are the only other furniture, though the room couldn't fit anything else. It wasn't decorated with gender in mind, the down comforter a plain white. I better not drink coffee in bed. I'd never be able to keep something like that clean for long.

"There's a lock on the door," he continues. "You won't hurt my feelings if you use it."

I lean against the doorjamb and look at him through the soft shimmer of the lights he didn't turn out in the sitting room. A nasty scar, puckered and red, starts at his temple, slashes his eyebrow in two, slithers over his eye and down his cheek, through the corner of his mouth, and stops at his chin. The surgeon stitched his lips together, but the skin there doesn't look quite right. I read the accident crushed the right side of his body. He'd broken his arm, fractured several ribs, needed a right hip replacement, and broken his leg in two different places. He was in the hospital for almost six months.

He stands and lets me stare. He must be used to it by now, because despite the scar, he's still a very handsome man, and once he's finished nursing his wounds, he won't be single for long. One of the questions I thought of while driving to Old Harbor was why his wife left him. It couldn't have been because of his injuries. Now, after having met him, I don't want to ask him that. It's too personal, and why she served him divorce papers isn't any of my business. The whole interview is starting to give me a bad feeling.

Rick reminds me of Talia. Fragile. Handle with care.

"Thank you. For letting me stay here," I say, squeezing his arm.

He jerks away. "You can help yourself to what I have in the kitchen. I get regular grocery deliveries, but Pete won't be able to drive up until it's done snowing and the roads are clear. What we have is what we have until then. Just so you know."

"As long as you have coffee, I'll be okay."

"I'd never run out of coffee. Goodnight, Devyn."

"Goodnight, Rick." I step into the room and flip the switch that turns the small lamp on. "It is Rick, isn't it?"

"That or asshole. It depends on who you're talking to."

With that, he shuffles down the hall, and the door to the stairs opens and closes.

I move my suitcase into the bedroom and trot back downstairs. Rick isn't anywhere, and I walk through the empty living room and kitchen and grab my phone that's in my jacket pocket. The coffeepot's still on, and our mugs and the bottle of Glenlivet are where we left them. I'm not comfortable enough to make myself at home like Rick said I could, but I find a small amount of comfort in the scent and warm kitchen. I sit on a bench at the table and call my sister.

The line rings for longer than I expected, and worried, I bite my lip.

She finally answers, a faint, "Hello?"

Relieved, I say, "Hey. How are you doing?"

She sighs, and her exhaustion seeps through the phone line. It's almost midnight and I woke her up. "Fine. Tired. Classes tomorrow as usual, group therapy after that, then the store called and said I could work a couple of hours if I wanted to. I'm not sure."

We can always use the money if Talia works extra hours, but her therapy sessions are hard on her and it's not uncommon for her to sleep all afternoon after one of them. "Do what you're comfortable with."

"Thanks. Where are you? Have you met him? Rick Mercer? Is he as scary as he looks?"

"I met him. It's blizzarding here, and if it moves that way, be careful. I drove straight to his lighthouse and now I'm stuck because the roads are bad. I'm lucky he's letting me stay with him."

"Do you think he'll talk to you?" She yawns, and I yawn too.

"I really don't know. He already said no, but maybe I can wear him down. I better let you get some sleep. Don't skip class."

"I won't. I promise."

"Goodnight. I miss you."

"I miss you too."

Reluctantly, I hang up.

"Boyfriend?"

Rick's leaning against the archway that opens into the living room with his arms crossed and a scowl on his face.

I could say yes, I could say no. It doesn't make any difference if he thinks I'm seeing someone or not. I won't be here long enough for it to matter.

He blows out a breath when I don't confirm or deny. "Right. I went up to your room to tell you if you want to shower in the morning, there are towels in the linen closet in the bathroom."

"Thanks."

He turns, walks through the living room, steps into another room, and shuts the door.

I help myself to another cup of coffee after all, adding another splash of whiskey. If we're rationing, I might as well not waste what we have.

I go back upstairs, and sipping my coffee, check out his books. I find a thriller I haven't read, and halfway through the first chapter, I fall asleep on the couch.

When I wake up, I'm covered with a thick blanket, and a bookmark saves my place.

CHAPTER FOUR

Rick

I toss and turn all night. I'm not used to having someone in my space, and I can't get the way she fell asleep reading out of my head. I'd only gone up—again—to ask if there was anything else she needed. I haven't had a guest in many years, and I've forgotten how to act.

Which is why, when I'm making French toast for breakfast the next morning and she walks into the kitchen, I'm gruffer with her than I should be. I don't function well on so little sleep, and it'll be a relief when the snow stops and the roads are cleared.

"Good morning," she says, leaning against the counter. "Thank you for the blanket."

"It's not a big deal." I look at her out of the corners of my eyes. I heard the shower turn on and shut off fifteen minutes later. Now she's barefoot and wearing black leggings and a light grey sweater, and her damp hair is twisted into a bun at the back of her head. She smells like roses, and she put on mascara and lip gloss. I don't know who she dressed up for, but if she did it for me, she could have saved herself the time. "Here. Eat." I shove a plate at her and nod toward the table where I already put out syrup and butter.

"Thanks." She sits and adds butter to the French toast, but no syrup. "What do you do all day?"

I flip my slices over and turn down the heat. "What do you mean?"

"Like today? If I wasn't here. What would fill up your day?"

"Nothing."

She pauses with her fork halfway to her mouth. "You can't mean that."

"Why? I'm not allowed to do nothing?"

"I suppose, but you don't seem like the type."

"Goes to show how much you know," I mutter. I put my slices on a plate, turn the burner off, and sit across from her. I try not to eat standing up or slap a sandwich together whenever I'm hungry. When I first moved to Old Harbor, I said I'd cook real meals for myself, not survive on junk food while living the life of a pathetic moron who couldn't keep his wife. Even if that means every time I make pasta I have to eat leftovers for days afterward because I dumped too many noodles in the pot.

"So, after breakfast you'd wash dishes, and . . . go back to bed?"

It sounds like a good idea to me, but I say, "Blizzards are different. I can't do anything today."

She looks down at her plate then back up at me, her lips pressed against a laugh. "You put me through all that on purpose."

"I'm contrary that way," I say, drizzling syrup over my French toast.

"Hmmm."

I wait for her to say more, but she only finishes her breakfast, washes her plate, and puts it in the strainer. She dries her hands and pours herself a cup of coffee in the mug she used last night. I wasn't around when she washed it. At least she'll clean up after herself.

She sips her coffee, and I eat my French toast and wash my plate. On a day like this, there wouldn't be much I could do with or without company. If Devyn wasn't here, I'd probably work. Just because I don't go to my office in Cedar Hill anymore doesn't mean I don't have a job. But the paperwork isn't going anywhere, and I ask, "Do you want to go up?"

"Up?"

"Up to the top? I'll show you around, and then you can go whenever you want. I can't very often. My leg and hip will always give me trouble."

She brightens. "Sure. Am I okay like this?"

"Socks would be good. The steps are cold."

We stop by her room, and I poke my head in as she digs for a pair of socks in the suitcase that's lying open on the floor in the corner. The bed hasn't been slept in. She didn't move after she fell asleep on the couch.

She tugs on a pair of white socks, and I open the door I told her to keep closed. There was no point in heating the entire lighthouse, and the air's chilly. There's enough light shining through the small windows to see by, the white snow blinding.

"You go first. If you trip, I'll try to catch you."

The staircase is safe—one side blocked in by the lighthouse's wall, the other guarded by a thick black railing. I tested the integrity of the entire staircase myself and reinforced the areas where it needed it. I didn't want to risk falling, either. I don't know how much more my body can stand before it shuts down for good.

She cranes her neck, looking to the very top, the meagre

light highlighting the delicate curve of her jaw. My mouth dries. She's beautiful in a classically elegant way. Clear skin, delicate eyebrows, bright green eyes, small nose, and lush lips. She's standing on the step above mine and we're eye-level, close enough I could kiss her without moving.

"I'll try not to, but heights have never been my favorite."

"You'll be okay once you get to the top. Don't look down." Halfway there, I have to ask her to stop. "Hold on. I need a break." I sag tiredly against the wall, my heart thumping against my ribs and sweat covering my skin, though it can't be warmer than forty degrees in here.

"Do you need to go back?" she asks, sitting on a step.

"No. It's good exercise, and I don't let myself avoid it. My doc says my body's still healing, but I think he doesn't want to admit that I'm not going to bounce back."

"You're lucky to be alive, from what I've read," she says.

"That's debatable."

Narrowing her eyes, she asks, "Do you go to physical therapy?"

"I work out at a gym in town. A physical therapist stops by once in a while and helps with strength training. I see a massage therapist. My stamina's shit. I'm not as young as I used to be. Come on."

She stands and grips the railing.

I'm out of breath again by the time we reach the top, but the view distracts her from my huffing and puffing.

The snow flies past us, and she presses her hands against the glass. If it was clear, she'd be looking toward town, not the lake. We have a three hundred and sixty degree view, the Fresnel lens centered in the middle. Encased in glass, we're safe from the blizzard, but it's cold up here, and I should have told her to wear her jacket.

"It's like we're in the middle of a snow globe," she says in awe, her voice soft.

"One shaken up by a vicious child," I say, slowly sitting on a folding metal chair I carried up just for this reason. I don't have another because I'm always alone, and I'm too tired to be chivalrous and ask if she wants to sit. She's younger and healthier than I am—if she needs to rest, she can sit on the floor. She'll be able to stand back up.

"Do you spend a lot of time up here?" she asks, looking over her shoulder at me.

"I used to, before the novelty wore off. It's…melancholy. More than you'd expect it to be. Especially if it's raining. I try not to put myself in situations that bring me down." For the most part, I succeed. I'm not the recluse the papers say I am. I have a handful of friends in town. Not many. Pete and his wife ask me to dinner sometimes, and I reciprocate because Pete's wife likes to come up and look over the lake. After nasty PT sessions, sometimes my physical therapist and I will go out for a beer, and a cute little thing at the gas station where I fill up asked me out once. I told her I wasn't looking for anything like that, but we went to dinner and had a nice time. I have a life, it just isn't the one I was living before the accident.

I'll never live that life again.

"Are you suicidal?"

Her question hits a little too close to home. "Is that one of your interview questions?"

She lifts a corner of her mouth. "No. Everything's off the record."

Her answer reminds me of who she is. She doesn't care about me, or the accident, or what the accident turned me into. She's the same as all the rest, only out for what she can get for herself. "Why are you here, Devyn?"

Frowning, she says, "You know why. To interview you."

"Yes, but, *why are you here?*"

I don't have to explain. She's intelligent. Has a degree in journalism. Maybe she double majored in English or Communications. Well-educated. I don't need to explain the nuance of the question.

She turns her back to the storm and rests her elbows on the rail running along the glass that years ago tried to keep tourists from plastering themselves against it like she did when we first came up.

"I got fired from the *Times,* and with my reputation, no one would hire me. I needed a job to take care of my sister—she's younger than I am and our mother can't help herself much less us. The editor-in-chief of the *Portland Pioneer* saw through the bullshit and gave me a chance. The owners, they don't like it so much, and every once in a while they tell him to assign me an impossible job so they can fire me when I don't come through. What they don't understand is, I've reported on some nasty shit, and so far, I've been able to do everything they've asked. Of course, that always made newspaper sales go crazy, and a couple of my articles were syndicated by the Associated Press. That only made them want to torture me more, and they told me to interview you. If I don't, they'll fire me." She sighs and presses her cheek against the glass.

I heft myself out of the chair and lean against the railing, my back screaming. I didn't rest long enough.

"I knew you wouldn't go for it, and that's why I was blubbering like an idiot last night. I wasn't trying to trap myself here. I had no idea a storm this bad was coming." She meets my eyes. "I really didn't. My sister and I have been okay in Portland, but, whatever, you know? They don't like me, and I shouldn't stay where I'm not wanted. We can figure something else out. Maybe a change of scenery would do us some good."

"Why were you fired?" She doesn't seem like the type to do anything dirty. Not like the players in my game.

"Sticking my nose where it didn't belong. She didn't like it and made sure I stopped doing it. It's all over online. I don't need to tell you the story. You can look for yourself."

"That's what reporters do though, right? Stick their noses in other people's business? I've had my share in my face." I try not to sound bitter about it, but it doesn't work.

"Yeah, well, harassing you isn't the same as what I was doing. I was trying to make a difference, make *change*. Cedar Hill is fucked—" she winces— "sorry, I can have a potty mouth —and no one wants to do anything about it. Or people are too scared to do anything about it, which amounts to the same thing. I don't care anymore. It's not my fight and I have more important things to worry about now."

"Like what?"

She scowls, but instead of looking angry, she looks like a spitting kitten—adorable. "I just told you. Take care of my sister and look for a different job. I can't force you to talk to me. I knew that driving up here, and I can't wait for you to decide you want to. As soon as the snow clears, I'll get out of your face."

"Will your boyfriend go with you?"

She turns away and swipes at her cheeks. "Yeah. We're just one big happy family. I'm going downstairs. Do you need help?"

It surprises me she cares enough to ask. "No."

Nodding, she pushes past me and trots down the staircase. I want to tell her to be careful, but she's an adult and can handle a set of lighthouse steps.

I'm not going to be sorry that I'm costing her a job. Her employment shouldn't depend on if she can get an interview out of someone. Whoever told her to talk to me has it out for her, and it's probably for the best she cuts her losses with that kind of attitude aimed at her. If it's not me, it will be something else, and it sounds like she's put up with that long enough.

I sit down again and my back thanks me for smartening up. I try to relax, breathe deeply, and release the tension in my body. The snow will keep me from going to my massage appointment, and I need to be careful I don't overdo it. An ambulance won't come for Devyn if she falls down the stairs, and it won't come for me, either, if I push myself.

The weather app on my phone says the snow will last two more days. Two days and maybe one more to let the snowplows catch up before she can go. That should be manageable if we stop having personal conversations. It sounds like she has it tough, but I don't have the emotional room to get involved in her life.

I stare at the snow whipping past the glass, the brightness of it still hurting my eyes.

A long and lonely hour later, my body is loose enough for me to go downstairs. I went through every relaxation technique I know, but I'm still going to hurt later. It must have been all the tossing and turning I did last night. I haven't had such a poor day in a long time. As with anything, going down is a lot easier than going up, but I sigh in relief when my feet are on solid ground.

I check in on Devyn, but she's not in her room. She's sitting on the couch, the blanket I gave her last night wrapped around her shoulders, staring into space, the thriller she was reading lying in her lap.

Letting her be, I go to my own room. I need to finish a library book that will be overdue with the storm, but I can't get comfortable, a knot in my back tightening until I'm moaning in pain.

Devyn finds me writhing and covered in sweat, and all I can croak out is, "Help me."

CHAPTER FIVE

Devyn

Things aren't that bad, and I try not to give in to a pity party. So what if everything I've worked so hard for is gone because Stevie Johansson discredited me, sicced her goons on me, and scared the fucking crap out of me. No one knows the truth about what happened, and I can't tell anyone. Talia would freak out, the cops wouldn't believe me, and Stevie "Sweetheart" Johansson might follow through with her threat. She took my career away from me. She said she'd take my life, too, and I believe her.

She's in control of the upper Midwest, and I was a fool to stay in Minnesota with Talia. We should have moved as far away as we could. California. Florida. Alaska. She wanted to stay in case she heard news about Mom, but the only news she's going to get is that her body was found in a ditch. I've tried my best to help her. Spent thousands of dollars to give her a place to stay and food she was too high to care about. I love her, God help me, I still love her, but there's hope for Talia. There isn't any left for our mom.

I don't need a password to connect to Rick's internet, and sitting cross-legged on the bed, I scroll through the job sites. I can't go back to reporting, even if we manage to move out of Stevie's reach. I'll have to change direction entirely. I can't even teach journalism. Though I have plenty of experience, after what happened, my reputation's shot. I could go back to school and get a teaching degree and teach high school English. It'd be a big enough career turn that Stevie would leave me alone.

The thought's depressing. Trapped inside a cube with thirty kids who didn't care where commas go. Oh, never mind. I know exactly where they'd want them to go, and it would be a very unpleasant experience for me. I'd rather ask Rick for another interview. I'd like the results the same.

My stomach growls, and I check the time on my laptop's screen. I said coffee would be enough, and my ass agrees with my brain, but unfortunately, my stomach does not. It's past lunchtime but too early for dinner. I could make do with a piece of cheese, a big one, or a peanut butter and jelly sandwich. I'm not picky, and when you're broke, you're not allowed to be.

I mark a couple of jobs as possibilities and set my laptop aside to go look for a snack. Rick doesn't seem like the kind of person who would sit back and enjoy a bag of Doritos, but if I found some snooping around, I wouldn't turn my nose up.

He isn't in the living room, and for the short amount of time I've been here, I've never seen him use the subtly elegant space. It's not a mancave with a huge TV, and along with the Doritos, I doubt he's the type to sit around in his underwear scratching his balls while he watches football.

We might have lived in the same city, but our lives couldn't have been more different. He was married and that knocked him off the Most Eligible Bachelor lists. I didn't care if he was married or single, but I've always respected him for the businessman he portrayed himself to be. He was never one to do dirty deals to get ahead, and he always appeared to have genuine affection for his wife, which made the divorce all the more puzzling to me and everyone who knew them.

I peek into the kitchen through the wide archway, but it's empty too. I'm thinking he has a private room he hasn't shown me or he braved the weather to get some air when a groan grinds its way from his bedroom. That room wasn't a part of the tour, and I instinctively felt it was off limits.

The door's cracked, and I push it open farther, hoping I'm not interrupting a rousing game of jerk off, but he's lying on top of his bed in a heap of pain. He's covered in sweat, and he can barely speak. "Help me."

"What is it? What's wrong?" I rush to the bed, but I don't dare touch him. I don't know anything about this man. His tortured gaze reminds me of my own expression after having nightmares about the night Stevie Johansson taught me to never meddle in her business again.

Rick could be going through withdrawal, or he could be having a seizure. The accident had given him a severe concussion, and he could still be suffering the side effects.

"My back," he gasps. "There's a knot—" A choke cuts him off.

"A knot," I echo stupidly. "You need a massage."

He can barely nod and closes his eyes against the pain.

I can do a massage, and I climb on the bed. "You have to turn over."

He's on his side now, and uttering a moan that twists my gut, he flattens onto his stomach. I sit on his butt, my thighs flanking his lower back, and yank his shirt's hem out of the waistband of his jeans. His muscles ripple like snakes under his sweaty skin.

I press the heel of my hand right where the knot is, and his shuddering stops immediately with the pressure.

"Fuck," he moans into his pillow.

"I know. I'm sorry. It will hurt more before it doesn't."

"Hmmm."

I rub my hands over his back, jagged pink scars criss-crossing his hot skin. "Why were you on the site that day?" I ask, partly to keep his mind off me working the balls of tension out of his muscles, and partly because I want to know. Several people have asked, and he never answered.

"I was always on site. I worked on every site. I was in charge," he snarls between clenched teeth. Not angry I asked, only still in pain.

I work as carefully as I can, but as forcefully as I need, and bit by bit his muscles loosen under my touch. "You have people for that."

"You sound like my ex-wife."

I stop my hands for a second. I know part of the reason why she left him now. She blames him for getting hurt. Blames him for being on the site that day, but he wouldn't do anything less because to Rickard Mercer, a good boss doesn't mean ordering people around. It means showing your workers you're willing to get your hands dirty doing the job they're doing.

From his neck to his lower back and up again, I tease the tension and pain out of his muscles. I work until my hands start to cramp and then longer still. Exhausted, Rick falls asleep, and it's only then that I pull his shirt over his scars and carefully climb off his bed.

In the kitchen, I pour a glass of Glenlivet, down it, and pour another glass for him. I find some ibuprofen in the cabinet above the coffeemaker and set both the glass and the little brown pills on the nightstand.

Sweat covers his forehead and his breathing is shallow. His bed is a king, and there's room for both of us. I lie next to him in case his back seizes up again and he needs me.

I'm still here, two hours later, when he opens his eyes.

———

"Fuck." He groans and barely moves. He's waiting to see if it will hurt, but I did a good job and his muscles felt like putty by the time I was done.

"Does that happen often?" I'm propped up on two pillows. I didn't want to fall asleep, and I dozed in that sickly space between sleeping and wakefulness that left me feeling muzzy and nauseated. I never found something to eat.

"No. I didn't sleep well last night. After the accident, if I don't get ten hours, it messes me up. That can happen."

"You didn't sleep because of me. I'm sorry."

"Not just you." His eyelids are heavy, and his whiskers have turned into a short beard. A lock of black hair falls over his eye and I want to push it back, but I don't dare. He's tolerating me in his house. Maybe he'd tolerate me in his bed too, if I wanted sex and he felt like giving it to me, but he wouldn't tolerate affection. Compassion. Sympathy.

I wiggle until I'm sharing his pillow, his scar hidden by his half. "But some of it."

"I'm not as social as I used to be." He lets out a sigh and his eyes drift closed.

"Before you go back to sleep, I brought you a drink and some ibuprofen. You should take them. It'll help with inflammation."

He lifts onto an arm just enough to swallow the pills with

the gulp of whiskey in his glass. Settling into the mattress, he asks, "Where did you learn massage?"

"In Cedar Hill. I took a few beginner's classes. My sister needs them sometimes. They help her relax, and I learned for her."

"Thank you." His voice is a mumble, and I'm going to lose him in a second.

"Do you want me to stay?"

He opens his left eye into a narrow slit. "Do you want to stay?"

I know before I say it how big of a mistake it will be, but I can't help myself. "Yes."

"Then stay."

———

It's dark when I wake up. The little rectangular window cut into the wall of the lighthouse doesn't offer any light. In Minnesota, that could mean it's five in the evening or midnight or later. I won't know until I get up to check the time.

Rick's body spoons mine, solid and warm, our figures touching from shoulder to toe. I didn't let myself miss companionship after Talia called and asked for my help. Before she came back into my life, I dated a little, someone at the *Times* who had the same career goals I did. That relationship faded away as she took up more of my time. Rick's arm is strong and rests against my stomach, his even breathing feathering over my neck, his lips centimeters away from my skin.

I wiggle closer.

It wouldn't be like me to roll over, press my lips to his, and ask for something to help get me through the next little while. I could unzip his jeans and push my leggings down to my ankles. We wouldn't have to undress. He could slide inside me, and with a light touch between our bodies, I wouldn't need much to come. It wouldn't be like me, but I wish it was.

Rick's out cold, and reluctantly, I roll off the bed, not worried about waking him.

My stomach's growling, and I pad into the kitchen to snoop around for something to eat. I open the large stainless steel fridge and scan the contents. There's ham and Swiss cheese, and I make a thick sandwich to tide me over until breakfast. Chewing the first couple of bites, I open cabinets and close them. Dishes, glasses, coffee mugs. Functional. Practical. Nothing whimsical. There's a floor-to-ceiling pantry next to the entryway, and laughing to myself, I find a bright blue bag of Doritos Cool Ranch.

He works with his employees and munches on chips. He suffers from pain that will never go away, but his arms are still strong enough to keep me close while we slept. He's angry, but underneath the rage is a wounded lion, roaring in agony and in warning. Can I be the brave little mouse that pulls the thorn from his paw?

What would that do for me? What would I hope to accomplish? Wanting to crawl into his bed and ask him to touch me isn't the same as having feelings for him, is it? No, that's not, but me wanting to touch him again, wanting to give him pleasure to experience instead of pain, that is. Those are feelings. And they couldn't have come at a worse time.

I check my phone after I eat. While I was massaging Rick's back, Walt texted me and said that Talia's all right. He asked if my drive to Old Harbor had gone okay and if I had any updates. I ignore his text but message Talia and wish her a goodnight. She answers right away and asks me to call her tomorrow, but knowing I'd think something bad happened, she says she's not in trouble. Between Walt's message and her promises, I'm not entirely convinced, but I keep my doubts to myself and tell her I'll call her in the morning.

I brush my teeth in the dark, not wanting to disturb Rick. If he needs that much sleep, I don't want to be the reason he's hurting. I was able to help this time, but I might not always, and in this weather, medical help could be hours away.

I'm not tired, but I change into pajamas and sit on the couch where I fell asleep last night.

I don't know how long I've been sitting when the door creaks open and Rick walks toward me dressed in the cotton shirt I imagined unbuttoning and the jeans I imagined unzipping.

"You're still awake? It's after two in the morning."

"I couldn't sleep," I say, watching him warily.

"Can I sit for a minute?"

"Yeah, sure."

He sits, and wrapping his arm around my stomach, pulls me to him, my back to his chest. He rests his chin on my shoulder. "Thank you for what you did."

I lean against him and let myself be weak for just a moment. I picture us in a relationship, him wanting to help me simply because he loves me. It's all I need. Just a delusional moment to pretend this broken man could hold my burden.

"You're welcome."

I stumble downstairs the next morning, the scent of coffee leading the way. Rick hadn't stayed long after that, brushing a kiss to my jaw before going back to bed. He'd wanted to stay. Or maybe that was my wish. I think he would have, if I would have asked, but after the snow stops I'll never see him again and I don't want a taste of what I can't keep.

There's a note leaning against the coffeemaker telling me there's cereal and milk if I like the cold stuff, and instant oatmeal if I want something hot. There's no evidence he made breakfast for himself.

The lighthouse feels empty. His bedroom door's open but he's not there, and his bed is made. He must have an office that he hasn't shown me, and keeping a secret place to hide is his right. He could be at the top, trying to see if the storm will stop soon, but I don't think he'd chance the stairs after what happened yesterday. No, he's around here somewhere—maybe working since he didn't say he quit his job or sold his company —but I have no choice except to let him be.

I pour a cup of coffee and use less milk than I normally do. If that's all Rick has, it's not very much. I skip the cold cereal and the oatmeal and eat a piece of toast over the sink. Trying to keep myself to a schedule, I shower and put on a pair of pajama bottoms, a tank top, and a cardigan. Cozy and comfortable. After I call Talia, I'll read and look for jobs for the rest of the day. I don't have an article to write, and I wouldn't anyway. I'm going to get fired when I drive back to Portland, and the *Pioneer* doesn't deserve any freebies.

I'm a little nervous about going up to the top alone, but I liked watching the snow whip past the glass. Without Rick's steady presence on the steps behind me, I go slowly. The railing feels secure, but unconsciously, I stay close to the concrete wall. The steps are wide but steep, and my heart's pounding by the time I reach the glass enclosure. The view is identical to yesterday's—snow, snow, and more snow. Visibility is near zero, and the weather app on my phone says more than a foot has already fallen since the night it trapped me here.

When this much snow drops on Portland or Cedar Hill, time stands still. Even after the snow stops, Old Harbor will need days to dig itself out. I'm fortunate Rick puts up with my company. It would be a very long week if he didn't.

I ignore the uncomfortable metal chair, sit on the cold floor, and bundle my cardigan around me. Maybe later I'll bring a book up here. The light brightens my spirits. I pull my cell phone out of the pocket sewn into the side of my leggings and bring up Talia's number. She quickly answers, and relieved, I say, "Hey. How are you? Is the weather still good?"

There's a burst of laughter in the background.

"Yeah. It's fine, blue skies. Walt stopped by and asked if I heard from you. He gave me a ride to campus, but it's nice enough I can walk home later. I just got out of class."

"Sorry." I wince. "I didn't look at the time."

"It's not a big deal. I have a few minutes until my next one. He's worried about you and said he's been trying to get his bosses to change their minds."

"They won't, and I'm not getting the interview, either. Rick won't talk to me, and the poor guy . . . he's had such a shitty time. I'd feel terrible if I badgered him. All I'm doing now is trying not to go crazy until I can get out of here."

The voices in the background fade, and sounding clearer, she asks, "What's he like? All his money . . . can you imagine it? Marry him and let it solve all our problems." She laughs.

"His ex-wife blames him for getting hurt. I don't think he's going to be jumping into a relationship any time soon." I don't like how disappointment pokes at my heart. It's not Rick Mercer I'm after. It's any good, stable man who could maybe help me for one fucking second instead of having to do everything alone.

"Did he say that? The blame part, I mean. They always looked so in love on the gossip sites."

"Not in so many words, but yeah. He's still in a lot of pain, and yesterday afternoon I had to massage a knot out of his back.

I asked him why he was on the site in the first place, and he said it was his job to work with his employees. I would imagine he'd feel even guiltier about it if he hadn't been hurt the day those two men were killed."

"You like him then." Talia has always been perceptive. I think after she graduates she'll be a wonderful therapist. She has so much compassion, and after years of rehab, empathy too.

"Yeah, I do. Underneath the anger, he's a nice guy. If he wasn't, I'd be eating snowballs and sleeping in my car."

"Did you explain why you wanted the interview? Walt really doesn't want you to go."

"I don't want to leave, but I've always reported with my heart, and I've never, ever, pushed aside my principles and integrity. I'm not going to pester him. He's had enough of it, and I've already told him anything he tells me is off the record. I think, more than anything, he could use a friend. So many people blame him for that accident, and it's not fair."

She sucks in a breath. "You more than like him."

I scoff. "What good would that do me?"

"Devyn."

"What?"

"Admit it." Her voice is soft and serious. I know she worries about what she'll do if I ever meet someone. Someone who wouldn't want her as a third wheel in our relationship. I would never let that happen. Talia will be in recovery for the rest of her life, walking that tightrope between sobriety and the need to get high, and I would never let her try to live on her own. The only way I'd ever loosen my grip is if she met someone and he promised to move heaven and earth to keep her safe. Until then, she's stuck with me.

We need each other.

"Fine," I say grudgingly, "there's something about him, but

that doesn't mean it's going to go anywhere. I'm sure women everywhere have that reaction to him."

"Not since the accident. Devyn . . ."

"You don't have to worry. Besides, with the way his wife left him, she probably soured him on women for the rest of his life. There's no way he'd give me a chance even if I wanted one. Can you imagine your husband, the love of your life, walking out on you when you needed him most? I wouldn't doubt if he wrote a vow in his own blood never to fall in love again."

"If you're sure."

"I am. I have more important things to worry about than Rick Mercer. I just want to go home. I never should have driven up here to begin with. Besides," I add lightly, "he thinks I have a boyfriend. He overheard me the other night telling you that I missed you."

Talia lets out a laugh. It sounds real and uninhibited, and it warms my heart. "Sneaky! You wanted to make him jealous!"

"That's not why I didn't correct him! A lighthouse sounds huge, but his actual living space isn't that big. There aren't a lot of places to be alone, and I thought it'd be better if he thinks I'm dating someone so he doesn't get any ideas."

"You did the exact opposite, and you know it. People always want what they can't have."

"All I want is a job I don't hate going to every day that can support us. It sounds simple, but hey, that's for me to worry about. I want you to focus on classes. Do you want to see pictures from the top of the lighthouse?"

Talia knows I'm trying to change the subject, but I don't want her thinking I can't take care of her or don't want to. She already feels like a drain, but we've been in therapy long enough that I understand when she says she's mentally and emotionally tired and can't do everything a girl her age should be doing. One day she'll graduate and she can open her own practice or work in an office with other psychologists, and all the scrimping will have been worth it. Until then, I'll do whatever I need to do.

"Yeah, sure. I'll look at them after class. I love you, Devyn."

Her voice is low, soft, and a little sad, and the words are full of so much more than love. "I love you too. Hey, I'm glad you called."

Confused, she says, "You called me."

"That's not what I meant."

"Oh." She pauses. "I didn't have a choice."

"You didn't have to," I say, looking down at my lap, "but I'm glad you did."

Talia doesn't say anything else, only hangs up, and I hope our conversation didn't bring her to a bad place. It's not the kind of talk I like to have if we're not with her therapist helping us through it, but I'll worry about her more than usual until I'm home. I snap a few pictures of the snow blowing by, and a selfie with my lips puckered in a kiss for her.

I linger for a little longer, finding a small sliver of peace alone in the white.

I go back downstairs near lunchtime, but Rick still isn't around. I grab a bag of chips out of the pantry and the book I found, and I settle in to read the rest of the day away.

CHAPTER SIX

Rick

Y*ou had to kiss her, didn't you, you dumbass,* I think to myself, paperwork wavering in front of me in a rush of frustrated anger. Of course I did. How could I not after feeling her hands roam my back, her touch a miracle, taking away the pain? How could I not after falling asleep with her, her inhales and exhales in time with my stupid heart? How could I not after sitting on the couch with her as she leaned against my chest, languid and trusting?

"It wasn't a kiss," I mumble out loud, my desktop's screensaver blinking on because I haven't been able to focus on work for the past twenty minutes. It wasn't a kiss. I brushed my lips over her jaw. The fact I did it with my lips and not my fingers would turn it into a kiss according to annoying people who focused on insignificant details. I didn't ask her to turn around. I didn't press my lips to hers, tease her with my tongue, asking her to let me in. I didn't push my hands up her sweater, warming them against her skin. I didn't pull her to me and ask her to let me make love to her, and I think with as lonely as she seems, she might have let me, boyfriend or no.

My scar doesn't bother her, and she saw plenty more yesterday.

I sigh and rub my face.

I braved the snow and the wind to work a few hours in my home office. It's small a cottage near the lighthouse where I set up a desk and my computer, filing cabinets and bookshelves, and a landline phone in case cell service ever blinks out. I thought after the day we both had, we could use some space, and I left Devyn on her own. She's a grown woman, and though I don't know her well, I trust her. Trust her not to email pictures of my bedroom to her editor in some strange *House and Garden* article instead of the interview she knows she's not going to get out of me, no matter how long she stays. Come to think of it, my living space may be of more interest to the paper's readers than rehashing an accident that's two years old.

Fuck it.

She said everything is off the record, and I believe her.

But I should pull my head out of my ass and ask her to sign an NDA before she leaves. Just because she doesn't take pictures or get her interview doesn't mean she wouldn't write a "The Week I Spent with Rickard Mercer and What He Eats for Dinner" article. There are several ways she could spin this snowstorm, and as a reporter, I bet she knows every single one.

Adding sex to the mix would muck it up even more and should be avoided at all costs.

My desk phone rings, and I pick up. Only a handful of people have this number, my ex-wife among them. We haven't spoken since the judge signed our papers and she ran off with thirty percent of everything I had.

"Mercer."

"Rick, how're you doing?" Beau Hendrickson, my co-CEO and good friend, asks cheerfully.

"I can't see two inches in front of my face, but it's going. What's up?"

"I saw on the Weather Channel you're buried in snow. Nothing here, just a dusting, enough to make people drive like they don't know how."

"I don't miss the traffic." The roads are nasty in a city of over four million people, but in Old Harbor, I learned to ease off the gas or the next thing you know you're hitting a kid chasing a ball or running over a dog.

"Sometimes I think you're a lucky son of a bitch, but I think I'd miss big city living."

He means he'd miss dining at five-star restaurants, his penthouse, car service, and his model of the week. Beau's a good guy, the best, or I wouldn't be working with him, but he parties how he works—hard. One day he'll meet a woman who knocks him on his ass. I hope I'm lucky enough to watch it.

"Is there a reason for this call? Did Renata reach out?" Reach out? I sound stupid, and I don't give a shit if she "reached out" or not. She knows how to get a hold of me. She can pick up a phone.

Beau pauses. "No. Did you want her to?"

Did I want her to. Now there's a loaded question. Yes, if just for the chance to ask her why.

She blames me for being on the construction site that day, said this never would have happened if I'd been doing my job from my office the way I was supposed to. That's only part of it. The other part, the part that's more the truth, is that she can't stand to look at me. She sure as hell wouldn't have jumped on the bed to rub me down like Devyn did yesterday. Hell, Renata's inked in for a deep tissue massage every Tuesday--she wouldn't know the first thing about how to give one.

She can't look me in the face, but I want her to. I want her to prove to me she's that vain, except, her leaving me already did that so there's no point in rubbing salt in my wounds.

Maybe I just want to see her again. I loved her once. When she loved me and not my money.

"No. Yes. Maybe. For old times' sake."

"I'm sorry, Rick."

"What for? You didn't make her leave me. Getting my face split in two did that. If she didn't ask you to call, what do you need?"

Beau changes the subject with his usual nonchalant attitude. "Declan Everett's been asking about the land."

"It's ours."

"He knows that, and he wants us to sell."

"No."

Everett's been a pain in my ass since day one. There's nothing I want that he hasn't wanted just as much. He turns every purchase, every business decision, into a pissing contest, and I'm so tired of it. The land in question looks like the setting of a post-apocalyptic movie. After the accident, I told everyone to drop what they were doing and walk. No one, including me, has been on that construction site since the accident. It must be driving Everett stark-raving mad to see land he wanted sit there covered in snow.

"Then what are we going to do with it?"

"Nothing."

The thought of stepping onto the property that almost took my life and did kill two of my men churns my stomach, the coffee sloshing around bitter and acrid. I'll never want to clear it out, or worse yet, finish the project. The site can sit there until I die. I don't care.

"Rick, you can't leave it the way it is."

The hell I can't. "Why not?"

"First of all, it's not safe. You don't live here anymore, you don't see the hazard it's become. Kids exploring, homeless people looking for shelter. Someone else is going to get hurt if you don't do something."

"It's supposed to be fenced in." I ordered the site locked down, but I was in the hospital, half out of my mind in pain, the other half in shock Renata didn't have the decency to wait until after I healed to walk out on me, and I couldn't see what type of fencing had been put up or how safe the area was. Beau had taken care of it, and that was good enough for me.

"It *is* fenced in, but you know people. Punks with wire cutters, jackasses brave enough to jump the fence. Come on. You know this. Don't play stupid because you don't want to face up to what's going on."

"Is OSHA done? The inspections?"

"It's been done for a long time. No fault." His voice is quiet.

There is fault. There is blame. It was all my responsibility, and I dropped the ball.

"I'll think about it."

Beau sighs. "I guess that's about as good as I'm going to get out of you, but Everett plays dirty. If he wants something, he won't let up until he gets it or hurts people trying."

"There's nothing he can do to me."

He scoffs, and now he sounds mad. "Seriously? Maybe you think there's nothing more he can do to you, but what about me? Renata. You may not love each other anymore, but I don't think you want him targeting her. If you care about your employees as much as you say you do, then think about them. If you don't want to do anything with that land, sell it. Doesn't have to be to Everett. At the very least, let me clean it up. It's dangerous."

"Okay, okay, but there's nothing we can do until April at the earliest, and that's if we have a decent spring."

"I'm glad you're seeing it my way. Don't sell it if you don't want to. It's prime land, and after the stink and the sting wears off, maybe you'll decide to keep going. It was going to be a fabulous hotel, Rick."

"And now it will be built on blood."

"You don't have to look at it that way."

"No, I don't, but I will."

"Yeah, you will." He agrees quickly because he knows me. This will haunt me for the rest of my life. "How are you feeling? Back still giving you trouble?"

"Yeah, some. I was in a tight spot, pardon the pun, yesterday, and Devyn was able to work it out. I would have needed the ambulance if she wouldn't have been here, and God knows if they would have been able to make it up the hill in the snow."

"Devyn? You have a woman staying with you? How did that happen? Did you meet her in town? Is it the pretty girl from the bakery you told me about?"

"No. That's Jessica, and she's married. This one's a reporter. She thought she could wrangle an interview out of me. I tried sending her back to town, but she sat outside crying, and you know how blizzards roll in. By the time I found her, there was no place she could go. She's not so bad."

"Devyn. A reporter. Why does that sound familiar?" Beau asks, then whistles. "You're not talking about Devyn Scott, are you? Jesus, Rick. Get her out of your house."

I lean forward, his words surprising me. "Why? What has she done?"

"Only royally pissed off the person closest to Declan Everett."

"I'm sorry, you're going to have to spell this out for me. I'm not as sharp as I used to be."

"That's obvious. Stevie Johansson? You missed their engagement announcement."

"Everett's engaged to Stevie Johansson? The owner of that huge candy store chain? Are you sure?"

"The very one."

Fuck. Devyn hinted at pissing off someone important, but I ignored it because I didn't care. No wonder the *Times* fired her.

"That doesn't have anything to do with me. She doesn't live in Cedar Hill anymore. She drove from Portland and the paper she works for said they'd fire her if she couldn't squeeze an interview out of me. I'm sending her packing the second the roads are clear. Don't worry about it."

"Well, I don't like that she happens to be there during a blizzard after being run out of Cedar Hill with torches and spikes for investigating a woman who's engaged to a man who would rather stab you in the back than shake your hand. That sounds like more than a coincidence to me, Rick. Don't trust her."

"I don't, but I think she learned her lesson. All she talks about now is moving and finding something that's not reporting."

"All right. Don't say I didn't warn you."

I scoff. "Everett's a pain in my ass, but he's never done anything but talk a big game. I'll send Devyn on her way and clean up the property. By this time next year, it'll all be blown over."

"Good. And get your pretty ass back to Cedar Hill. Quit hiding."

"I'm not hiding."

"Yes, you are, and I'm tired of covering for you. I want my friend back. Take care and stay safe."

He hangs up before I can retort. He doesn't get it. I'm not going back to the city.

As the wind beats against the cottage walls, I try to go through more email, respond to the requests that Beau asked me to look at, and sign contracts that need to be signed. It's not that difficult to conduct business from Old Harbor, even if Beau acts like it's the most inconvenient thing he's ever had to put up with.

Maybe one day I'll be comfortable enough to drive into Cedar Hill occasionally for a business meeting, but that's a long way off. I hate that fucking city.

I put in a couple more hours' work and call it a day.

What Beau told me about Devyn didn't exactly worry me. I had doubts about her already, but he gave me another reason why I shouldn't trust her. On the other hand, she helped me yesterday when she didn't have to. She could have stood there and watched me suffer, made a half-hearted attempt to call 911 knowing the poor chances of an ambulance being able to drive up to the lighthouse from town in the snow. No, she'd jumped right in, literally.

That had to mean something, didn't it?

Before I log off, I send a quick email to Beau apologizing for our phone call. He's stood by me, and I owe him more than a surly attitude.

I step outside, and the wind immediately knocks the breath out of my lungs. The drifts are taller now, and I sink past my knees in the snow.

With my head down, I trudge toward the lighthouse. I slam gratefully into the entryway, choking, ice already frozen in my beard. It isn't far, but even a few feet in wind like that can smash you to the ground, and my skin stings from the snow pelting against my face. Leaning against the wall, I pull air into my burning lungs. It was worth it to stare at a different set of walls, and I'll do it again tomorrow. And every day after that until Devyn can leave, because I can't stop feeling her hands pressed against my back.

I kick off my boots and hang up my jacket next to Devyn's.

It's been a long time since I've hung up my jacket next to someone else's, and a longer time than that since I've stepped into a kitchen with a woman waiting for me and something hot on the stove.

The kitchen smells like heaven, and I close the second door behind me, keeping the winter storm outside.

Devyn's sitting at the table, her hair plaited into a braid, the shoulder of her sweater sliding down her arm, revealing soft skin and the lacy strap of a tank top. Her foot is propped on the bench, and her chin is resting on her knee. She's using a mouse to scroll a website, and she looks at me, her eyes widening in surprise.

"Where have you been?"

"I have an office next door. You might not have noticed it when you drove up. I was doing some paperwork. The internet," I say, nodding in her direction as I assume she's using it, "is still strong and I was able to get a little work done. What smells so good?" I shuffle to the stove and lift the lid to a large pot I don't remember owning.

"Chicken soup. I was going to ask if you had plans for the two chicken breasts in the fridge, but I couldn't find you and I took a chance. I hope it's okay."

"This is a lot better than what I had planned for them. Thank you. You cook a lot?" I stir the soup with the wooden spoon lying near the stove. Chunks of chicken swirl around with egg noodles, onion, celery, and carrots. If it tastes half as delicious as it smells, I'll be a happy man. She made enough for a couple of days, and I won't get tired of eating the leftovers.

"When I worked for the *Times,* no. You lived there, in Cedar Hill, I mean. You know what a rat race it is. Leave for work at six-thirty, don't get home until seven. Rinse and repeat. There's not a lot of time for cooking. That changed when my sister moved in with me and we had to move so I could find work. If there's one thing I can say about Portland, it's that I like working nine to four and having a life again. I learned to cook, started reading for pleasure, planted a garden. I hang out with my sister doing useless things like shopping at the mall and eating ice cream while we look at ugly clothes. It's different."

I tap the spoon against the edge of the pot and put the lid back on. I don't know anything about soup and don't know if it's done. The oven is on as well, but I don't risk opening the door and peeking inside. I don't want to ruin whatever she's baking.

"My business partner called while I was doing paperwork. He knows who you are."

She winces. "Everyone in Cedar Hill knows who I am. The only reason I slipped by you was because you happened to be in the hospital fighting for your life."

I lean against the counter and cross my ankles. "Stevie Johansson? You've got balls."

She lifts a shoulder, and the sweater falls farther down her arm. Whoever her boyfriend is, he's one lucky son of a bitch.

"I'd do it all over again. She's dirty, and I was trying to prove it."

Laughing, I fold my arms over my chest. "She owns a chain of candy stores. What do you think she's doing?"

"Nothing. I don't think she's doing anything. That was two years ago, and all I care about now is watching out for my sister and making ends meet the best I can. Like eighty percent of the American population, I'm in debt up to my eyeballs, and getting fired from the *Pioneer* isn't going to help fix that. I was looking for a new job, and I might have found a lead or two. Surprisingly, I still have a few friends at the *Times* willing to give me a reference, and Walt said he would too."

Jealousy stabs at me again and I try to push it back, but I'm not successful. "The boyfriend?"

She rolls her eyes. "Forget about him. Walt's the editor of the *Pioneer*. I'll go back to Portland empty-handed, but it's not his choice to fire me for it. I'm good at my job, and he knows that."

I wait for her to mention the interview, maybe in exchange for what she did for me yesterday, but all she does is continue with, "Things happen for a reason, and I'm going to take this lesson and run with it. It has nothing to do with you."

"It shouldn't. I've only known you for three days."

"Huh." She turns back to her laptop and starts scrolling.

"Can I eat? Is it done?"

She picks up her phone. "The biscuits have two more minutes. If you want to wait, wait. If you don't, don't."

"Biscuits?"

"Your flour looked questionable, but I made it work."

"I had flour?"

She looks up from her laptop and smiles, and I swear, just for a second, I feel like I'm back outside unable to breathe. "We're in trouble if you didn't."

———

We talk while we eat, but nothing heavy.

I don't ask about Stevie Johansson again, and she doesn't ask what kind of work I was doing in the cottage. I find out she *does* have a degree in journalism with a minor in English. She's well-read, knows a lot about the state of the world, and she cares about her sister. She briefly mentions her parents but speaks as if they've never been around. Maybe that's why she needs to take care of her sister, but I don't feel comfortable asking and she doesn't offer the information. We talk a lot about life in a small town compared to living in Cedar Hill. Our lives weren't that different in the city. We were rats in a different race, but we were still running, and we compare notes about the simplicity of small town living.

We talk for nearly an hour, but it occurs to me as we clean the kitchen together that everything she told me I could have found out online. She didn't get personal, didn't say anything about her boyfriend, either. She could be engaged and planning her wedding.

She didn't say anything about the kiss.

Not that I expected her to. If she's in a relationship, she'd want to ignore it and hope I don't pursue it.

I liked spending the time talking to her, but I came away from our conversation empty, wanting more and not knowing how to get it, not knowing if I should.

The snow's supposed to stop in a couple of days, and what seemed like too long suddenly feels like not enough.

I lean against the sink, my hands braced on the edge of the counter.

"Are you okay?" she asks, pausing near the refrigerator.

I'm a lot of things, but okay hasn't been one in a long time.

With my back still turned, I straighten enough to say, "Yeah. Thanks for dinner."

"It wasn't a problem. I'm going to go, ah, read for a while. Is that okay?"

"Yeah."

I feel her turn toward the living room. One more step and she'll disappear from the kitchen.

"Devyn," I say, turning around, and she pauses and meets my eyes.

I want to ask her if she feels it, or if I'm only imagining the pull between us. If I say something, would she blame the snow-storm? Being trapped together? Would she say I only feel this way because I needed her help yesterday? That's what Beau would say. That this is all made up because I haven't been with a woman since Renata left me. That besides a nurse, she's the only woman to have touched me in years and I'm lonely. There's no reason not to believe it.

She saves me from having to say anything.

"We shouldn't." Her eyes search mine, waiting for me to agree.

But I don't. "Because of how I look?"

I know what the accident did to my face and my body. Renata was my *wife*, bound to me through sickness and health. She promised when she said her vows in front of our friends, family, and God, but that hadn't been enough after seeing what happened to me.

Silently, she pads across the hardwood floor in her white socks and stands in front of me. Her hand trembles as she traces the scar that starts at my temple, snakes down my cheek, and ends at my chin. The scar tissue is raised and raw and puckered in places. The surgeon had done a good job with what she'd had to work with and after I healed, I had no complaints. I didn't want plastic surgery . . . I deserve to look like this.

Her fingertips skim my skin, her other hand resting gently on the side of my face.

She licks her lips, leaving a sheen of saliva.

I swallow, her touch setting my nerves on fire, but not from pain.

"Never because of how you look. We shouldn't start something we can't finish. I have responsibilities and so do you. How would it work?"

I stare into her green eyes that are framed by lashes the same color as her hair. It's true, on many levels, that starting something now would only cause problems later. I may have accepted the blame for the accident, but I'm nowhere near facing it, or fixing it. I made sure the families of the men who were killed would never need anything, but the site's abandoned and until Beau called me this morning, I had no plans for that to change.

Her hands linger on my face, but she drops them when I say, "But you feel it." I insist because I need the validation. Proof it's not all in my head, that Renata hadn't broken me, that she hadn't ruined me.

I think she's going to run away or lie, but instead, she closes what little space is left between us and says, "I feel it."

"Christ," I mutter, a knot of tension loosening in my chest. I can't stop myself, and resting my hand on the nape of her neck, I lower my head and press my lips to hers. A sigh escapes her mouth and her breath is warm and gentle against my skin.

I shouldn't be doing this. She's going to leave, and I'll be right back to where I was when Renata left me.

Reluctantly, I lift my head. "What if I asked you to stay?"

Rubbing her thumb over my lips, she says, "I can't."

"You said you're in debt. Is it money?"

She steps away from me and tugs her cardigan closer around her body. She's shutting me out.

"Not all of it. I can't lie, some of it is, but that's not all of it."

"Is it your boyfriend?" I can't let it go. I want to know the truth. If she's already in a relationship, her rejection won't hurt so much.

Huffing a quiet laugh, she says, "You don't give up, do you? I don't have a boyfriend. I was talking to my sister. I called her this morning too, and she knows. She could hear it in my voice when I talked about you, and it scared her. Talia's several years younger than I am and she's had it rough the past few years. She needs me. I'm sorry."

"You don't have to be sorry for taking care of your family."

"Thank you. I'm going upstairs."

She lifts a corner of her mouth in barely a smile and steps into the living room.

I stay in the kitchen and put on a fresh pot of coffee. I want to follow her and ask what happened to her sister, try to work something out, but I don't have room in my life for her, either. Not if I'm going back to Cedar Hill and . . .

And what?

Head the clean-up crew? I'd need to face all my demons to do that. Go back to the office like Beau wants me to? My priorities shifted after the accident and what used to be important isn't anymore. The life I was living in Cedar Hill doesn't appeal to me, but running my company from Old Harbor will only last for so long before I get bored or I frustrate Beau to the point he quits. He accepted the co-CEO position to work with me and this isn't what he had in mind.

The coffee drips, and I lean tiredly against the counter. Even if Devyn's obligations keep us from having a relationship, I'm glad it wasn't all about money. Then I would have offered to keep her with me and resented her for taking it, and she would've resented me for giving it to her. She would have been obligated to me then, and I don't want her with me like that. I want her to stay in Old Harbor because what she was feeling in my kitchen while we kissed turned into something more.

It won't if she leaves.

I want more time.

I try to read too, but a normal evening reading a good book isn't as satisfying with Devyn upstairs. I'm not going to turn into a stalker, and I stay in my bedroom despite my need to simply be in her space. Ten o'clock rolls around and I hear her shuffle through the living room to the bathroom. I imagine her getting ready for bed—washing her face and brushing her teeth. I don't poke my head out to even wish her a goodnight.

Not tonight, but tomorrow night, the snow will stop. The city works with me and plows the road up to the lighthouse first. They know I need to go to my doctor's appointments and

Pete will remind them I haven't had a grocery delivery in close to a week. I'll be plowed out, and she'll be on her way in forty-eight hours at the most.

Maybe a trip to Cedar Hill will be what I need to forget she was ever here. She wouldn't have been here long enough for memories of her to bother me when I come back. I can't do anything with the site right now, but I can look at what needs to be done and put a plan together. The cleanup that can start at the end of March or beginning of April, depending on how slowly spring decides to stroll into the city.

Near one in the morning, I give up on my book and go into the kitchen for a glass of water. Through the wooden door at the top of the stairs, a muffled shout drifts through the lighthouse.

I forget the water and run across the living room and up the stairs as quickly as my hip and leg will let me. My sweaty fingers grapple with the doorknob, and desperately, I twist it enough to open the door.

"No! Please don't!" Devyn cries, and her voice is louder now. She didn't close her bedroom door, trusting me not to hurt her.

She's thrashing on the bed, the comforter wrapped around her legs. Her hair is spread over the sheet and a pillow is on the floor.

Everything I know about waking someone up while they're having a nightmare advises against what I do next. I jump on the bed and wrap my arms around her. She kicks and claws at me, her fingernails raking over my clothes.

"Please don't," she sobs, and her body bucks against mine. "I promise, I promise."

"Devyn. Devyn, wake up." I tighten my hold. "You're safe, baby. You're safe."

Her rigid body slightly relaxes, but she cries, her hot tears wetting my skin. She curls into a fetal position, her ass snug against my dick. I mold my body to hers, but I don't want her to feel trapped and I loosen my grip.

She smells like roses, and her pajama set is a soft, thin fleece. A quiet mewling comes from the back of her throat.

"Baby, you're safe. I won't let anything happen to you." A blatant lie. I won't be able to do anything after she leaves Old Harbor.

I lose track of how long we lie like that, her shuddering easing with every minute I hold her.

She twists in my arms and presses her face into my neck, her leg over my hip. "Rick," she murmurs into my ear.

"I'm here, baby." The endearment sounds natural, like I've been saying it to her for years. I push my hand up her pajama top and spread my hand over her back. Her skin is soft and warm, and she's not wearing a bra. I want to touch her everywhere, but I only hold her and pray she never asks me to stop.

CHAPTER SEVEN

Devyn

The nightmare comes out of nowhere.

That's not true. I know exactly where it came from. What triggered it is puzzling, though I can only guess it's from telling Rick about why I had to leave Cedar Hill without telling him why I *really* had to leave Cedar Hill.

He says he won't let anything hurt me, and I believe his intentions. He'll try not to let anything hurt me, but even with all of his billions, if Stevie Johansson wants to get me, she will.

He's still strong, and lying in his arms is the safest I've felt in a long time. If I could bottle up this feeling and take it with me when I go back to Portland, I'd be the luckiest woman in the world.

What did he think he was offering me after we ate dinner? A relationship? Marriage? A future? It would've made me angry if he hadn't looked so depleted. That doesn't sound right, but it's the right word. He looked empty of love, hope, and the fight to keep going. He never answered me when I asked him if he was suicidal. Maybe he used to be. Maybe he still is. Therapy keeps Talia's head above water, but I don't know if Rick has seen anyone to help him deal with the accident and his wife leaving him.

His hand is warm against my back, and I wish he'd touch me everywhere. Make love to me and help me forget my nightmare. He won't, though, not unless I make the first move, but I don't have the energy to give him anything.

Reluctantly, I let go and settle on the mattress. There's no pillow. I must have pushed it off during my nightmare. Rick tugs me against his chest and keeps his hand splayed over my belly. I like how he can't stop touching me. I could get used to it. Too fast. He props his head on his hand and looks down at me, a frown creasing the skin between his eyebrows. There's a little light in here—he turned the lamp on when he came into the room. It helps. For a long time, I was scared of the dark.

"What was that about?" he asks, his thumb moving back and forth near my belly button.

It's truth or lie time, and I've never been a great liar. "If I tell you, I'll have to start at the beginning. Either you'll believe me or not, but it's the truth, Rick."

"I'll believe you." His voice is firm, but he hasn't heard the story yet.

I sigh. "Talia was addicted to Sweet."

Rick sucks in a horrified breath. "Jesus Christ. I'm sorry."

"Our mother lives in Cedar Hill. She's addicted too, and all she does is sell herself to pay for the next fix. There's thirteen years between us, and Talia lived with her while I went to school and started working. Talia did her best, but I gave up on Mom a long time ago. At a party one night, Talia got hooked. Six months after that, she was arrested during a drug raid and spent three years in rehab. When she was clean enough to leave, she called me. She didn't have anyone else."

"How long ago was that?"

I turn toward him and meet his eyes. "About three years ago. That's what started it."

"Started what?"

"I wanted to know where in the hell it was coming from. I wanted to know who was bringing it into the city and ruining the lives of thousands of people. Do you know why it's called that? Sweet?"

"It's short for swetexopril, and from what I've heard, it tastes like bubblegum," Rick says.

"That's only part of it. It's called Sweet because Stevie 'Sweetheart' Johansson runs the drug operation that brings it into the Midwest through her candy stores."

He pulls his hand out of my shirt and sits up. "Devyn—"

I lost him. I knew I would, but I plow on. "For close to a year, I dug. I talked to dealers, snitches, and prostitutes, trying to find out where they got it. Stevie doesn't make it here—it's made in drug labs in Mexico. She has ties to gangs there who smuggle it across the border and pass it on to gangs in California who run the supply up here. She has connections to people in the postal service and shipping companies who deliver it to her warehouses. The gangs in the city help her distribute it."

Rick pauses. "Can you prove any of that?"

I scoff. "Of course not. Why do you think the *Times* fired me? Would I be working at the *Pioneer*? Stevie found out I was sniffing around. I wasn't that discreet, so it's not hard to imagine word getting back to her. You want to know where my nightmare came from."

"Yeah. Devyn, are you in trouble?"

"Not as long as I leave her alone and stay out of Cedar Hill. One night, I was near Camden Way talking to a snitch. A white van pulled up next to us, and one of Stevie's goons shoved a pillowcase over my head and knocked me out. When I woke up, I was duct-taped to a metal chair. They threatened me all night."

Rick shoves his fingers through his hair and says, "Fuck. What did they do?"

I sit up and search his face. He's not going to believe what I say next.

"They held a bit of Sweet near my lips and told me if I didn't stop asking questions, they'd hook me. All it takes is one time, one little taste, and I'd be like my mother, fucking anything that moves hoping to score. Finding my next fix would become my entire life, and Talia would end up on the streets again, same as Mom, same as me, if they did what they threatened to do. They came so close, and I've never been so scared."

He wiggles his arm under my back and cuddles me to him. "They let you go?"

"Yeah. They left me taped to the chair in her warehouse. It took me hours to get loose. The first thing I did was wash my face in the first bathroom I found. Stevie called the *Times* personally and said if they didn't fire me for harassing her, she'd stop advertising her stores in the paper. People think I'm an idiot for accusing Stevie Johansson of being the Sweet queenpin of the upper Midwest, and maybe I am. I talked to so many people, but nothing I heard was rock-solid evidence, and that's what made it so impossible." I swallow. "If I had a million dollars, I'd still bet it all that she uses her stores to launder her drug money. I just couldn't prove it."

"How did you end up in Portland, then?"

I pull away and sit up, needing the space. "We should've left the Midwest altogether. It was stupid to stay in Minnesota, but Talia doesn't want to leave in case she can help Mom somehow. I don't know how she, we, can. Talia has enough on her plate with her own sobriety. Even after three years in rehab and three years living with me, every day is a challenge. Every day is a new day for her to slip up. A friend of a friend knew Walt, and he took me on as a favor. Now you know why the owners of the *Pioneer* hate me. They don't want my stink on them, and I can't blame them, really. After this blizzard blows out, I'm going back to Portland and I'm moving us somewhere far away from here. The farther Talia is from Cedar Hill, the better off we'll be."

"What about your mother?"

I feel guilty for being so callous, but I have no choice. "There's no hope for her. It sounds heartless, but I've tried. She doesn't want to clean up. She's been arrested and put in drug rehab programs, but they're never long enough. Talia needed *three years*. They wanted to release her after four months. She begged them to let her stay and after she was finally ready to go home, she owed half a million dollars. I was able to sign her up for medical coverage through the state, but they back paid her bill only six months. That saved me a little bit, but . . ." I shrug. "I'd do it all over again. She goes to school now. She wants to be a therapist like the ones who helped her in rehab. She'll make a good one, I think."

"Devyn, I don't know how to say this without making you upset. It's not Stevie Johansson. She's opened stores on my properties. She sells her candy everywhere. She *is* Cedar Hill's sweetheart. Everyone you spoke to lied to you."

So much for keeping me safe. So much for believing me. It shouldn't hurt so much, but it does. I've been on my own since Stevie called the *Times*. The only people who have shown any kindness toward me and Talia at all have been Walt and the people at Talia's small college who don't know who we are. Pretending I don't care, I roll off the bed and pick up the pillow. It doesn't matter what he thinks, but it sure would have been nice to have someone in my corner for once.

"It's over and done. I don't care if you believe me or not. She can sell Sweet all she wants. She ruined my mother's life. She almost ruined Talia's. I'm lucky she showed me a little mercy, or I'd be on the streets right now hooking like my mom. You know, when I was digging for evidence, anything I could bring to the cops, I'd see her standing on a corner, gouges dug into her face from going too long without a hit. I'd get out of my car and give her a fifty. She'd see me, but she didn't know who I was. You think I liked seeing my own mother on a corner, not having showered for God knows how long, and longer still since she ate a decent meal? Talia would always ask me if I saw her, and I would always say no. She'd want to go look for her, and I can't have my sister out there around that. I need to get some sleep. The weather app on my phone says it's supposed to stop snowing soon. I'll get out of your way the second I can."

I turn off the lamp and crawl into bed. He doesn't go, but there's enough space that I don't touch him.

After a moment's hesitation, he lies next to me and pushes his arm under my pillow, spooning me.

I should kick him out, but it's nice to have someone close. Sometimes Talia crawls into my bed like a child who doesn't want to sleep alone. It's difficult for me to be away from her, but I know it's good for her, too. She can't learn to stand on her own if I'm always propping her up. One day she'll want to go out on her own and I'll have to let her live her own life.

"Where did they threaten you?" Rick asks, his mouth close to my ear.

"They brought me to a warehouse on 120th Avenue and Pike."

Rick freezes. "That's where Stevie stores her candy. That's her distribution center."

"Oh," I say bitterly into the dark. "Did I forget to tell you that part? They thought they scared me enough I wouldn't say anything, and they were right. Besides, I took a chance and looked around. That's not where they're running the Sweet from, at least, not that I could tell. Just before the shit hit the fan, I asked a contact at the police station to get his hands on the security footage around the warehouse. There was a power outage that night, at almost the exact same time that I was there, and all the cameras in that grid were down. I didn't have any proof they'd taken me there, and after that, I swore I'd never look into Stevie Johansson again. And I haven't."

He nudges my shoulder, and I roll over onto my back. He's still dressed in jeans and a shirt and has socks on his feet. Without the light, I don't understand what he wants until his lips are on mine and he's pulling me close.

I don't have room in my life for this, but I kiss him back, needing the comfort, his hand once again splayed under my back, his touch soothing. I wiggle closer, and he slips his tongue in my mouth, lazy licks that stir something deep in my belly that I haven't felt for a long time.

I hold his face in my hands, and his scar is a bumpy ridge under my fingers.

He leans away just as I think he's going to take it further. I would, if he wanted to. Kissing me on the forehead, he mumbles, "Get some sleep."

"Are you sleeping with me?"

"If I told you I wanted to, would you let me?" he asks, tugging the comforter to my chin.

"If I said yes, would you get undressed? Your jeans feel uncomfortable."

"If I get undressed, would you feel safe with me in your bed?"

I laugh a little, the last of the nightmare fading. "Yeah, I would." He's been a perfect gentleman since the second he pushed me into the lighthouse, giving me shelter in the storm.

He might not believe me and that might hurt my feelings, but that's the only way he'll hurt me.

"Okay." He rolls off the bed and unbuttons his shirt. I hear him push his jeans to the floor, and he shifts from one foot to the other to take off his socks.

I have no idea what he was wearing under his clothes. He molds himself to me under the comforter, and I pat his hip, discovering the soft cotton of his boxer briefs.

"Still good?" he asks.

"Yeah. It's perfect."

CHAPTER EIGHT

Rick

It took a lot of willpower to sleep next to Devyn and not peel every inch of material off her body and make love to her all night. She would have let me, too. Her body was quivering with it, but she was emotionally drained after her nightmare and I wasn't going to use that. I didn't want to leave her alone in case she had another one, and it might not have been because I was with her, but she slept peacefully through the rest of the night.

I got out of bed before she woke up, made coffee, and left her another note saying to help herself to breakfast. Today's my last full day with her, but I'm spending the morning in my office, the wind howling past the windows just as strongly as yesterday.

The snow doesn't show any sign of letting up, and I find it hard to believe this will be over by tomorrow morning, but the Weather Channel's reliable. It's only because I don't want to say goodbye to Devyn that I'm hoping the meteorologists are wrong.

She needs to leave. I get that.

It's my own fault I let myself fall a little bit in love. The sooner she leaves, the quicker it will fade. I was happy alone before she drove up, and I'll be happy again after she drives back down.

I can't concentrate on work, and on a whim, call the editor of the *Times*, Bill Newsom. Back in the day we belonged to the same gentleman's club in Cedar Hill and attended the same fundraisers and other functions, bullshit parties Renata wanted to go to that I couldn't have cared less about. We haven't kept in touch, but he'll still answer his phone.

I use his private number I have saved in my cell, and he answers with a gruff, "Newsom." I see he hasn't lost his grumpy teddy bear act.

"It's Mercer."

"Hey, you in town?" His voice is muddled, and I think he's talking around a cigar.

"No. I have a couple of questions for you, though."

Clearer now, he says, "Yeah? What can I help you with? Going to offer me an exclusive on what you've been up to for the past two years?"

"No."

"Oh. This isn't about Renata, is it?"

That throws me off. "No. Why?"

He clears his throat. "I thought maybe you heard that she and I are seeing each other. Nothing serious, just a couple parties here and there."

"No. Beau hasn't mentioned it." He'd be the only one to tell me something like that.

"You don't mind, do you?"

I lean back in my chair and watch the snow fly horizontally past the cottage window. Three days ago, I would have minded. Two days ago, I would have minded. After sleeping in Devyn's bed last night, my body warm against hers, my hand resting beneath her breasts, I don't mind. "No. She's single and can do whatever she wants, but a word of warning, she's not that loyal."

"Noted." He sounds amused, but if he falls in love with her and later becomes involved in a situation she finds inconvenient and leaves him, he won't be that amused. "You didn't call to talk about that."

"No, I didn't. Tell me about Devyn Scott."

He sighs. "That was some fucked up shit. My best goddamned reporter, and I had to fire her. She was better than this fucking city. It's what made her a great reporter. Stepping in the shit, and not afraid to do it. Unbiased. I could count on her to tell the truth, and you know what," he asks, ranting now that he has an audience, "she was one of few, one of the fucking few, who wouldn't take a bribe. Just let one rookie go last week for taking a payoff to slant a piece. It's ridiculous no one's honest anymore."

"But Devyn was."

"Hell yeah she was. She cleaned out her desk and I was fucking sobbing."

"Why'd you fire her? What'd she do if she was that good?"

Newsom lowers his voice. "She stepped in the wrong pile of shit. Fucking Christ. You couldn't have called me in the afternoon so I could drink while we talked about this bullshit?"

"It's that bad?"

"Look, she was sniffing around Stevie Johansson, and you know she's got the city by the balls."

Frowning, I say, "No, I didn't know that. In fact, when I lived there, I thought I did."

He laughs. "You're too soft. You know only Hendrickson's

timing landed you that property when Everett wanted it too. You beat him by a half second, and he'll never forget it. No, you're not cutthroat enough to rule this city, but Stevie, especially since you've dropped out of the game, she's in it to win it."

"Devyn was snooping around her for a reason then." People don't call you cutthroat for nothing.

"She said Stevie's selling Sweet, and using her candy stores to launder the money."

I lean back in my chair and rub my finger over my lips. "Is she?"

"Hell, it wouldn't surprise me. The shit's coming from somewhere. We just ran a piece yesterday. Hundreds of people in the hospitals from overdosing on the stuff. Twenty to fifty people a day drop dead. Overtaxing our medical services, funeral homes have a wait list, a fucking wait list, for a fucking funeral. Cops can't keep hookers and dealers off the streets. Crime is on the rise. We've got serious problems here, and no one cares."

"It sounds like Devyn did," I say dryly. "If it's that bad and you think you know who's doing it, why aren't you doing something about it?"

"Stevie's pinkie-swearing with the mayor, and she's engaged to your buddy Everett. With him behind her, she's untouchable. But here's the thing, Mercer. There's no proof. It doesn't matter what the word on the street is. It doesn't matter if a million people can say the same thing. We need proof to run a story, the cops need proof for a warrant. The DA needs proof to bring to trial. The jury needs proof to say she's guilty. Devyn didn't have it. It's that simple. Stevie started squealing slander, and we had to cut her loose. It broke my heart, it really did, and I hear she's still reporting up in some little hick town.

Maybe she'll make a comeback, but she's better off lying low and hoping it blows over."

"Did you talk to her about it?"

"Who? Devyn? Yeah. She investigated on her own time, but I knew she was sniffing around. As long as my reporters aren't getting hurt and not hurting anyone, I let them do what they need to do. Devyn could've stumbled onto something big. Maybe she already had but just needed time to keep digging. Stevie didn't give it to her, but that's not a fucking surprise, not if she's guilty. I defended her, and you have to believe that, Mercer, but Stevie threatened to cut off advertising dollars and direct it to the *Chronicle,* and the guys upstairs went fucking ballistic. My hands were tied."

"You do any damage control?" I ask.

Newsom scoffs. "It turned into a fucking nightmare. We had a leak, maybe we still do, and it got out I had to fire Devyn for pointing a finger at Stevie for selling Sweet. Devyn couldn't go into a grocery store without someone harassing her. She picked the wrong woman to piss off, and I'm sorry for it. The paper issued a public apology to Stevie and said we handled the situation the best way we could. It wasn't long after that I heard Devyn moved out of the city with her sister. It probably would have been better for her if she'd moved out of the fucking state, but I think they have family here."

"Their mother," I say vaguely, thinking how close Devyn came to being taken out of the picture permanently. It sounds like what Stevie wants, Stevie gets, but it's strange that when I lived in Cedar Hill, the woman wasn't much on my radar at all except as a person I occasionally did business with. "How long have Stevie and Everett been engaged?"

"We ran their announcement two weeks ago. So, who knows. A few months? They've been on the social scene for a couple of years. At least since you've been laid up. They look good together, not that it matters. They were doing okay separately. Together, they'll rule Cedar Hill. There's already talk that nabbing an invite to their wedding means you're in. That's not a club I want to join, if you know what I mean. What's the sudden interest in Devyn, anyway?"

"She contacted me and asked for an interview. I said no."

"If you're feeling charitable and you want to help a girl down on her luck, an interview with you would probably boost her up a bit. She's a good girl, she really is, and I hope she lands on her feet. I gotta get going. The next time you come into the city, let me know. I'll buy you a drink. Take care, Mercer."

Newsom hangs up leaving me with more questions than answers.

Devyn wasn't lying then. I didn't think she was, but I thought maybe she was exaggerating. It sounded over the top that a couple of goons would drag her to a warehouse and threaten to hook her on Sweet just because she was nosing around and asking questions, but Newsom didn't even hesitate when I asked if Stevie could be running Sweet around Cedar Hill.

It doesn't change anything. Stevie's still the sweetheart of the city, Devyn's still fired from the *Times,* and the *Pioneer* is still going to let her go. I do a quick internet search and find that the *Times* and the *Pioneer* aren't owned by the same conglomerate. Maybe Devyn had thought of that too and felt safe applying at any paper MediaCorp didn't own. I could buy the *Pioneer* and tell this Walt guy to keep her on, but that wouldn't stay a secret and Devyn wouldn't thank me. She'd hate me for interfering.

The bottom line is her sister needs her, and with Talia being a recovering Sweet addict and Devyn running from Stevie and needing work, they won't hang around Minnesota.

I'm going to lose her.

The weather app on my phone says the snow is predicted to stop in twelve hours, and it's starting to thin, though the wind's still strong. I don't know what I can do to keep her here. My ultimatum didn't go anywhere. The interview was only a means to an end and she doesn't care if I give her one or not. I could call the city plows and ask the crew chief to plow me out last, but I don't want them to get into the habit of doing that. I could ask her to stay, but she's worried about her sister and wants to check on her. I could ask for her phone number, but that wouldn't do me much good if she decides to move to Hawaii.

Or I could grow the fuck up and realize we weren't meant to be.

Timing, circumstances. It happens.

I shoot off a quick email to Beau and tell him that I won't be online for a few days, then I brave the wind and trudge through the snow to the lighthouse. There isn't soup on the stove like there was yesterday, but she made a fresh pot of coffee, the carafe full and hot. I pour a cup and add a little milk. We'll, I mean, *I'll* be completely out by the time I can run into town. Pete will have his own shit to do after the storm, and I'll need to do something to keep my mind off the fact Devyn's gone.

Sipping on coffee, I change my clothes. My jeans are wet, and I switch them out for sweats and a t-shirt. Devyn hasn't bothered to dress up, preferring to stay in comfortable, casual clothes, and I might as well follow her lead. There's nowhere to go and nothing to do.

I try to resist looking for her. I should stay in my room and read or nap. I didn't get much sleep last night between her nightmare and rolling out of bed early to put in a couple hours of work. My back has been holding out okay, but I'll be in trouble again if I don't get back to my normal routine. Knowing our time together is almost gone, I'm drawn to her, and I find her in the guest bedroom, sitting on the bed and scrolling on her laptop.

"More job hunting?" I ask, my throat scratchy. Maybe I'm catching a cold.

She's beautiful, dressed in different pajama bottoms than yesterday, and a different colored tank under the same robe-like cardigan. She left her hair down, and it's a damp mess of waves down her back. Her rose scent drifts to me, and like a moth to a flame, I walk toward the bed. She doesn't tell me no, and I sink onto the soft mattress.

I frame her face in my hands and turn her head.

"Rick—"

I don't let her finish. I press my lips to hers and everything fades into the background. She clutches at my wrists as I nudge the seam of her mouth with the tip of my tongue, asking her to let me in. She does, and she tastes like coffee and something sweet I'll never find anywhere else. I push her backward and cover her body with mine, never once breaking our connection. My leg rests between her thighs, and I nudge my cock against the side of her hip. Through the thin material, she'll know I want her.

I drag my mouth away from hers and nibble at the delicate skin under her jaw.

She moans. "Rick."

"Tell me to stop, and I'll stop."

She meets my eyes and skims a fingertip down my cheek. I shaved this morning, and my scar stands out against my pale skin. I want her to *see me*. I want her to look at me without flinching. Unlike Renata who visited me in the hospital and could barely meet my eyes.

"Tell me something first," she says, her finger lingering near the corner of my mouth.

"What is it?" My hands itch to undress her. I want to

touch. I want to taste. I want to feel and save it all up for when I'm at my lowest.

"Would you still be here, in this room, if I was just anyone?"

The question hurts, and I want to hurt her back. "Yes."

She lifts onto her elbows and brushes her lips over mine. "Thank you for telling me the truth."

"Move your laptop or we'll break it." I lean away from her, and she scoots off the bed and puts her laptop on the dresser. Her small suitcase is still open on the floor, her clothes piled messily on each side. She didn't unpack, but I wish she had.

She takes her cardigan off and steps near the bed. "It's been a long time for me. I dated a guy at the *Times* before Talia called me from rehab. Since I picked her up, there hasn't been anyone."

I pull my t-shirt over my head and toss it on the floor next to her suitcase. "I haven't been with anyone since my wife left me. You can see why."

If I'd thought this through, I would have asked for this in the dark where she couldn't see. Devyn didn't turn the lamp on, but there's a small window in her room that lets in just enough light to see by. When the boom fell on me, the impact broke my bones and tore my skin. The scars are there, from the stitches that held me together. More stitches from surgery to repair my broken bones and evidence of my hip replacement.

She sits next to me and reaches out a hand. "Can I?"

I shrug. "It's a mood killer, isn't it?"

Lightly, she smooths her fingers over the bumps, over the patchwork that saved my life. "It's beautiful."

It's the last thing I thought she'd say.

"How long were you pinned under it?"

"Three hours."

"And you lived."

"There are days I wish I hadn't."

"Why do you say that?"

I scoff. "Seriously? I can rarely move without pain. I sleep in the wrong position for five seconds and I need hours with a massage therapist. I get headaches, and winters like this are hell on my bones. I lost my wife, my friends, my life. I can't look at myself in the mirror without hating what I see."

She rests a hand on my shoulder and presses her other hand to my cheek, forcing me to meet her eyes. "Have you seen someone addicted to Sweet?"

"No. What the hell does that have to do with anything?"

"It's the most terrible thing you will ever see in your life, and that's including your reflection. The addiction controls you until you can't think of anything else. If you can't afford it or you can't find a dealer, you slowly go crazy. You pick and tear at your skin—physical pain feels better than the mental withdrawal. You don't want to eat, you don't sleep. You stop caring about being clean. There are sick people out there, Rick. People who prey on addicts, men who like to beat on women, or rape them. These women, they need the Sweet and they *beg* for it. You have no idea how lucky you are. No idea. Talia . . . she doesn't talk to me about what she did for Sweet. She tells her therapist who says addiction is a disease and that it's okay. But it's not okay. It shouldn't be around in the first place."

Fury shimmers around her, and I want to reach out and touch it.

She sucks in an angry breath, and she traces the scar that destroys my face. "You are still beautiful, and it's a shame you can't see it."

I don't have time to blink before she's on me, her mouth fused to mine, my arms full of the fury that could burn me and kill me just as easily as it could thaw me out and save my life. I shove my hands up her tank top. She's not wearing a bra, and I fill my hands with her breasts. Her skin is so soft, her breasts heavy and full, her nipples already hardening under my touch.

I yank my mouth away and push her top up. Greedily, I suck on one of her nipples and bite, needing to consume all of her.

She whimpers and pushes on my shoulder. "Slow down. We have time."

"No, we don't," I growl, frustrated she doesn't understand the desperate urgency I'm feeling. Using more force than necessary, I tug her tank top over her head and throw it on the floor. "The snow will stop tonight, and you're leaving tomorrow. This is all the time we have."

"No, Rick—"

With my chest heaving, I grab her upper arms and squeeze. "This is all the time we have," I repeat.

I let her go and she steadies herself with a hand to the mattress.

"That's not . . . Okay." She nods and slides off the edge of the bed.

I can't keep my eyes off her as she strips her pajama bottoms and panties off and stands in front of me with nothing but the fear I won't find her good enough. Her skin glitters like pearls in the white light that floats through the window. She's perfect compared to me, a delicate beauty to my ferocious beast, and I know I should leave. I won't be able to come back from what we do on her bed, and she'll always remember making love to a man who lives in the shadows, too ashamed to show his face.

I get off the bed, trying to decide what will hurt me the least.

She steps forward and rests her hands against my chest. "I know what you're thinking. Don't go."

I twist my fingers in her hair and say, "And if I say those words to you tomorrow? Would you stay?"

Shaking her head, she slides my sweats down my thighs, and her strands slip through my fingers as she kneels. I step out of them at the same time she reaches for the elastic of my boxers. She pulls them down, and my cock springs free, thick and heavy. I haven't been with a woman since before the accident, when Renata and I made love hoping for a baby. Afterward, we laid in the dark and threw baby names back and forth at each other, laughing.

"I can't," Devyn says, jerking me from the past to a future I want but don't know if I'll be able to keep. "But you can ask me to come back."

I didn't consider a compromise. When I've thought about her, it's always been all or nothing. She'd stay or she'd leave. I never thought about asking her to move to Old Harbor once she's done with what she needs to do, and I never thought I could leave Old Harbor and go with her. "Would you?"

Holding my hand, she sits on the bed, and she lays back, her thighs slightly spread. I follow, covering her body with mine. Her legs cradle my hips, and she brushes some of my hair off my forehead. "Do you want to date?" she asks, a smile playing with her mouth. "Take me to the movies? Buy me popcorn?"

I skim my fingertips along her seam until I find what I'm looking for. I slip two fingers inside her, and she sucks in a breath, arching her back. She's hot and wet, and so tight. My cock surges and I don't make him wait.

She moans, and it's the sexiest fucking thing I've ever heard. I glide into her with one, smooth stroke and cover her mouth with mine, pushing my tongue between her teeth the way I'm sinking my cock inside her until I can't move another centimeter.

"I want the movies." I begin to rock, lacing her fingers with mine, my other hand under her ass. "I want popcorn. I want conversations in front of a fire on a cold winter's night and walks along the lake. I want to learn something new about you every day. Yes, I want to date you."

What I want doesn't sound like dating. It sounds like a helluva lot more than that.

She licks at my mouth, and I forget about talking.

Her nails scratch my back, and I pant, trying to hold off. "Devyn, you're not with me."

"It's okay," she whispers.

It's not, but it's going to have to be. Over two years of abstinence have taken their toll and her lush body is all the invitation I need.

Pumping viciously, I come, my face pressed into the curve of her neck as I ride out my climax. She hugs me, her legs tangled with mine, her fingers grabbing at my hair.

My body aches from the strain.

Sex is a lot of work.

Needing to rest, I gently settle on top of her and breathe deeply, willing my body to relax. I'm going to be stiff tomorrow, but having this beautiful woman under me is worth it.

"Why did you let me do that?"

Laughing, she says, "You're not off the hook. You can still help me out." She wiggles away from me, and my dick slips out of her. I already miss how she feels, and I'm already looking forward to having her again.

I roll onto my side and skim my fingers down her belly. She's thin but not overly so. Not like Renata who counted calories within an inch of their lives. Her pubic hair is neatly trimmed and blonde, like the rest of her. "Like this?" I ask, my lips near hers.

"Yeah." She closes her eyes in anticipation and arches her hips, encouraging my fingers.

I find her clit and suck one of her nipples into my mouth. This time, lightly, I nibble. It wouldn't be difficult to become obsessed with her breasts. They're as beautiful as she is, and I love how she trembles as I tug and suck.

She widens her legs and moves under my hand. I shove two fingers inside her and press my thumb to her clit. "Faster," she whispers.

"Open your eyes and look at me," I tell her, pushing three fingers inside her, filling her. I'm getting hard, but I won't take her again until she comes. I'm only selfish in the conference room.

Her eyes blink open, a hazy green. "Rick," she breathes, "kiss me."

I do. Anything she asks of me, I would have to do. There's nothing I would deny her.

She comes under my hand the second our lips meet, and wrapping her arms around my neck, she cries against my mouth. She trembles as the orgasm rolls through her. Her muscles hug my fingers, and I twist them, hoping to make it as good for her as it was for me.

She quiets, almost to the point I think she could fall asleep, but that doesn't stop me from wanting her again. "Can I?" I ask, nudging my cock against her hip. "I want you, Devyn."

"Then you're going to have to throw in a box of Milk Duds," she says, rolling on top of me and positioning herself over my cock.

With my hands to her ass, I guide myself inside her. "If you need *anything*, all you have to do is ask. I mean it. Anything."

Rubbing my nose with hers, she says, "Just you. Right now. That's all I need."

She didn't mean it the way I took it, but I'm deathly afraid she told me the truth.

———

Lazily, she kisses my chest, dragging her lips over my skin. I'm propped up in bed, playing with her hair, hoping she'll let me nap, but her eyes are bright and her hands are all over me. She's not sleepy, and if I know females like I think I do, she wants to talk.

"Out with it then," I say, tugging on the ends of her hair.

She sits up and covers her breasts with the sheet.

"If this is going to be a serious talk, you could at least let me have the view," I grouse, hoping to get her to laugh. I don't want our last hours together to be somber.

It earns me a smile, but she doesn't let the sheet drop. "Why did your wife leave you?"

It's not the question I expected, but it's bad enough. "I think that's obvious."

"Is that truly why? Because of how you look after the accident?"

Her question makes me mad. It brings up things I'd rather forget. "How the hell am I supposed to know? I had a few surgeries. My arm, leg and hip, and patches of my skin. They didn't do it all at once, and I was in and out of consciousness for weeks. The anesthesia made me sick and fogged my brain, and I was on a lot of pain medication. She waited until I was barely with it enough to have a conversation, and she dropped her wedding ring on the bed. She said she loved me, but she needed more than what I was going to be able to give her. Maybe she thought I wouldn't recover, or a doctor told her I'd always live with pain. We were trying for a baby, and maybe she thought I wouldn't be a good father anymore. She never said." My voice fades along with my annoyance that Devyn asked the stupid fucking question in the first place. I don't see her bedroom, only the hospital blanket and the ring glittering in the sun shining through the window. I was in too much pain to pick it up. After she left, a nurse came in to check on me, and I had to ask her to put it in the hospital's safe.

It's still there.

I never claimed it.

"You wanted kids."

It's not a question, more of a sad statement. It's difficult for me to think of it, too. If Renata had gotten pregnant, our baby would be a year old.

"Yeah, we did." I grip her chin and say, "I didn't use anything."

She raises a shoulder, exposing the top of one of her breasts, and lifts a corner of her mouth along with it. "I know. I have an IUD. Some months my cramps are really painful, and it helps. I don't use it for birth control, but in this case, it's a perk. I would've told you if I wasn't on anything. Besides, I don't have room in my life for kids. Until Talia's on her feet, I don't want children."

So if you want them soon, find a woman who does.

She doesn't have to say the words for me to hear them. I shrug. I haven't thought about kids, about having a family, since Renata left me. "Maybe she's right and it's better if I don't have anyone depending on me."

"If you talked to her, maybe you'd get back together. You didn't turn out as bad as she thought you would."

I scowl. "You don't know that."

"You don't either. Has she seen for herself how well you've recovered? When was the last time you saw her?"

"In mediation. The woman who divorced me isn't the woman I married, Devyn. I don't want to say the money changed her because it's not true—she wasn't like that. She enjoyed the parties and the clothes. She liked redecorating the penthouse every year. She liked the lifestyle, but I think if my company hadn't taken off, she still would have been happy. She's not a bad person."

"No, she only left a man who loved her high and dry. Do you still?"

I lose the question in the anger flashing in her eyes. Devyn fights for what she believes in, will stand by the people who mean something to her. That's integrity, that's honor. That's why she's a good reporter. That's why she's a good sister. When she marries, it will be for life. No matter what. "Do I still what?"

"Love her."

"I wouldn't be with you if I did." I pause and let my fingers skim along her arm. "I lied, you know."

She leans into me. "About what?"

"It wasn't just anybody. I know in the end it's not going to work out, but that doesn't mean I don't wish it would. It would've been nice to have more time, that's all. Come here."

She snuggles between my legs and rests her head on my chest, and I wrap my arms around her. Tomorrow, she'll be free to go. I'll have to watch her drive away knowing she won't come back.

She'll have good intentions, promise to visit if a free moment pops up or when she and Talia are on their way out of town, but she wouldn't let me support them while she looked for something different and she's too driven not to want to work.

"I talked to Newsom this morning," I say, brushing my knuckles back and forth along her spine.

"What for? Did you tell him I was bothering you?"

"Not exactly. I asked him about Stevie and Sweet, and he

told me how that played out. He said he tried to keep you on, if that means anything."

"About as much as Walt saying he's trying. It all comes down to fear and money, but then, I can't blame them. Why make an enemy if you don't have to? If I never see Stevie again it will be too soon. I just want to forget she breathes the same air I do and get on with my life. She's taken so much from my family, all for money and power. Talia will always have that noose around her neck, and we've lost our mother." Her hair tickles my chest as she speaks, and when she looks up at me, her nose grazes my jaw. "Don't waste your life hiding here, Rick. You can do more than this."

"I don't want anything more than what I have."

"Why? Don't you want to know what caused the accident?"

"I know what caused the accident. It rained the day before, and the crane was parked on shaky ground. I should have postponed the lift and waited for it to dry out. I was in a hurry because we were behind, and good men lost their lives that day. OSHA investigated, and they cleared me. I couldn't have known the earth was going to move, literally, under my feet. Haven't you watched the footage?"

She sits up. "They filmed it?"

"Sure. A big lift like that, it was a major piece of the building. That night, we had plans to go out and celebrate. The crew was looking forward to having a few beers. It was a big deal, and the OSHA rep recorded it on his phone. After the accident, more clips popped up online—people who stopped to watch but started filming when they realized something bad was going down. It was all over social media, just Google it."

"Have you watched it?" she asks, rolling off the bed.

"I don't want to watch it. I lived it. Where are you going?"

"I have to go to the bathroom, and I need coffee. Why?"

She gives me an impish smile and tugs on her pajamas. She knows I wanted to spend the afternoon in bed.

"I'm not done with you yet."

"I'll come back. I promise."

She dashes out of the room, and I miss her already.

Fuck. After she leaves, I'm going to have to do something or missing her will eat me alive.

Reluctantly, I yank on my own clothes and follow.

In the kitchen, I trap her in my arms and breathe her in, memorizing this moment, her hands under my t-shirt, her lips roaming along my neck. I sear these precious seconds into my brain. Winter has just begun, and they'll be the only things that will keep me warm.

CHAPTER NINE

Devyn

I wait until he's sleeping to watch the clip.

He's insatiable, and we've made love twice more since he generously gave me ten minutes to grab a snack and a cup of coffee. He said the coffee is okay—the caffeine will keep my energy up. He has a sense of humor under the gruff, and I think he likes to make me laugh.

Making love wore him out, and he's dead to the world now, lying in his bed, the comforter pulled up over his chest. His bedroom's closer to the kitchen, he said, and I couldn't argue with that. He didn't bother to put his clothes back on either, before falling into a heavy sleep, his kiss still warm on my lips.

Quickly, I yank on my pajamas, run upstairs, grab my laptop and earbuds, and settle back onto his bed to watch. Listening to him talk about the time he spent in the hospital chilled me to the bone, his wife abandoning him when he needed her most. I don't want him to wake up and not find me here.

I'm falling in love, and it scares me. I don't want to leave tomorrow any more than he wants me to go, but I have responsibilities that won't disappear hiding in Old Harbor. He denies it, but I think once he's done licking his wounds, Old Harbor won't be enough for him, either. It will be natural for him to move back to Cedar Hill, but I can't live in the city and Talia can't be around Sweet. That's not to say Portland doesn't have its own share of drug problems, but kids smoking pot in their parents' basements is far from having Sweet available on every street corner. The temptation is too much, and it's best to keep her away from it and find a small town that still has everything we need.

I brush my fingers along his jaw, and in his sleep, Rick turns his head toward my touch.

The video's cued up and ready to go, and I push the earbuds into my ears and press Play. The information for the clip states it was posted by OSHA rep Fred McAllister who was on the site that day overseeing the lift. There are other clips from various angles, nosy people filming, hoping for their fifteen minutes of fame, but thankfully nothing that shows Rick and what happened after the crane's arm fell from the sky.

I've never seen a crane up close, and around the time of Rick's accident, I'd been desperately trying to keep my head down and out of the news while finding Talia and me a place to go as quickly as I could. I still heard about the accident, everyone had. No one could avoid it. When Renata Mercer filed for divorce four months after Rick almost lost his life, it was big news. I'd skimmed the articles over bites of breakfast thinking they were nothing but rich people problems and moved on, dealing with my own aftermath, settling Talia in school, and finding a niche at the *Pioneer*.

Construction workers stand in a thin layer of mud and watch the crane move a large piece of framework off the ground and into the air. It looks like part of the insides, curved metal beams welded together forming an enormous arch, too heavy for a crane to lift. It does though. The crane slowly moves the framework off the ground, and the workers clap and hoot.

It looks like everything will go smoothly until the truck starts to tip, just a little, and exactly like Rick described. The OSHA rep zooms in, and the crane's operator scrambles with the controls, the light bouncing off the glass partially blocking him from my view.

The truck begins to fall over, and there's nothing anyone can do. The men on the ground start to scramble out of the way, and the huge frame sways from side to side, hanging from a hook several feet off the ground. The truck gives in to the soft earth, and as if in slow motion, it tips over, and the—I open another tab and look up parts of the crane—boom, the long arm extending from the truck, crashes to the ground, the framework smashing into part of the building already in place.

Because of the angle, I can't see who's hurt or where, except for the crane operator. I found out later that he lost eight months of his life in a medically induced coma to treat a cerebral hemorrhage and brain swelling caused by his head slamming against the glass window of the operator's cab.

Rick had stayed too close trying to warn two ironworkers to get out of the way. It hadn't helped, and the frame killed them when the boom collapsed and the framework dropped.

The video ends, and I wipe my tears away. I'm glad whoever was filming hadn't filmed Rick too. I couldn't watch as emergency crews worked to free him.

There are other views, and most focus on the truck tipping, the wind whipping ahead of another storm. The truck slants, the boom sways, and the frame swings back and forth. I try to calculate when the operator should have stopped the lift, but there doesn't seem to be any indication until it's too late. The wheels sink in the mud and that might have been just enough with the wind to cause the accident. Rick's right about one thing—they should have waited until the next storm passed and the ground dried out. But . . .

I watch the video again.

Why did the crane tip in the opposite direction of the framework? I don't know how much it weighed, I would have to ask Rick, but it looks like it should have been more than enough to counteract the wet ground.

My reporter's mind searches for clues, but I don't know enough about construction sites, cranes, or weather conditions to argue with what Rick told me. OSHA investigated—hell, the rep was right there—and if they didn't find anything wrong, then it must have just been poor timing and poorer luck.

Still, I watch the video again. The crane operator should have known something was going on. He should have known something wasn't right, but he moved forward. He should have been able to feel when the balance shifted.

Shouldn't he have?

Or had he been so focused on the framework that nothing else mattered?

I sigh.

"That's why I don't watch it," Rick says from behind me. "All I'd do is beat myself up for not waiting until the ground dried out. I was stupid, and it cost people their lives. Let it go, Devyn."

"But have you seen what happens?" I insist, wiggling my earbuds out of my ears and frowning. "Something isn't right."

He sits up and closes my laptop with a sharp snap. "You know more than OSHA? You know more than my foreman? You know more than the crane operator? You're just a reporter pointing fingers at the wrong people, pissing them off until they run you out of town. Let. It. Go."

There's so much pain on his face that I don't want to keep arguing, but it doesn't excuse the crappy things he just said. I don't want to give him the power to hurt my feelings. People have said worse to me, and he's not wrong. I *am* a reporter, and it *is* my job to point fingers, but Stevie Johansson isn't the wrong person. She's into Sweet up to her eyeballs, only it's not up to me to prove it anymore. She forced me out, and I'm never going back.

"Okay," I say, scooting off the bed and snagging my laptop along the way. "I need to call Talia and check in on her. She should be out of class by now."

"Fuck. Devyn, don't. I didn't mean it the way it sounded." He sits up, his eyes bleary with exhaustion.

"You might not have, but it doesn't change the fact that you're right. Snooping fucked up my life, and it fucked up Talia's. I can't take care of her the way I should be able to. She needs me, and I don't even have a fucking job. It's cool."

I slip out of his room, blinking back tears.

"Devyn," he calls after me, but I ignore him. Not to be petty or mean, but I need a few minutes.

I put my laptop in my room and layer my cardigan over my pajamas. I climb the steps to the top hoping Rick doesn't feel good enough to come after me. We'll have tonight and maybe a few hours in the morning, but the snow's lightening up and the plows won't wait until the weather's completely clear to start doing the roads. There's too much work to do.

While we were in bed, visibility improved, and I can see parts of the lake now, the angry pewter waves crashing against the brown, craggy rock. I walk around to see the entire view, and the metal floor chills the bottoms of my feet. I stop and look out over Old Harbor.

I didn't drive through town the day I drove from Portland, taking my chances and coming straight here.

I'm falling in love with Rick Mercer, but I think, knowing what I know now, I would rather have been snowed in at a hotel instead.

I'm not ready for this.

Sitting cross-legged on the floor facing Harbor Lake, I call Talia, and she answers the phone breathless and happy.

"Hey, how are you?" she asks.

"I'm all right, but not as good as you, it sounds like. What's up?"

"Oh, nothing. Walt called and invited me to dinner with him and Colleen, so I'll be doing that later. I'm drying some clothes and just finished vacuuming. I don't want you to come home to a mess. Homework later, and after dinner at Walt's, work asked me if I could close since the girl who was scheduled has the flu. I said sure, it's only two hours and it's nice they trust me to do that."

Talia works at a women's clothing store in the Portland Shopping Center, a tiny mall that has only a handful of stores. They work with her schedule and her mental health, and she likes her boss. She doesn't bring in much money, but it's a positive experience for her and that's what counts.

"That's great. Sounds like you have a full evening planned."

"Devyn, I know we haven't been close and I haven't lived with you long, but I know if you're sad. What's the matter?"

I pick at my cardigan. I have to tell her, but I don't want her to worry about what it means. "I'm in love with him."

She sighs. "I knew when I talked to you yesterday that it would happen. You want to stay there, don't you? I can figure something—"

"Don't you dare! If that's how you're going to think, I shouldn't have told you. That's *not* where I was going with it at all."

"It has to be because falling in love isn't something to be sad about. I'm happy for you."

"Yeah, don't be so quick. He knows a little bit about you and what happened. He knows a lot about why we had to move to Portland, and that when it's done snowing, I need to get back. He's hiding, but I don't think he's here to stay. He has a lot of unfinished business in Cedar Hill, and we can't live there."

"*You* said we can't live there, but if you're saying that because of me—"

"I'm not. I'm saying that because of me, and you know it. I can't get a job there, and Stevie won't leave me alone."

"Are you going to ask Rick for the interview? Does he feel the same way you feel about him? He'll give it to you now, won't he, if he knows that you need it to keep your job?"

I brighten, but then I let my shoulders fall. "He probably would, but I don't want to use him like that, and he's had it bad enough as it is. I'm not putting him through the attention it would drop on him. Anyway, the owners of the *Pioneer* would only give me another impossible assignment. It'd delay the inevitable, that's all."

"So, what if Rick takes care of his business in Cedar Hill, and then you two figure out where to live?"

"You mean us three."

She scoffs. "You're not going to want me as an extra. Especially after you two get married."

I laugh. "Who said anything about getting married? He said he wants to date me and go to the movies."

"All right, well, they say, movies, sex, marriage, babies. You're on the first step."

"Actually, we did the sex part already," I mumble, my cheeks heating.

Talia squeals, and I jerk the phone away from my ear. "How was it?"

"Truthfully?"

"No, I want you to lie about it. Of course I want the truth."

"He's a bit stiff—"

She giggles.

"Not like that. His accident hurt him pretty badly, and he's always going to have to be careful with how he moves."

"Meh. You're not adventurous anyway."

"You might have a point, but yeah, it was nice."

"Don't tell him that," she teases. "Now what? You aren't going to leave Old Harbor and not look back. You're in love with him. I'm not going to let you."

"It wouldn't be that easy even if I could. The snow's letting up, and I'll be able to get out of here before noon tomorrow. When I get back to town, I'll clean out my desk at the *Pioneer* and then I want to look into something." Rick can get mad at me all he wants, but there's something strange about that accident, and until I know the logical reason behind it, I'm not going to let it go.

"Ooh, I sense a mystery. I want in."

"Talia . . ."

"What? Let me help. What is it?"

I blow out a breath. "Okay. He doesn't want to hear any more about it, and we had a fight before I called you, but something isn't right. I was looking at a video clip of his accident. I never claimed to have a sixth sense, but I have decent intuition and I think I'm on to something now. When you have time, look at all the clips you can find of that accident. I watched a few from different angles, but Rick got annoyed and told me to let it go."

Talia laughs. "That's not the way to get you to leave things alone."

"You have to give him a break—he doesn't know me that well yet. Probably not tomorrow, but the next day, we need to drive to the city. I want to talk to a few people. Can you miss class?"

"I'll let my teachers know I'll be gone, and I'll make it up online. You think Rick's accident wasn't an accident?"

"I'm sure it was, but I don't know very much about cranes. I just have a couple of questions, then I'll forget about it like he asked."

"And then what?"

"What do you want me to do? Map out the rest of my life?" I say it like I'm joking, but her insistence is irritating. I don't know what I'm going to do after we come back from Cedar Hill. I don't know if Rick's still going to want to see me. I could make him so angry he doesn't want to talk to me ever again. If that doesn't happen and he does want to date, how are we going to do that?

"No, but my therapist is always telling me to have a plan. Life feels better with a plan."

She's not wrong. Life does feel better if you know what you're doing and have a backup in case things go to hell. I didn't have a backup when Stevie went after me or when Walt said he had to fire me. I'd put it off in the hope that something better would come along.

It did, in a way. I fell in love, but that, in all its forms, did not go according to any plan.

"Let me do a little digging. We can't decide anything until I find a job. It doesn't matter what kind of plan I have if I can't pay the bills."

"I understand, but it's love, Devyn."

"Yeah. It is. How do you feel about living in Old Harbor?"

Carefully, I walk down the stairs, and in my bedroom, I toss my cell on the bed. I peek into Rick's room to see if he's sleeping, but the bed is made and I follow the scent of coffee into the kitchen. He's sitting at the table, his eyes closed and his forehead pressed against his clasped hands. He looks like he's praying, but his shoulders are hunched and waves of sadness threaten to drown me.

"Are you okay?" I ask, stepping into the room. "Are you feeling okay?"

He snaps his head up. "I'm sorry, Devyn. I am so sorry. I didn't mean what I said earlier." He lowers his hands, and he looks so bleak, I can't help but sit next to him on the bench and wrap my arms around him. He's wearing the same clothes as before, and I breathe him in. He feels so solid, so safe. I'm going to miss him while I'm gone.

"I know you didn't, but you were right. I've found plenty of trouble. If you want me to forget about it, I will."

He covers my face with kisses, his whiskers scratching my skin, and I laugh. "I want to move on. Christ, you don't know how much I want to move on."

I think he wants to believe that, but how can he move on if he's hiding from everything he's lost? I have no problem moving to Old Harbor if I can find a job and if Talia can find a little slice of life she can call her own and we can be happy, but Rick has a lot of decisions to make and he never will if he thinks he has none.

"Okay. We can do that. What should we do for dinner?" I ask and brush a kiss over his mouth. I slide off the bench, stand, and head to the fridge. A hot meal and hot sex through the night sounds like a lovely way to put off thinking about tomorrow. It's going to wreck me to drive away, but I can't let him know it.

"There's a package of hamburger in there. If you can make something with that, I'll be yours for the rest of the night."

"Aren't you already?" I ask, quirking my mouth at him.

He comes up behind me and presses a kiss to the top of my head. "Thanks for not being mad."

I turn around and let him trap me against the fridge. "It's not my way to be mad or I'd be a shriveled up old shrew by now. But I think," I say, pushing my hands up his t-shirt, "that maybe some of the things you've been fighting with since you moved here will go away if you confront them. You don't know why your wife left you—" He opens his mouth to interrupt, but I speak over him— "not really. You haven't gone to your office in Cedar Hill since you moved to Old Harbor, right? What about your employees? What about your apartment? Is it still full of your things? When I moved to Portland, I left things behind too. My mother's on the streets. How can I help her? Should I write her off as a lost cause? I had friends in the city, people I stopped talking to who would've stuck by my side through the whole Stevie scandal. I hide and say it's better for Talia, and in some ways it is, but it's an excuse, too, to keep my head in the sand."

His eyes turn stormy, and I know he's at the end of his patience.

"I'll stop talking about it now. I promise. I was poking around your kitchen when I made soup and I think you have ingredients for spaghetti. How's that?"

He braces his arm against the fridge above my head and rests his hand on the back of my neck. He's frowning, and his scar twists his lips into an ugly grimace. I could be scared of him, but he won't hurt me. He's wounded, and he's used to people kicking him when he's down. A rich, powerful man, he could have let it turn him hard, merciless, ruthless, like Declan Everett, another rich and powerful man always in the news and always, it seems, one step behind Rick. Instead, he let it turn him into a vulnerable puddle and I love him all the more.

His voice is rough. "I hear what you're trying to say, but like I have to remind Beau, you need to let me do things at my own pace. I'm still healing. Mind, body, and spirit, as my massage therapist likes to say, and I need time, Devyn. You can't rush Talia through her recovery, and you can't rush me through mine."

"You're right. It's your life, and you need to live it how you need to live it." I dig the package of hamburger out of the fridge and face him again. "But no one said you had to *stay* there, did they?"

He scowls.

My eyes bright, I twist my fingers in front of my lips and throw away an invisible key.

"I need a drink," he mutters.

"And a pan," I add. "Can I have a drink too?"

He swallows, and instead of going for a pan or a drink, he cuddles me to him. We stand in his kitchen for I don't know how long and I'm near tears by the time he lets me go.

Together, we make dinner without speaking, sipping on a shared glass of Glenlivet.

We go to bed early, but we're too busy to sleep.

Rick

The beeping of the snowplow wakes me. It's too early, too soon. I didn't expect it until later today, and in denial, I cuddle Devyn closer. There isn't a millimeter of space between us, but that doesn't mean I don't try. She's warm and naked in my arms, our legs tangled under the blankets.

She's mine, for the next couple of hours.

Am I a selfish bastard for wanting this for the rest of my life?

"Hmmm," she mumbles against my arm, and I'm hard in an instant.

I nudge her onto her back and nestle my hips between her thighs. Her eyes blink open as I gently slide inside her, and she sucks in a breath, lifting her hips. I go slow—I know she's tender after a long night of making love. She let me have her over and over again. She knew I was trying to block out this day, what was coming, and I was rough with her.

Giving her all my weight, I nuzzle her neck, and she plays with my hair.

"Good morning," she says, her lips tickling my ear.

"It's morning, but it's not good. The snowplow's outside."

I ease out of her tight body and gently slide back in, taking my time, letting it build. I bet the plows have been at it most of the night, and there's no reason for her to wait. She'll be gone before lunchtime.

Reaching between our bodies, I rub her clit and help her come with me. She squeezes my cock as she orgasms, mewling into my ear. It pushes me over the edge, and I come too. It's incredible I have anything left to shoot inside her, but I fill her again, my small claim of her body that won't last nearly as long as I want it to.

She indulges my mood and holds me, slicking her fingers up and down my sweaty back.

"I don't know why you're acting like you'll never see me again," she says, kissing my cheek and down my jaw to my neck. "Or is that what you want? Are you trying to figure out how to say goodbye? You don't have to worry about hurting my feelings, Rick. You didn't want me here."

I lift up onto my forearms and smooth the hair away from her face. I can see her clearly, though the small window cut into the side of the lighthouse isn't giving us any light. It's early enough that it's still dark outside. It's the weak glow from the kitchen stove that lets me devour the delicate curves of her face.

The thought of telling her goodbye for only a few days threatens to break me. I can't imagine if later, in a few hours, I'd be telling her goodbye for good. I can't think of it.

"I've known you for four days." I stop and clear my throat. "It wouldn't be fair to ask you for the rest of them."

She kisses me, slow and gentle, brushing her fingers over

my face, her fingertips catching my scar. "Then it's a good thing I know life isn't fair. Rick, things are going to be okay."

I don't know how she can say that unless she knows something I don't. She's leaving, and as soon as she leaves our happy bubble, she'll forget about me.

"Let's get up. If the roads are clear, I need to get going."

Reluctantly, I let her go and slide out of her in a warm gush. I sit on the edge of the bed, not knowing what to do first. I go through the steps of my morning routine. Put on some clothes, make coffee. But I can't move.

Devyn leans into me and presses her forehead to my temple. "It's going to be okay," she repeats.

"I was barely hanging on when you turned into my driveway. What am I supposed to do after you leave?" I'm bitter. I found something in her arms, and she's going to yank it away.

"What you should have been doing," she says, but I don't know what that means.

She bounces out of bed and a few moments later the water in the shower turns on. With my feet dragging, I get dressed and fill the coffeemaker with grounds and water. She'll be puttering around, packing, getting ready for the drive, and I don't want to be here while she does that.

I layer up, go outside, and assess the damage of seventy-two hours of heavy snow.

The sky's lightening, the clouds finally gone, and the stars glitter against a hazy purple and pink.

The snowplow operators know where I like them to push the snow, and luckily, with the plow's bright lights, he saw Devyn's car and didn't block her in. In fact, he cleared behind it and on both sides, giving her all the space she needs to turn around and head for the road. I suppose it would have been too much to ask that he'd pushed her car off the cliff and into the lake. Knowing Devyn, that wouldn't keep her here.

I go back into the lighthouse's entryway and search Devyn's coat pockets for her keys. My truck's parked in the garage attached to the cottage, and I get my ice scraper and clean off her car. When I can open the driver's side door, I start it, and the engine turns over and settles into a smooth purr. She doesn't have much gas, and she'll need to fill up before heading out of Old Harbor, but she'll appreciate sitting in a warm car on her way to town.

I do a bit more shoveling, as much as my back can tolerate. I'll have plenty to keep me busy in the next few days. My doctor's appointments, running to town for groceries. Laundry. It'll be nice to have the lighthouse to myself again. I've missed the seclusion.

Yeah, sure I have.

She finds me staring over the lake, the surface calm after the blizzard. The rocks are covered in snow, and the rising sun shimmers off the white. It's beautiful, and I wouldn't trade it to go back to the city. I may have unfinished business there, but there's nothing left that would make me stay.

"Thank you for starting my car. Did she give you any trouble?"

"No. It didn't get that cold."

She shuffles beside me, her winter jacket brushing against mine. I look at her out of the corners of my eyes, and she's dressed how she was the night I met her: hat over her hair, winter coat, mittens, and winter boots. She's an adorable snow bunny, and she's going to dart off any second.

I want to tell her that I love her, but she wouldn't believe that after four days and the conversations we've had about Renata. I'm not sure I believe it myself. I've never fallen in love so quickly. With Renata, it was slow. Months of seeing her around Cedar Hill, the same parties and fundraisers I was expected to go to. We had a long courtship until one day I knew

I wanted to marry her. This thing with Devyn, it hit me out of nowhere, and I'm trying to turn it in my hands and study it, but I can't. It's a feeling, an apprehension, an anticipation, and trying to hold it is like grabbing at air.

"You'll text me when you make it back to Portland?" I ask, kicking at some snow.

She looks a little surprised I asked, but she says, "Sure. I should drive in sometime early this afternoon."

"Don't push it if the roads are slippery."

"I won't. I better go. Talia's waiting for me."

I pull off my mitten and graze her cheek with my fingers. "It was good, yeah?"

She tugs my hand, walking backward to her car. Her suitcase is already in the back seat. Lifting up on her toes she whispers in my ear, "You're worrying about the wrong things. I'll text you when I make it back, and I'll call you tonight." She kisses my cheek, her eyes bright and a smile on her mouth. It isn't hurting her to leave.

With a wave, she climbs into her car and slams the door shut. She doesn't give me a chance to say anything else, as if she didn't want to hear the hopeless "I love you" that threatened to tumble out of my mouth in a desperate attempt to get her to stay.

I watch as she backs around and heads toward the road, and I stand there in the cold and the snow at a loss long after her car is gone.

Shake it off.

I have plenty to keep me occupied until I can forget about her.

Carefully, I finish shoveling around the garage and the

cottage. The snow drifted, and it takes me a long time to clear a path from the lighthouse to my office.

Inside, the silence hits me. No, not the silence. Devyn wasn't loud, quiet as a church mouse scampering along, even when she came, she would with barely an audible moan. No, it's the emptiness that used to be a comfort after the long months in the hospital, a nurse in my face every five seconds, and then after that, when I met with my attorneys to give Renata what she'd be happy with in the divorce. We had a prenup, but I earned the bulk of my wealth during our marriage and she sued me for more. I didn't argue. It's only money, and I gave her most of what she wanted. We signed on the dotted line, and by then, I was heartsick and tired of people. My body was still battered and bruised, worse than I am right now, and being left alone was a blessing I'd needed at the time.

Devyn helped herself to the coffee, and the mug has a smear of her light pink lipstick on the rim. The glass we sipped Glenlivet out of while we made spaghetti last night is still on the counter. I've never cooked with a woman before.

I straighten the kitchen, putting her mug and our glass in the dishwasher. I pour my own mug of coffee and use the rest of the milk. I'll run into town later today, and I'll check on Pete and ask if he or his family need anything.

I check the guest room, and Devyn's things are gone. I didn't expect her to leave anything behind, but it still hits me that the room looks the same as it did before she drove up hoping for an interview. I strip her bed, and mine too, and shove the sheets and pillowcases into the washing machine I installed inside the cottage. There wasn't a practical place to add a washer and dryer set in the lighthouse, but I didn't want to drive into Old Harbor every time I needed to do a load of jeans. It's still inconvenient in the winter, but it's better than using the public laundromat in town.

I linger in my office for the twenty minutes the wash cycle needs to finish, and I think back to what Devyn said about her bills. I can't buy her. She never asked me for help, and I didn't want to offend her by offering. Living off the divorce settlement, Renata doesn't have to work a day in her life if she doesn't want to, but even if Devyn had all the money my ex-wife does, I think she'd still need something to do, a reason that would get her out of bed in the morning besides wanting a cup of coffee. I'm not comparing the two women, except that they *are* different and what makes Renata happy wouldn't necessarily make Devyn happy. I never minded that Renata didn't want to work, and I don't care that Devyn does.

It doesn't change the fact that Devyn's in a tight spot, and it'd be an easy thing to pay off Talia's rehab bill. I call my attorney and ask him to do the digging. I assume her sister shares her last name, but I could be off base. It could be she and Talia have different fathers. I didn't ask her that either, and it could explain why there's an age gap between them. I'll let my attorney figure it out. That done, I email Beau and tell him I need another day or so to get back up and running. That killed the time I needed to waste, and I put the sheets in the dryer and use extra fabric softener to get rid of Devyn's scent.

I want to do more, and I sit down at my desk and open an empty Word document. I make up nine questions I think Devyn would have asked me in an interview, given the chance. She never pressed, even after we became lovers, even after I would have said yes to help her keep her job at the *Pioneer*. I answer them and search for her work email address on the *Pioneer*'s website.

I wait for the interview to pop up, to cause a stir on social media. Devyn Scott, the one and only reporter to get an interview with Rickard Mercer after the horrific accident that crushed the right side of his body and turned him into a beast.

It doesn't.
But something else does.

CHAPTER ELEVEN

Devyn

Brushing tears off my cheeks, I drive away from the lighthouse. It was so hard to pretend leaving wasn't a big deal. He never asked when he'd see me again, never asked me to come back, never offered to drive to Portland to see me. Damn him for thinking these past few days didn't mean as much to me as they did to him.

Before I turn onto the highway that goes into town, I text Talia and tell her I have a few things I want to do before hitting the road. She's at school arranging her absence for the next few days, though I don't know how much time I'll need. A day to be proven wrong. Weeks, maybe, if my suspicions are accurate.

I'm not familiar with Old Harbor, though I know it's quite a bit bigger than Portland. Rick's lighthouse is fifteen minutes out of town, and I crawl along the slippery road hoping I don't slide into the ditch, my tires searching for traction against the ice. I stop at the first gas station I see and choose to pay inside.

I fill up my tank, shivering, and gratefully push into the convenience store to pay.

"Morning," an older man says, looking up from a newspaper spread out on the counter. "Just gas?"

"I'll grab a coffee too, and I have a couple of questions if you have a second."

He laughs, and his eyes dart around the empty store. "I think I might."

I fill a Styrofoam cup with hazelnut-flavored coffee, add a good amount of cream, and press a plastic lid over the top. I walk to the counter, my boots squeaking over the tile. "Can you recommend a close realtor? And the name of the newspaper here is the *Harbor Herald*, right?"

He runs my card and the receipt prints, the ancient machine grinding and spitting out a narrow strip of paper. Nudging a thick stack of today's paper lying next to a dish of pennies, he says, "Take one, free of charge. There's a Century 21 down the street a couple blocks to the south. You thinking about moving here? Need a job? I could use a dependable night manager."

I grin my thanks and slide the paper off the counter. "I might be moving here, but during the blizzard I was snowed in with Rick Mercer."

He chuckles. "Pretty thing like you won't need a job then. Nice guy."

"He is. A little sad."

Two teenagers stomp inside, laughing, and the old man looks their way. Shaking his head, he says, "Let that be a lesson to ya. Doesn't matter how much money you have if you can't be happy."

"I'll do my best to turn him around. Thanks."

"Have a good day."

"Thanks, you too."

I drive to the *Herald*'s offices and ask the receptionist if I can talk to the editor-in-chief. Luckily, he's not in a meeting and I introduce myself to the serious man wearing a dress shirt, his sleeves already rolled up to his elbows and his tie loose around his neck. He knows who I am, and unsurprisingly, he's heard about my fiasco with Stevie Johansson. I explain that in the next few weeks I'll be moving to Old Harbor and if he'd be willing to take a chance, I could really use a job.

Barney Rubens studies me with interest. "That blew up in your face, didn't it?" He leans against his desk, takes his glasses off, and catches the earpiece between his teeth.

Sucking in a breath, I prepare to tell him something I didn't tell Walt when I applied at the *Pioneer*. I don't know which company owns this paper, but maybe one day I can redeem myself and what happened won't be such a stain on my résumé. Then it won't matter who owns what. "Mr. Rubens—"

"Barney."

"Barney. I was on to something. After a year of digging, I knew it, but Cedar Hill's a cesspool, and they all watch each other's backs. Bill Newsom's a decent guy—he fired me because he had to. I get it. Everyone loves Stevie and no one wants to think badly of her. But, if she's innocent, I just don't think she would've hit me so hard. I hadn't announced anything publicly, and it's not like I was writing articles full of accusations for a gossip site. I was investigating on my own time, and she heard about it. She stopped me before I could find evidence of the truth."

"And what truth is that?" Barney asks, a curious gleam in his eye.

"That she runs Sweet out of her warehouses and she uses her stores to launder the money she earns distributing it. She's dirty. I just didn't have time to prove it. I left the city for other reasons than just her, but she was a big part of it."

"You're taking a chance that *I'm* not in her pocket," he says, scowling. "For a reporter, you're too trusting. She owns Minnesota, Devyn, and North Dakota, South Dakota, Iowa, Illinois, Wisconsin, and Indiana. She's looking to branch out into Nebraska, Wyoming, Montana, maybe more. We have Sweet on the streets here, and, coincidentally, we also have one of her candy stores. After you were chased out of Cedar Hill, I started looking into it. You were on to something big, I agree, and if she falls, she's going to drag a lot of people down with her."

I wilt in relief. "Then you believe me."

He nods. "I believe you. I saw it for myself when my niece went into her store for candy and came out hooked on Sweet."

I pause for a moment to give his niece the respect she deserves. "I'm sorry. My sister was addicted. She spent a lot of time in rehab. They were able to get her off it, if you want the name of the facility."

"Where did your sister pick it up?"

Shrugging, I say, "At a party, but she doesn't talk to me about it much."

"You let me know if she did the same as my niece. Went in for those dipping sticks— Devyn. If she's doing what I think she's doing, she's creating her own addicts from candy she sells in her stores."

My mouth drops open, and I sag in my chair. "Of course. Why didn't I think of that?"

"You were thinking bigger, and in Cedar Hill, that was the right thing to do. In Old Harbor, I was looking a little closer to home. She can't drug all her customers—that would make it too easy to pin her down. But I think one out of every three, four hundred customers, eventually she'll get everybody who wants a sugar fix now and then. All it takes is a taste."

I wince. I know how true that is.

"What are your plans?" he asks.

"I was snowed in with Rick Mercer during the blizzard. The *Portland Pioneer* sent me up here to get an interview, and he was kind enough to let me stay."

Barney grunts. "He doesn't talk to anybody. I'm surprised he didn't throw you out on your ass."

"It was close, but by then it had already started snowing."

"Did you get your interview?"

I quirk the corner of my mouth. Our relationship turned into so much more, I forgot about asking. "No. I fell in love and I wouldn't have printed it even if he would've talked to me."

"I like it. But what are you telling me for?" he says, turning his hand that's still holding his glasses in a circle, urging me to continue.

"Because when I go back to Portland, I'll go back empty-handed and I won't have a job. My sister will have to transfer—she's taking classes at Portland's community college—but before we do that, I'm going back to Cedar Hill. Rick told me about the accident, and my reporter's nose started twitching. I want to ask a few questions before we move here."

He lifts an eyebrow. "You're relocating for Mercer?"

Poking my tongue into my cheek, I say, "Well, it's difficult to get married when you live in one town and he lives in another."

Barney laughs, his teeth gleaming against his dark skin. "I suppose it would be. What time frame are we looking at? January?"

I have enough savings to last me until then, but it'd be great if I didn't have to rely on it. "I can spoon feed you stories remotely for a couple of weeks. I've got a bunch of 'Life in Minnesota' articles that would be okay for your Lifestyles section. Otherwise, while I'm looking into Rick's accident, I'll keep my ear to the ground and write some gossipy Cedar Hill stuff. Filler."

He sinks into the chair behind his desk. "Okay. I'll put you on the payroll starting tomorrow. Email me your CV—I need it for HR. I'll hire you on salary. Less than what you were making at the *Times,* but more than what they're paying you at the *Pioneer,* I bet. The second you get a chance, send me what you have. I'll have my Lifestyles and Entertainment editors take a look." He pauses. "My Lifestyles editor is going on maternity leave in February. She isn't coming back. What would you think of that?"

"Would I still be able to work on my own things?"

"Devyn, I didn't just hire you to sit around and proofread someone else's articles. Get yourself situated, and then I'm going to need your help getting Sweet off my streets."

I stick out my hand. "You've got a deal."

———

Buzzing with relief and excitement, I step into Century 21's offices and introduce myself to a realtor who said she'd be more than happy to help Talia and me find a place to live.

Our living situation is tricky right now. Love is strange. I can love Rick, want to be with him so desperately that I'm willing to settle my sister into a new college and find a new job for myself, yet, I barely know anything about him.

We'll need to date—I'm holding him to those Milk Duds— and once we know for sure this is going to work, decide what we'll do. He likes the lighthouse, but it'd be too small for the three of us. I know Talia could live on her own, but I don't want her to if she doesn't have to. Building a house that has an apartment attached would be the best of both worlds, but that will be something I'll need to talk to Rick about . . . if he's not so spitting mad he doesn't want anything more to do with me.

He told me to leave this alone, but I can't.

It's the way I am, and he's going to have to love that part of me if he's going to love me at all.

I slide the woman's card into my wallet and promise to call when I'm ready.

I text Talia and let her know that I'm on the way home.

My coffee's cold, but the progress I made was worth it.

The roads are clear, and with each mile I drive farther away from Old Harbor, my heart feels heavier and heavier. I miss him like crazy. The tender way he'd hold me, or the way he'd slowly push inside me. He went at me hard last night, trying to show me what he couldn't say.

Rick won't chase me, and that's okay. I understand. Maybe he would have if his ex-wife wouldn't have left him the way she did, but the damage is done. He doesn't think she hurt him, but I think she hurt him more than the crane's boom did when it fell and crushed him into the ground. I'll have to prove that I'm in it for good, but it's not like I haven't had to prove myself in other ways.

When I'm close to the Portland city limits, I call Rick, wanting to hear his voice. His cell rings and rings, and after it goes to voicemail, I hang up. I don't know what I'd say in a message. I text him instead, using voice-to-text to let him know I made it safely and to have a nice night. If he's already starting to pull away from me because he thinks this isn't going to work, we're going to have a problem. I'm rearranging my life to be with him. The least he can do is be on board.

We should have said the words.

He wanted to.

I wanted to.

It would have made this easier.

And a lot harder.

I drive straight to the *Pioneer*'s offices.

The parking lot's almost empty, but I know what Walt drives and he's still here. I have to stop and use the bathroom first, instead of doing what I really want to do—waltzing into his office, saying what's on my mind, and swiping everything off my desk in a fit of anger—but now I have time to think about what I want to say. I'm not going to shove my job at the *Herald* in his face or point out that Barney cares more about taking risks and printing the truth than he ever has. He took a chance and gave me a job for the past two years. If he hadn't done that, Barney might not have been so quick to take me on.

"Hey," he says, turning away from his computer monitor. "How'd it go? Did you get it?"

"Nope. He didn't talk to me." That much is true. He didn't give me the interview. "I'm quitting before you can fire me. I'll work something else out."

Walt sighs and rubs his eyes. "I'm sorry, Devyn. I didn't want it to be like this."

"I understand. I've worked with plenty of dirty people, and your bosses will just be added to the list. No hard feelings. I appreciate all you did for Talia and me. You didn't have to do the things you did for us, on a personal level, and it means a lot to me." My thanks are sincere, and Walt can hear it.

He nods. "I'm sorry I couldn't do more."

"You fought to hire me, and I hope I proved it was worth it." I shift on my feet. There's no point in dragging this out. "I'll clean out my desk."

"Check your email and wrap up your business," Walt says. "You won't have access to anything come tomorrow."

"Thanks for the reminder. Take care of yourself."

"You too, Devyn. You're a helluva reporter."

"Thanks."

I sit at my desk, but I don't have any attachment to it. I liked some of the people I worked with, but they'd all stayed somewhat aloof, as if they were afraid to get too close to me. Walt would say they were intimidated, but I don't think like that. Passion to tell the truth drives me, and if I'm a better reporter than others because of it, then I am. I care about making the world a better place, but that's nothing to brag about. Everyone should feel that way.

I've been offline for a few days and my inbox is full of article leads, answers to requests for interviews, City Hall meeting times, and activities schedules. There's also something from Rick, and my hand trembles against the mouse as I open the email. I read what he did and my eyes fill with tears.

He sent me an interview.

God.

He never said the words, but he does love me.

As much as I love him, or he never would have sacrificed his privacy.

Quickly, I skim his answers, but I don't want to learn anything about him from a fake interview. I want him to tell me while we're taking walks, lying on the couch, cuddling in bed after we've made love. I want to hear it all, but from his lips fluttering against my ear.

I delete it.

Then I go into the trash and delete that too.

I restart my computer and refresh my inbox just to make sure it's gone.

There are some things I print, and I empty my desk drawers. Everything I told Barney I had that's up for grabs is on my personal laptop. I don't want Walt accusing me of giving the *Herald* articles I've written on the *Pioneer*'s time.

Once my computer is wiped clean, papers are shredded, and the generic information like City Hall meeting times are all that's left for the next reporter who will sit at this desk, I put the few knickknacks I had sitting next to my computer in a small cardboard box.

This isn't as bad as when I left the *Times*. Then, I was scared and humiliated. I truly believed I would work there for the rest of my life, and I mourned. I thought I was on my way to the top, and I was devastated when Bill fired me.

Now, I walk out the *Pioneer*'s front doors without looking back. I have better things to look forward to.

The drive from the paper's offices is quick, and ten minutes later I step into the little house I managed to find us to rent. With a job that barely paid anything and Talia's rehab bill, every bank I applied to for a mortgage turned me down. Renting was a better option for us anyway, and all I have to do is email the property manager and give him the two months' notice required to leave. The house has been fine, and the man in charge of maintenance is always prompt and friendly. Compared to the apartment I lived in, the tiny house with its small patch of grass was an upgrade.

I wouldn't mind another yard, but nothing will compare to Rick's lakeside view.

Kicking the snow off my boots, I wrestle with my suitcase and keys and open the side door. I hang my jacket in the closet and leave my wet boots on the mat.

Talia's packing in her bedroom and chirps, "Hi." She drops a handful of panties into the half-full suitcase lying on the bed. "How was the drive back?"

I was worried about asking her to go to Cedar Hill with me. There are so many bad memories attached to that city for both of us, but she looks excited to see something other than the four boring walls of Portland.

Leaning against her dresser, I tell her I already found a new job and that I'd gotten in touch with a real estate agent who's going to help us find something in Old Harbor. "You really don't mind moving?"

"I really don't. It's a nice place?"

"It's beautiful." What I saw of it.

"Then I'm sure I'll love it. A dress, do you think?" she asks, holding a little black dress above her suitcase.

"Sure. We might as well go out and celebrate."

"Cool." She drops it on the pile and flicks a glance at me. "You don't have much to say about Rick."

"I texted him that I made it back to town, but he didn't answer. He's got this strange idea that I left for good."

Talia lifts her eyebrows. "You didn't tell him you were coming back?"

"Not in so many words. I'm waiting to see how mad he's going to be at me for poking my nose into his business."

"Your stubbornness takes a little getting used to. You're like a dog with a bone when you know something isn't right."

"Yeah, well, sometimes that's paid off, and sometimes it hasn't. I'm hoping to get on the road by eight. It'd be nice to have half the day to start."

"You mean go to bed at a decent hour."

I laugh. "Yes, that's what I mean."

I try not to act like her mother, giving her space to be herself and stay sober in the way she needs, but we both learned through therapy that Talia is most comfortable with rules and a schedule, which is why I'm nervous about leaving. I should have given Walt more thanks than I did for checking on her. While I was working for him, he hadn't turned into a friend, but he did more than a boss needed to and I should have let him know how much I appreciated it.

Talia decides to soak in the tub and read before lights out, and I take my laptop and a legal pad to bed with me. I start a list of the things I know about Rick's accident. It's not very much, and I watch the clip again. The way the crane tips over gnaws at me.

Rick still hasn't answered my text, and he doesn't have his read receipts turned on. All I know is that my message from earlier was delivered.

I ask him a question, hoping to get him to answer me. *Where in Old Harbor will we live? Talia and I should have our own place for a bit, don't you think?*

We'll see what he thinks about that. We have plenty of time to decide. Talia needs to finish out the semester and it doesn't end until Christmas break.

That reminds me to open my file of unpublished articles, and I send Barney what I have. I've written quite a few pieces about northern Minnesota living, dealing with the cold, safety precautions, things like that. I participated in a snowshoeing class last winter and took pictures with my phone, thinking the *Pioneer* could use the piece at some point, but Walt never expressed an interest in what he thought was a boring activity. The *Herald*'s probably printed articles about those particular topics several times before, but a new writer offers a new slant and he might find something useful, even just for the digital edition.

I have a difficult time falling asleep, and I toss and turn all night. Talia crawls in bed next to me and links her fingers with mine. She knows I'm nervous, but it doesn't help.

The next morning, I wake up with a ball of tension in my chest that a cup of coffee and a hot shower doesn't help. I fill up the car, and we head out of Portland just a little after eight. I'm worried the city will be a trigger for Talia, and I'm worried that Stevie Johansson will hear I'm back and sniffing around.

Rick didn't believe me when I told him that she had her goons kidnap me and threaten to hook me on Sweet if I didn't leave her alone, and I have no way to prove it happened. But it did, and I'm hoping that enough time has gone by she's forgotten about me and has other things to worry about than a disgraced reporter.

What I'm going there for has nothing to do with her.

We sit in silence for about twenty minutes, and I try to relax, loosening my grip on the steering wheel and shaking out my shoulders. The highway's empty, and the roads are clear of ice and snow. To make conversation, Talia asks about Old Harbor, the newspaper, and the university. We chat, and I try to answer her questions, though I don't know much about the town I'm asking her to move to all for the sake of my love life. She brings the university's website up on her phone, and we talk about transferring her credits, the paperwork involved, and the deadlines she'll need to keep if she wants to enroll in spring semester. They have a full psychology department and internship opportunities at a mental health facility that the community college in Portland doesn't have. She skims, and I stare into the bright orange horizon. The sun is coming up, and I hope the beautiful sunrise is an omen of good things to come.

I want to ask Talia about something Barney mentioned during my interview, for lack of a better description, but I wait until we go to the bathroom and buy cups of coffee at a gas station just off the highway. This is shaky territory, and I say her name cautiously, "Tal?"

She looks up from her phone. "Yeah?"

"When I was talking to Barney about a position on his paper, he said his niece was going to rehab for Sweet addiction. He asked me how you got hooked, but I had to tell him I didn't know very much. You went to a party on campus? Is that right? Can you tell me?"

People blame addicts for their own problems and say to just stop. Cold turkey. Stop drinking, stop smoking. If you were strong enough, you could stop if you wanted to. You're weak.

Selfish. Talia and I have heard it all, and I have *never* met a stronger person than my sister. She's been clean for six years and every day is a struggle. Every evening that she goes to bed sober is a triumph. I couldn't be prouder of her. I ask, my voice soft and without a hint of accusation.

She shifts uncomfortably and looks out her window, unable to meet my eyes. I know she's ashamed of what she's done, ashamed she needs me, ashamed she shouldn't live alone because having free time would be too tempting.

"Yeah," she mumbles. "I went to a frat party, and I got drunk. I woke up hooked." Embarrassment stains her cheeks. "Someone must have given me some without me knowing, or I thought it would be fun to try it and don't remember."

I nod. Six years ago she was in her first year of college, trying to attend classes and do homework around working part-time and cleaning up after Mom. I helped when I could and told Talia several times to live with me, but she didn't want to give up on our mother. Going to a party with friends would have been natural. When I was in school, I partied too.

"You didn't get hooked living with Mom?" I ask.

"No. I knew not to touch it, but she didn't bring it home very often, Devyn. She kept it on the streets."

If there's any friction between us, it's that she wants to keep trying to help our mother. Mom's been addicted to Sweet for years, and the longer you're on it, the harder it is to get clean. Talia was hooked for only a few months, and she needed three years in rehab. I can't imagine how long it would take someone like our mom, or how long it would last before she's on the street, licking the bubblegum-flavored powder off some guy's cock because she couldn't score any other way.

"Do you remember what else you did that day?" I ask without trying to lead her. I don't want to put any ideas in her head.

She twists in her seat and frowns. "What's this all about?"

A huge semi-truck passes us and the car shakes. I slow down a little and let him speed ahead. "Just humor me, okay?"

"Yeah. It was a Friday, and I went to class. I remember I did because that's when we were invited to the party. My friends and I decided to go shopping at the mall to look for something to wear. It wasn't a shit party—the frat guys were having something fancy, and a friend of Serena's said she could get us in. We went to Bloomingdale's, and Serena bought me a dress I wanted because I couldn't afford it."

Talia wouldn't have asked me for spending money. I was already paying their rent, the utilities, and grocery bill.

She sips her decaf—we stay away from anything that could be habit-forming—and sighs. "We bummed around, you know? We were kids, excited for the weekend."

"Yeah." It makes me so angry. She should still be a kid, not a twenty-four year old who has seen more than anyone should in their lifetime.

She stops talking and we spend the next few minutes in silence, but then she says, "Serena got munchy."

I glance at her in surprise. I thought she was done.

"I told her I'd buy her lunch in exchange for the dress, but she said she wanted something to bring to the party that night, and we went into Stevie's candy store."

My heart starts to slam against my ribs.

Barney was right.

"Did you buy anything there?" I ask, trying to sound like I couldn't care less.

"Yeah. A pound of gummy worms. I didn't eat them until we were at the party, though."

"Did Serena buy anything?"

"Some Sour Patch Kids, I think, and . . . I thought it was

funny, but she bought a few of those dipping stick packets. I didn't think I'd like it, but it wasn't bad. Tart."

"You had some of Serena's dipping sticks at the party?"

"She passed them around. A frat guy pretended the powder was coke and started sniffing it up his nose. Everybody thought it was funny."

Hysterical. I wonder if he's hooked on Sweet. It's something I add to my list. To ask Talia if she can remember anyone who had been there and if she knows how many were addicted after that night.

"How's Serena doing?" I ask. Talia hasn't talked about her friend in a long time. Serena got hooked at the frat party and was at the same party the cops busted too, but she wasn't as lucky as Talia. Serena didn't have the support system a recovering addict needs to stay sober, and after her short stay in rehab, she ended up on the streets again.

Talia picks at some white fuzz on her black leggings. "I don't know where she is now. I lost touch with a lot of people when we moved to Portland."

"I'm sorry," I say, but I'm not. Portland was what Talia needed, and it's been good for her. I can't feel bad for the people we left behind.

I focus on the road, the traffic picking up as we get closer to the city. We still have another two hours, and my plan is to drive straight to Rick's office building. His partner, Beau—I don't remember his last name—should be there and hopefully if I tell him what I'm doing and that I'm doing it for Rick, he'll help us out.

"Are you mad at me?" Talia whispers.

"No, sweet—" I was going to call her sweetie, but God. Sweet ruined that endearment for a lot of people. "I have something I want to talk to you about, but I wanted to wait until I could find a place to stop."

Two minutes later I turn into a roadside rest area and park at the end of the parking lot. We both get out and stretch. It's a beautiful day. Old Harbor's blizzard never came this far west, and several people are getting some air before driving the last couple of hours into the city.

Through the snow, we walk past a playground where children are playing, and we sit on a bench that looks over a wooded area. A short distance away, a man is throwing a red Frisbee to an excited German shepherd.

Quietly, I tell her what Barney told me, how he suspects his niece went in for candy and came out with something else.

"It sounds a lot like what you and Serena did," I say, staring straight ahead and giving her privacy to think about what I just told her.

She lets out a strangled cry, a hand over her mouth. "It's not my fault."

"Hey," I say, grabbing her arm, and she looks at me. "It was *never* your fault. Maybe you shouldn't have gone to that party and maybe you shouldn't have gotten drunk, but what you did that night, thousands of kids do everywhere, all the time. It wasn't your fault. I know you think you deserve the blame, but all you did was go in and buy some candy. How many children has she hooked? How many kids go through withdrawal after eating something from her store and their parents don't even know what's happening?"

Talia falls into my arms, sobbing against my chest. I hold her for a long time, brushing my hand over the back of her head.

I know this theory might not be correct, or even provable, but the way it makes sense is scary.

After several minutes, Talia lifts her head and rubs her wet cheeks. "You have to stop her."

She's not even done speaking and I'm already shaking my

head. "Nope, nope, and nope. I tried, and I failed. I'm not going up against her again. I'm in love with Rick, and I want to marry him. I'm not going to do anything that could keep that from happening because I was stupid and got hurt."

"But—"

"No. You remember how she ran me out of Cedar Hill. She turned everyone against me. I don't have the power to go after her alone, and no one believes me except for an old newspaper editor in a small Minnesota city. Those aren't great odds."

She sags and leans back against the bench.

"Sometimes you have to learn from your mistakes. I learned from mine. I can't think about everybody, all the time. You know that. I have to take care of the people close to me. That's you. And now Rick. I wouldn't even be spending time in Cedar Hill at all if it wasn't important."

"I wish there was a way."

"I wish there was too, but not at your expense, and not at mine. Okay? She's dangerous, and she's playing a game we can't win. Come on. We have a couple hours left, and I need you to call and make a hotel reservation somewhere for the next few nights. I don't know how long this is going to take. The less time, the better. I already want to go home."

"To Old Harbor, you mean," she says, a hint of a smile on her mouth.

"Yeah," I agree softly.

"I love you, Devyn," she says, pushing her face into my arm.

"I love you too, and you will *always* have a place in my life. I promise."

———

"Now what?" Talia asks as we stand in the lobby of Rick's building, M&H Development. A bank of elevators is at the rear, four of them busy around the lunch hour. Going through security was a familiar experience, reminding me of the years I worked the *Times,* and Talia, too, was quick. The rehab facility had a zero-tolerance policy, and the residents were checked frequently for weapons and drugs.

Now we stand with visitor badges hanging around our necks, trying to figure out what to do and where to go. Beau's office is located on the eightieth floor. Co-Chief Executive Officer, Beaumont Hendrickson.

"Go up and ask. That's all we can do. If Beau won't see us, then we'll have to do some investigating on our own. I still have a few friends at the *Times,* but going to the public library first might be a better bet. I don't want to involve anyone I don't have to."

I tried to dress the part of a professional reporter: black high-heeled boots, black wide-leg slacks, cream blouse and black wool jacket, my hair twisted into a bun fastened with a black elastic. Talia dressed up too, in her school clothes—over-the-leg boots, new black leggings, dressy sweater, black coat, her hair pulled back into a sleek ponytail, and earrings glinting at her ears.

We look like we belong, so that's a start.

I never used to feel claustrophobic in an elevator, but I twitch, remembering the last few days I was in Cedar Hill, and I imagine everyone is staring at me, knowing exactly who I am and what I did.

It's a relief when the lift stops on the top floor and I'm able to get out and breathe.

There's a long counter of receptionists answering the telephones, and we wait impatiently for one to free up. "Is Mr. Hendrickson available?" I ask.

"Do you have an appointment?" She tilts her head and smiles.

"Unfortunately, no." I should have made one, but I didn't want Beau to call Rick and tell him I was coming here.

"Let me see if he's in. What's your name, please?"

"Devyn Scott."

"One moment."

She punches a couple of buttons and murmurs into her headset. Turning to me, she says, "You're in luck, Miss Scott. He just came back from a meeting. Go through those doors, and then to the right. His assistant will show you to his office."

"Thank you."

Talia and I push through the glass doors that separate the other departments on the eightieth floor from the executive offices. We take a few steps inside the luxurious space, the vibe not unlike the *Times'* offices. Everyone's excited, happy to contribute to projects that mean something to them and enjoying the company of their coworkers. M&H is a good company to work for.

A young woman not much older than Talia greets us, and she's just as cheerful as everyone else. "He just went to freshen up. Have a seat," she says, pushing the door open and revealing a huge office done in dark greys and teal.

"Thank you," I say, glancing around, the sun streaming through floor-to-ceiling windows.

"Can I get you anything to drink? Coffee? Tea? Water?"

"Decaf coffee with cream would be great."

She looks at Talia.

"Same, thank you."

I didn't order decaf primarily for Talia's benefit. I feel like I'm going to have a heart attack.

A few moments after Beau's assistant serves us our coffee, he strides into his office wearing an immaculate black suit and red, black, and silver tie. His eyes are warm, and he holds out a hand. "Devyn Scott. I admit, this is a bit of a surprise. The last I heard, you were snowed in with Rick and badgering him for an interview. How did that turn out?"

"You know, or you wouldn't have asked. Thank you for seeing us. This is my sister, Talia Scott."

Beau's eyes land on Talia, and if he were a cartoon, his pupils would have turned into big, throbbing red hearts. He holds her hand and squeezes, his eyes searching her face.

For crap's sake.

Talia's no better, her lips popping open and her purse landing on the carpet with a soft *thud*.

I'm amused and a little concerned. Not because of their ages. If anything, Beau being older than she is—by a good fifteen years if I had to guess—would help keep her steady. All she needs is a young jerk who hasn't gotten partying out of his system. Beau's been there—not finished with that, as I think he still has a pretty active social life—but if he gave it up for a woman, he'd have no regrets.

No, I'm not quite sure if *she's* ready for something like that. As her sister, I can only support her and hopefully guide her into making smart choices, but Beau Hendrickson is a good guy or Rick wouldn't work with him. I'd bet my life on that.

They're still staring at each other, and I let them have at it, taking off my coat and helping myself to the coffee service set out on a gleaming metal cart.

I drink half my mug, and needing to break it up or we'll be here all day, I sigh audibly. Beau jerks his gaze away, but, I notice, doesn't let go of her hand until he says, "I'm sorry, Miss Scott, let me help you with your coat."

"Talia's fine," she says, easing out of her jacket as he tugs it from her shoulders.

Beau hangs it on a coat rack near the door, something I could have done with mine, but I laid it over the arm of a loveseat instead.

Talia sits on a loveseat across from me, leaving space for Beau to sit next to her.

Even I wasn't this goofy with Rick. We'd shown restraint.

For a couple of days.

"What can I do for you?" he asks, leaning back and resting his arm along the top of the loveseat's cushions, his hand conveniently close to Talia's hair.

"I want to go over the accident," I say.

He frowns. "What do you mean?"

"I mean, I watched the clip, and I need you to explain what happened."

"If you've watched the video, then you know. The ground was sagging due to the rain, and the crane tipped over. We should have postponed the lift."

"That's what it looked like, but can you watch it with me?"

"Sure, if you want, but I don't know what you're getting at, Miss Scott."

"Devyn's fine, but you can keep the gooey eyes to yourself."

Beau flicks a glance at Talia who pushes back a smile.

A laptop is lying on his desk, and he carries it to a small black conference table near the wall of windows. I stand on his left side and Talia stands on his right. We've both seen the clip that's on social media quite a few times now, and Beau brings up the same one that has reached over two million views.

"Don't you have one that's proprietary to your company?" I ask.

"It's this one. This is the one the OSHA rep filmed. We have other angles on file, one that catches the boom falling—" and crushing Rick, but he doesn't have to say that— "but this is the one we have, it's just more easily accessible."

He clicks Play, and we watch the beginning, the workers cheering as the framework is lifted into the air. The OSHA rep sweeps from the framework hanging on the hook attached to the boom to the truck and the cab, but the operator is only partially visible because of the glare against the glass. The truck starts to tip, and it's clear the ground is giving way under the truck's tires.

"Stop right there," I say, and he clicks Pause.

"What?"

"Why is the truck tipping that way?" I ask.

Beau's voice is patient and maybe a little condescending. "You can see the ground, Devyn. It's not clearly visible in the video, but it was also very windy that day, and it created a force that contributed to the truck tipping."

I suck in a breath and ask the question that's been bothering me since the first time I watched the clip while I was sitting on Rick's bed. "I get that, but why is it tipping over *that way*? Even *if* the ground was giving under the tires, because of course, I can see that," I point to the screen where I *do* see the tires sinking into the mud, "isn't the framework heavier than the truck?"

Beau rubs his lips. "No. The framework weighed two tons, and the crane is always counterbalanced with weight," he says, pointing to the area underneath the boom. "We rent out the size of the truck we need based on the weight of the load. This truck was an average fifty-ton truck."

My heart sinks. I was wrong. "Then the counterweight balances the load."

"Yes."

"It really was just an accident," I murmur.

"Not just an accident," Beau says, playing the clip until the OSHA rep stops filming, "but an avoidable one. We should have waited. It's why Rick took it so hard."

I chew on my lip. I completely understand what Beau's saying. Everything he said makes sense. No, it's more than that.

Everything he said can be proven, and that's what's hanging me up. I need proof.

"She's going to need proof," Talia says, her hand skimming over Beau's to play the video again.

We watch it in silence, imagining the boom falling and Rick yelling at his team to get out of the way.

"The proof is right here," Beau says, gesturing to the tires sinking in the mud.

I sigh. "It falls over so fast."

"Trucks do that," Beau says dryly. "They're heavy."

The clip plays out.

"Who's in charge of putting the crane together?"

"The crane operator directs a team."

"Rick said OSHA investigated. What was the official cause of the accident?"

"Inadequate bearing capacity due to rain from the previous day, and inappropriate weathervane into the wind."

"Can I look at the investigation reports?" I don't know very much about any of this, even after Beau's explanation of what happened and why it did, but I still believe if the truck was balanced with the framework, it shouldn't have fallen over as quickly as it did.

Beau narrows his eyes at me. "Does Rick know you're here?"

I wince. "Not exactly. He told me to leave it alone."

"That's the last thing he should have told her," Talia says, stepping around Beau and elbowing me in the arm.

"I can't help it," I say irritably. "If nothing's funky, then us looking around shouldn't cause anybody any problems."

Beau scratches the back of his neck looking handsomely undecided.

Talia swoons by my side, and I return her painful jab.

"What the hell," he says, planting his hands on his narrow

hips and glaring at us. "I can set you up in Rick's office. Look over what you want. When I'm ready to leave, I'll drive you out there."

I blink. "Drive us out where?"

"To the site."

"You mean he hasn't done anything with it? It's still sitting there after all this time?"

"That's what I mean. Even the crane's there. You can poke around until your heart's content. It'll be good for me to look around too. I called Rick a couple days ago, while you were there, incidentally, and told him Declan Everett wants to buy it. He either needs to clean it up and do something with it, or sell it. Maybe you can talk some sense into him."

That's not likely, but I say, "I appreciate it."

"Come on."

Beau asks his assistant to bring the boxes full of the paperwork that has to do with the investigation to Rick's office.

Talia and I follow him, leaving our purses and jackets in his.

"Where are you ladies staying tonight? You're not driving back to . . .?"

"Portland. No. Talia made us reservations at a hotel not far from our old apartment."

"Don't waste money on that. Stay with me. I have a couple of guest rooms." Beau opens an office door that has Rick's name etched into a black placard. His office is a mirror image of Beau's, but it feels abandoned. "I'd offer you Rick's penthouse, but it wouldn't feel right. He hasn't been in it since Renata left him."

I step into Rick's office and glance at Talia who shrugs but has a grin on her face that could light up Cedar Hill for a month. "Thanks. That's nice of you."

"Well, I do have an ulterior motive," he says as his assistant and her helper set large cardboard storage boxes on the same kind of conference table that Beau has in his office. "I want to keep an eye on you. I know the muck you raked up with Stevie Johansson. I don't want you out there by yourself."

"Let's . . . not talk about that."

"I'll take care of it. Is there anything else?"

"Not that I can think of," I say, looking around the room.

"Okay. Let Lola know if you need something, or if you have a question, I'll be in my office. Door's always open," he says, winking at Talia who fangirls as he steps into the hallway.

He closes the door behind him, and I say, "Seriously?"

"Seriously what?" she asks, crossing the room and lifting a lid on one of the boxes. "He's cute."

I follow her and take the lid off the other box. "He obviously thinks the same."

Talia sinks into a chair. "I never thought about, you know. After."

I sit next to her and squeeze her arm. "I did. The second he looked at you. If he's steady, if he understands what you've gone through and what you need, he could be good for you."

"Do you think so, really? He wouldn't think I'm . . . icky?"

"If he did, he wouldn't be the right man for you."

She sighs. "Yeah."

"Let's look through this stuff. I don't care what Beau says. Something isn't right, and God help us, I'm not going to be able to quit until I figure out what it is."

CHAPTER TWELVE

Rick

I needed the entire day to scrub the lighthouse down, and my back was killing me by the time I was finished.

There isn't anything left of Devyn Scott.

It doesn't get her out of my head, or my heart.

The hours after she left were the emptiest and longest hours of my life. Every second felt like a million years, and at about ten, after knocking back half a glass of Glenlivet, I collapsed into clean sheets hoping sleep would finally put me out of my misery. But I tossed and turned so much I didn't get any sleep at all.

I get up irritable and pissed off, and with the sun shining in my face, I drive to town for groceries and more booze. I see my massage therapist who says Devyn did a great job and that I'm lucky she'd been around.

Lucky.

Yep.

I don't want to go home, but there's no reason to hang

around town. After I put my groceries away, I go to my office, sit at my desk, and stare at the texts Devyn sent me. The first telling me she made it to Portland, and the second, asking my opinion on where she and Talia should live. I hadn't meant to miss her phone call. I should have called her back, but I can't bear to hear the sound of her voice when I can't hold her, and I took the coward's way out and didn't respond at all.

Her question about her living situation didn't help.

Sad, lonely, and needing a friend, I call Beau on his cell.

"Rick. What's up?"

He sounds happier than he usually does, which takes me by surprise because Beau's one of the happiest guys I know. He must have a hot date tonight and is already looking forward to it.

"She's gone."

She's gone and didn't tell me when she was coming back. *If* she was coming back.

"I know. She's here."

I lean forward in my chair. "She's there? You mean, in Cedar Hill?" I don't know what she'd be doing in Cedar Hill, don't know why she would risk going to the city with Stevie Johansson on her ass.

"Yes and no. She's in the city, but she's here. In your office."

"*My office?*" The office I haven't been in since the accident. "What is she doing?"

"Looking through the accident reports. You know, I thought she was crazy, but she might be onto something. I'm giving her whatever she wants. Maybe she'll find something, or if she doesn't, it'll call her off. Either way, she's here with her sister. She's a looker. Did you know that?"

I bristle. I don't like him gawking at her. "Devyn's gorgeous. Keep your hands off her. She's mine."

Beau chuckles and I want to punch him through the phone. "Not her. Talia. Delicate little thing. What's her story?"

Devyn might not like me sharing, but if Beau has his eye on Talia, he needs to know the truth. "She was hooked on Sweet. She went through rehab and now Devyn keeps her on a tight leash. She can't party with you, Beau."

"No, I don't suppose she could," he murmurs. "Still, she's pretty. Anyway, they're staying at my place tonight. I don't like the thought of them running all over, and I'll put a couple extra men on them too, in case Stevie hears she's in town and decides to cause trouble."

"Thanks."

"You bet. You wouldn't want to drive in, would you? You'd make it in time for dinner. We could double date. Better yet, order the plane. We could hang out all afternoon."

"Devyn isn't there to hang out."

Beau laughs. "You're right about that. She's got a bug up her ass, but she's a solid reporter, so if there's something to find, she'll find it."

"I already told her OSHA went over it. She's not going to find anything."

"So that's a no about coming to the city?"

"I'll think about it, but it's not in my plans for today." Or any day.

"Right." He pauses, and I can hear him shift behind his desk. "You fell for her, huh?"

"Yeah." I don't sound happy about it.

"Do you want my opinion?"

I scoff. "Not especially."

His voice drops, and he's as serious as I've ever heard him. "For what it's worth, she loves you too, or she wouldn't have risked coming back here. You were in the hospital when all of that went down and you don't know how ugly it got for her. Think about that before you get angry at her for being here."

"I wasn't going to get mad."

"Yeah, you were, if you aren't already. She's digging into a situation you want to forget, and it's going to piss you off. Don't let it. There's no harm in it. When she's done, put it away and move on. With her, without her, whatever you need to do. You've been healing. I understand more than you give me credit for, but you can't live like this forever. I mean that with every honest intention I have."

"I hear you." I don't like what he's saying, but there's more truth to his words than I want to admit.

"Good. I'll let you know if she finds anything. Do you want me to pass along any messages?"

"Tell her I have room. She'll know what that means."

"Got it. Have a good night and look at the contract I emailed you this morning. I think we can get more out of him if we squeeze a little harder."

"I will. Keep them safe, yeah?"

"Nothing's going to hurt them. You have my word. She's a looker."

Beau hangs up on my laugh.

Talia could do a lot worse than Beau, if he decides love is enough to slow him down.

Tiredly, I rub my hands up and down my face. Devyn's in Cedar Hill. At least I know where she is, what she's doing, and that she's safe, but that doesn't make me miss her any less. To give myself something to do, I look into adding on to the cottage for living space for Talia and plan my own unwanted trip to Cedar Hill which comes a lot sooner than I thought it would.

CHAPTER THIRTEEN

Devyn

"What are we looking for?" Talia asks, scanning several sheets of paper in front of her. "I can't help if I don't know."

"I have no idea. Something, anything, that proves the truck tipped over when it wasn't supposed to."

"But we've watched the video clip a hundred times now. The mud made it tip over. According to the instructional videos we watched online, they were supposed to be using outriggers and bearing plates, and they weren't."

"Right." I dig through a pile of photographs.

Throughout the stack are pictures of Rick as he lay pinned under the boom, paramedics and engineers standing near him and arguing about the safest way to free him. I set those aside without looking at them. I find the one I want and point at the truck before it tipped over. The wheels on the driver's side have sunk into the mud, causing the vehicle to become unbalanced. "So, first, the wind was against them. Second, the mud and the earth settling under the tires because of rain the previous day. Third, no outriggers or bearing plates which could have prevented the whole thing. But, think of a car. When you're driving and you slide into the ditch. You don't flip over because you're at an incline, not unless you're going over the speed limit, and the truck wasn't moving. If the framework and the boom were balanced, why did the truck tip over?"

Talia bites her lip. "You're asking why the mud was enough to make it do that. Besides the wind."

"Exactly."

"Maybe the wind was enough."

"Maybe it was." Trying to keep my tears from falling, I push my fingers to my eyes. I'm not successful and one drips down my cheek.

"Devyn, what is it?" Talia asks, putting a hand on my arm. "It's okay if this was an accident."

I sniffle and wipe the tear away. "I wanted to give him something, you know? He's lost so much in the past two years. I wanted to give him something back."

"You don't think you're enough? I bet if you asked him, he would say you are."

"I'm not enough though, that's the problem. He was run out of Cedar Hill just as much as I was. If we asked Beau, I have no doubts he'd say that Rick hasn't been in this office since the accident. He lost his business, his wife. His social life, everything. I wanted to give it all back to him."

"You want to give his wife back to him? You *don't* want a relationship with Rick then? Why are we moving to Old Harbor if that's true?"

I stand, dig through the box in front of me, and pull out more sheets of loose paper. A booklet of some kind with the front cover torn off is lying on top of more photos, and I flip through it. It's the crane's manual, and it has pages and pages of diagrams and tables. I set it aside in case we need it later.

"She left him because she blamed him for getting hurt. I thought if I could prove this wasn't an accident, that someone sabotaged the lift, maybe she'd go back to him and he'd be happy. It's stupid."

"It's not stupid. Does he still love her?"

"He said he doesn't, but they were trying for a baby."

Talia tilts her head. "And you don't believe him?"

I shrug and dig through the box again. "We've only known each other for a few days."

"You don't believe in love at first sight? I do. I believe the second you meet someone you'll know if it can be more."

"Like you and Beau?"

She quirks her mouth. "Just because there's a spark doesn't mean it will turn into anything."

"I think you just proved my point, little sister. Anyway, the whole thing is pointless if I can't figure this out."

"Okay, forget about falling in love for a minute and think back to what you said." She stands up and leans against the conference table. "You said sabotage, but that's not where I thought we were headed. I thought we were looking for a mistake, an error in judgment, or an idiot not paying attention. Now what you're trying to do makes more sense. You're searching for a way someone could have deliberately made the crane tip over."

I blink. For a reporter, sometimes I can be blind to my own way of working. "I guess I am."

"But I don't see how. There were a hundred people on the site that day. Rick was there overseeing everything and so was his foreman. OSHA was there filming the lift. There's no room for sabotage, is there?"

"We need to talk to someone who would know."

"Beau?"

"No. We need to talk to the crane operator."

———

"Not possible." Beau's frowning, his hands on his hips, shaking his head.

"Why not?" The more I think about it, the more I'm sure that the crane operator is the key to it all.

"Because he was injured. Because the whole thing did to him what it did to Rick. He won't talk to anyone, hasn't given one interview. OSHA cleared him of fault, but the accident messed with his head and he's been hiding ever since."

"Out of guilt?" Talia asks, sitting in a chair in front of Beau's desk.

He blows out a breath. "It's true he should have listened to the warnings going off in the cab, but he'd been operating a crane for years and knew how far to push the limits to get the job done. He overestimated the ground's stability, that's all."

"Then talking to me shouldn't be an issue. I don't want an interview. I just want to ask him for his side of the story."

"You're bullheaded, you know that?" Beau stomps to his desk and snatches a pen off the blotter. He scrawls a name and address on a piece of paper. "Do not tell him where you got his name, and don't tell him why you want to talk to him. Not in connection with M&H Development, at least. We let him go with a generous package. He doesn't work anymore because of the accident, but he doesn't have to."

"Thank you. I'll be discreet, I promise."

"Do that tomorrow. It's close to quitting time. I want to go out to the site, and then we can talk more over dinner."

I push back my annoyance at the delay. I *do* want to see the site, but eating dinner and getting settled into Beau's penthouse will feel like a giant waste of time. I need to find some of the patience I had when I was finding, or trying to find, evidence on Stevie Johansson. I'm not going to figure this out in a day, and Beau's saving us a lot of money giving us a place to stay.

Talia rides shotgun, and I sit in the backseat of the elegant SUV.

While they chat, I check my email. Barney has gotten back to me saying the articles all looked good and were worth my pay so far. He says I'll add a little sophistication to the *Herald,* and I smile. I couldn't feel any less sophisticated.

Beau laughs at something Talia says and eases out of his lane much to the annoyance of the other drivers.

"Can you at least keep your eyes on the road?" I ask over the horns blaring.

He laughs and winks at me in the rearview mirror.

Talia blushes.

For crap's sake.

"Rick called earlier. I told him you were here," Beau says, staring straight ahead.

Shrugging deeper into my seat, I say, "I suppose he didn't like hearing I was checking into things." I can imagine how their conversation went. "Does he want me to go home?"

"No. I've known Rick for a long time. He hates talking about any of this and you being here had a good chance of royally pissing him off, but I told him to let you do your thing. It's good for him, Devyn. I've been trying to get him to see that this doesn't have to put his life on a permanent hold. You spent time with him, more time during that blizzard than I have since the accident. How is he?"

I weigh what I want to say. As Rick's business partner, Beau has the right to know how he's handling things, but if Rick wanted him to know, he'd tell him. I don't want to be in the middle. "He's in pain. Physically, I mean. His back and hip give him trouble. I upset his schedule, and he didn't get a lot of rest while I was there. It threw him off."

Beau's lips twitch. "I doubt he minded."

"Not like that. You asked, and I'm trying to be serious. He's angry, and he carries a lot of guilt on his shoulders."

He nods. I didn't offer any new information.

"I don't know if he'll ever be able to let it go," I say, almost to myself. If the past keeps Rick from looking into the future, where does that leave me?

"He won't. He won't let himself. He'll live with it, and hopefully what he's feeling will fade in time."

It's been two years, and his pain is a constant reminder. I think that will be easier said than done. "Did he say anything else?" I ask.

"He asked me to tell you that he has room." His eyes meet mine in the rearview mirror. "He said you'd know what that means."

I press my fingers to my lips to hide a smile. He's been thinking about my text then. Good. "I know what that means. Thanks."

Beau turns his attention from me to Talia, and he asks how she likes living in Portland. I tune them out and imagine what Rick has planned for our living situation. I think I'd like living in the lighthouse with him, but I don't want Talia to live by herself, especially since I'm the one asking her to move.

My daydreaming comes to a stop when Beau pulls up alongside the construction site.

The bleak look of it quiets all of us. He parks, and we stare at a building that's barely just begun.

"This was supposed to be a hotel?" I ask, climbing out of the backseat. Before we left, Beau asked if I would change my shoes, and I'm grateful I'm wearing ballet flats instead of my high-heeled boots.

"It was going to be the best in the city. Fifty floors of luxury. The city put the land up for sale instead of preserving it for a park and playground, and we bought it right out from under Declan Everett's nose. We only had an advantage because I used to date one of the administrative assistants working at City Hall and she kept a soft spot for me. Cedar Hill made a killing—we paid a lot more than it was worth, even for a location like this. But the hotel would have brought in a hundred times over."

From the back of the SUV, he takes out three bright yellow hardhats. I adjust mine, but Beau pulls out Talia's ponytail and puts the hat over her hair himself. She beams at him, and I rein in my need to caution her. She can be in a healthy relationship, and telling Beau about her past addiction and explaining her boundaries will be for her to do, not me.

I turn away from them and study the building. "Rick has more than an MBA."

"You bet. He also has a bachelor's in architecture and a BS in construction management. He can do it all. This accident shouldn't have happened."

Majoring in journalism with a minor in English kept me plenty busy. "He's smart."

"Smart enough to hook up with you," he says, taking a set of keys out of his jacket pocket and looking at me over his shoulder.

"Don't wink," I warn. "You're charming, but it can turn creepy real quick."

He scowls. "You know, you're the first woman to have objections."

"Then luckily for you, I'm already taken."

We cross the sidewalk, and Beau unlocks a huge padlock that's holding a thick chain together, keeping a door in the wire fence closed. He jiggles the door and yanks it open. The hinges squeal, and I step onto the site.

I make a sweeping gesture at Talia. "Smarm away."

As I walk away from them, Beau mutters, "You don't think I'm smarmy, do you?"

"Maybe a little," she says, and I cover my mouth to muffle a laugh.

Shifting my attention to the hotel, I try to figure out what's already been built, but I can't. The foundation, of course, but what they had been working on is a mystery to me. "What's this part supposed to be?" I ask Beau as he and Talia come up behind me.

He points to what's in front of us. "This would have been the lobby, then the sleeping rooms, west wing, east wing, set in a V. In the middle, we planned a giant ballroom. We'd just completed what would have been the fourth floor. As you can see, we had months yet before it would even resemble a hotel. Which was a good thing for us, otherwise even more damage could have been done when the crane tipped over."

I need all my willpower not to snap at him. I understand where he's coming from, in regard to time lost and the cost to fix any damage, and if Rick hadn't gotten hurt, he very well could have decided to keep the construction on schedule. Beau didn't mean to make it sound like the building was more important than the men who were killed that day and Rick's injuries, but it's callous just the same.

After Beau explained what I was looking at, the layout is clearer now, the metal skeleton raw and abandoned in the snow. It would be interesting to see the rendering of what the completed hotel was supposed to look like. Closing my eyes, I can hear the laughter and the music. How many wedding receptions would have taken place here, how many parties? Is it odd to hear the murmur of voices from guests who haven't yet stayed here? And maybe never will?

"It haunts me too, every time I have to come out. It would've been magnificent."

"Why doesn't he want to finish it?"

"You'd have to ask him that. I suppose a lot of it has to do with Renata. They were going to renew their vows here. Their party was going to be the first in the ballroom to bring us good luck."

I meet Talia's eyes, but she shakes her head. I know what she's thinking. The past is the past. You can't live in it. She can't, or she would always live with her addiction. I can't either, or I'd still be mourning my job at the *Times* and where my career would be right now if I'd been able to expose Stevie, or better yet, had never gone down that path at all and found my claim to journalism fame investigating something else.

"Do you want to see the inside?" Beau asks.

Talia agrees, but I stay behind. Holding her hand, he helps her cross the site and they step into what will be the ground floor. One day Rick will finish it, but I'm not so egotistical to think that I'll be the one to help him forget about his ex-wife.

I take a pen and little notebook out of my purse. There's a light dusting of snow over the ground and equipment, and the hem of my pants drags over the frozen mud. The crane is still here like Beau said it was, and I note my impressions as I pick my way through the site. It hasn't been completely abandoned —at some point, cleanup had taken place, if only to make the site as safe as it can be. Homeless people, bored kids, gangs, and drug dealers all gravitate toward construction sites like this. Beau must have more connections at City Hall than just an administrative assistant for them to let Rick leave the property this way. Not only is it an eyesore in one of the most upscale parts of Cedar Hill, but it's dangerous, and sooner or later someone is going to kill themselves or find themselves at the wrong place at the wrong time.

I take pictures of the poor crane lying on its side. It makes me think of a dead dinosaur, and feeling sorry for the inanimate object, I rub the cold metal. I note the company's name and the make and model of the vehicle. Rick must have bought it so it could stay here. So much wasted time and money on this land. So much pain. I step back and take a picture of the entire thing. The boom is still attached to the truck and the framework is still lying on the ground.

Studying the crane, I compare it to what I've seen in the videos. Where the counterbalance weight would go. The wheels that had sunk into the mud. The broken glass of the operator's window where he hit his head when the truck tipped over. He was experienced and knew when to push the limits, Beau said.

He wouldn't have hurt himself deliberately. He wouldn't have caused the accident unless he thought he could escape uninjured, but if he was that experienced, he'd know that would be practically impossible, and it had been. He's lucky he's not dead.

I follow the boom lying in the dirt and drop to my knees where I imagine Rick had lain trapped. Did he think he was going to die? What had gone through his mind? Did pieces of his life with Renata flash before him? Happy times, things they hadn't done yet? Did he think he'd never see her again? Or was he in too much pain to think about anything at all? I rest my hand on the metal, and it's nothing but cold. Maybe that's all that can be trapped in it. The misery, what it had stolen from those people that day.

Tears run down my face, though I try not to cry. He deserves so much more than this.

I wipe my cheeks.

Suddenly, the dirt near my side explodes.

I know exactly what that whisper is, the silent whip of a bullet as it slices through the air.

Chips of rock pelt against my jacket's sleeve, and I don't give them another chance to shoot me. I shove my pen and notebook in my purse and sprint with all my might toward the building, my lungs heaving as I struggle to draw in a breath.

I need to find cover.

A foot in front of me, frozen mud flies into the air, and this time I swear I could feel the hot bullet hum past my cheek.

I race toward the lobby. Beau has Talia backed up against a wall, his arm braced above her head, his other hand playing with her hair. "Beau," I scream as I get closer, my hardhat tumbling off my head.

His gaze collides with mine, and he reaches for his cell phone at the same moment Talia breaks away from him and starts running toward me.

"No!" he yells and jerks her back by the collar of her jacket. "Stay out of sight."

She fights him, but by the time she's able to get loose, I'm sheltered by the thick beams and I fall to my knees gasping for air.

"Fuck." He starts hollering at whoever answered his call, his face red.

Talia drops by my side and cuddles against me. "What's happening? Are you okay? What's going on?"

"I'm okay," I say, but she doesn't let me go.

"We need to get out of here," Beau says, shoving his cell back into his pocket. "I had two men with us and neither of them are answering their phones. This way."

He hustles us through the rear of the structure, a possessive hand pressing against Talia's back, and an SUV similar to Beau's is waiting on the street. There's a door chained shut in this part of the fence as well, but we don't use it. Instead, we crawl through a large hole cut in the metal that shouldn't have been there. It adds to Beau's temper, and he swears under his breath as we step onto the sidewalk.

The SUV's windows are tinted too darkly for me to see who's driving, but Beau trusts him. He opens the back door, takes off Talia's hardhat, and pushes us inside. With anger glinting in his eyes, he slams the door shut, rounds the hood, and flings himself into the passenger seat, shoving his and Talia's hardhats by his feet. "To my penthouse." He looks back at us. "Rick told me to keep you safe and he's going to have my ass for this."

I lean over, press my forehead to my knees, and breathe in and out.

Talia curls into herself, tears streaming down her cheeks. On the streets, she was exposed to violence in a different way than I was. It's still a shock, but something I'll process a lot easier than she will.

I've seen gunfire before—gang members warring for territory, loan sharks collecting their dues when money isn't paid—and snooping for evidence on Stevie, I've been around a lot of weapons. For an article I wrote for the *Times,* I took a firearms class, and I can imagine the kick and the odor. What I could never imagine is aiming at something other than a piece of paper, intending to take someone down, maybe forever. I don't have it in me to kill anyone.

Someone wants me dead, and it's easy to guess who. She knows I'm in the city and waited until I was out in the open. I won't be able to go anywhere now without looking over my shoulder. Talia should go home—it was stupid to bring her with me. I don't want her getting hurt, but I'm not leaving until I know what caused Rick's accident.

Beau lives downtown, and during rush hour, traffic clogs

the streets. We blend into the crush, and I feel safe, the tinted windows keeping us from view. I lift my head and pull Talia into my arms. "It's okay."

"You could have died," she says, tears in her voice. "Then what would I have done?"

I squeeze her in a fierce hug and tell her the truth. "You'd be just fine. I have no doubt about that."

The SUV stops behind the building, and it would be like Beau, from what little I know of him, to live in the most luxurious penthouse Cedar Hill has to offer. He probably owns this building, and possibly every building on the block. The security will be top-notch.

"Come on," Beau says, climbing out of the truck. He opens our door and we both slide out the back. Talia stumbles, shaking, and instead of impatiently pushing her forward, he picks her up and cradles her against his chest.

I don't pretend to dislike his attention toward her now.

Beau calls the private elevator, and silently, we step inside. In the quiet, he holds Talia, his grip strong and steady, and I lean against the wall, trying to find my bearings. It's silly, but it isn't the getting shot at part that worries me. It's that she'll try again, and again, and again. That's the part that freaks me out. I'll always have an enemy in Cedar Hill. "Fuck," I whisper.

"You can say that louder," Beau says, "because I agree with you."

The doors open revealing a beautiful foyer done in creams and greyish-blue. Beau doesn't stop until we're in a spacious living room, and he gently sets Talia on a huge cream couch. He frames her face in his hands and kisses her forehead. She puts on a brave expression and tries to smile.

He brushes his fingers over her cheek and turns to me. "Drink?"

"No. Thanks. Talia and I need our things."

"I'll get a guy on that. You have luggage in your car?"

I nod. "Yeah."

"I need to make a couple of phone calls, then I'll be back with you. We'll order in."

"Thanks."

I take my jacket off, drape it over the arm of the couch, and sit next to my sister. Squeezing her arm, I ask, "You doing okay?"

"Yeah. I was just a bit overwhelmed."

I laugh, letting out some tension. "You and me both." I pause. "You know I can't stop looking into this, right? I can't let her stop me from looking for proof Rick's accident wasn't only an accident."

She unbuttons her coat and slides her arms out of the sleeves. "I know. I think I've been as well as I have because you're strong, and I've needed that. I can't be selfish and keep all your strength for myself. If Rick decides to do something with the hotel and moves back to the city, he's going to need you. I don't want to stop you from being who you are, even if I'm scared."

"You don't have to be scared. Beau won't let anything happen to us."

"He's sexy when he's mad."

"All the good-looking men are."

She laughs.

"I'm going to clean up. I'll be right back."

I pat her leg and pad down the hall to find a bathroom. Beau's voice drifts to me, and that's when I know there's going to be a lot more mad and a lot more sexy sooner than Talia and I thought.

Beau's telling Rick what happened, and he's furious.

CHAPTER FOURTEEN

Rick

I don't take it out on Beau. I could yell, and I could scream, but it's my own damned fault that Devyn was in danger today. The second Beau told me she was in Cedar Hill, I should have gone too, but I still didn't believe that the candy store sweetheart who's worth millions of dollars for selling licorice and gummy bears would care that much about a woman who was in town doing business that didn't concern her.

I was wrong.

It takes me longer than I want to reach the airport because I hit every fucking red light, but the pilot has the Cessna ready to go and I don't have to wait. I'm not wasting time driving, and I'm too rattled to fly myself even though I've had my license for years. He greets me, briskly shaking my hand, and we waste no time boarding the plane. I don't have a bag.

I sit in a passenger's seat instead of the cockpit, and as I fasten my buckle and fidget, he does a quick pre-flight check. We're in the air ten minutes later.

The flight doesn't last even forty-five minutes before he's landing at the Cedar Hill airport. I barely say a thank you and goodbye, and I trot across the tarmac and jump into an SUV Beau has waiting for me. The drive from the airport to Beau's building is almost as long as the flight, and I'm shaking with anger, anxiety, and fear by the time Mack lets me off on the sidewalk. I need to get Devyn out of Cedar Hill, but that's not where the fear comes from. She won't come with me if I ask. She'll stay in the city until she's done what she's come here to do, and not a second sooner.

The concierge tips his head at me. I'm the only one on Beau's guest list allowed to go up without him calling ahead.

Impatiently, I wait for the elevator to carry me up to the top floor, sweat dripping down my back, and I burst through the doors before they glide fully open.

Devyn's sitting on the couch wearing what she wore when she stayed with me. Lounging pants, a matching tank top, and the cardigan that looks more like a robe than a sweater. A young blonde woman is curled up next to her, looking, I bet, like Devyn did at that age. Beau hovers near them still wearing a suit.

Her beautiful green eyes meet mine, and she tentatively stands from the couch. I don't give her a second to say one damned word. I yank her to my chest, twist my fingers in her hair, and press my lips against the top of her head. I don't care that Talia and Beau are watching. I don't care about anything except that she's okay.

She melts against me and wraps her arms around my waist.

"I'm sorry, Rick," Beau says. "I had men with us. They were knocked out, both of them."

I unclench my jaw enough to speak. "Did you report it?"

He shakes his head. "Didn't bother. If Stevie Johansson is after Devyn, getting the cops involved will only piss her off more. We'll keep a closer watch on her and Talia."

Devyn leans away from me. "I want Talia to go home."

Talia's gaze shoots straight to Beau. So there's more there than Beau just gawking at Devyn's sister.

"No," she says. "I don't want to go back to Portland without you."

"That's not necessary. She can stay here," Beau says to Devyn as he rests a hand on Talia's shoulder. "Now that we know she won't leave you alone, we'll tighten security. We won't let her chase you out of the city. You have every right to be here."

"And she wouldn't leave regardless," I say, nudging Devyn back against my chest. She was only a step away from me, but it was too far. "We'll talk about this tomorrow. I'm bringing Devyn to my place."

"What about—" she starts.

"I'll be fine," Talia interrupts.

"It's not far from here, Devyn." I'm impatient. I want to be alone with her.

Meeting my eyes, she swallows, searching my face. I don't know what she's looking for, but she must find it because she says, "Okay. I need to get my bag." I tighten my grip on her arm. She nods, and I let her go.

She disappears down the hall, and I hold out my hand to Talia. "Rick Mercer."

"Talia Scott, Devyn's sister. Thank you for paying my bill. The billing department at the center emailed me, but I didn't tell Devyn. I wanted to thank you somehow without her knowing." She looks at Beau out of the corners of her eyes. She hasn't told him and doesn't know he already knows. She's more concerned about her secret than my scars, and she doesn't flinch when she shakes my hand.

"You're welcome. Devyn told me a little about the situation, and I never want her to be worried about money."

"Thank you."

Devyn steps into the living room carrying the same suitcase she used when she stayed at the lighthouse. She gestures to Talia, and huddling in a corner of the living room, they whisper to each other. I can imagine the conversation is full of sex, consent, birth control, and good choices.

Beau won't hurt her, and if he were the type of man who could, he wouldn't be my friend.

"I'm sorry," he says again.

"Don't be. You were right. I should have been here. That might not have stopped it, but I wasn't here. She's stubborn, and she won't let me tell her what to do. Did she look through everything?"

"Yeah. She's going to talk to Tony Kelly in the morning."

I chew that over. I don't like her traipsing all over the city looking into an accident that was only an accident, but the quicker she realizes that, the sooner we can go back to Old Harbor. "Okay. I'll do some work at the office and Talia can hang out with us."

Beau raises his eyebrows. "You're not going with her?"

"I doubt Devyn would let me, and Tony won't talk to her if I'm there. It'll be easier all around if I just accept it. We'll see you at nine." Devyn and Talia walk toward us, and I turn in their direction. Holding out my hand, I say to Talia, "It was nice to meet you."

She places her hand in mine, and Beau watches, his eyes narrowed.

For fuck's sake.

"It was nice to meet you too. I'll see you in the morning,"

she says pointedly to Devyn, and my mouth twitches in amusement.

I crowd Devyn to the elevator, picking up her suitcase to hurry her along.

We step inside and the doors close. I jerk her against me and breathe her in. I didn't realize how much I missed her scent. Roses will always make me think of her.

The elevator bumps to a stop in the lobby, and Devyn tries to step away from me.

"Can you stop for one fucking second?" I growl, trapping her in my arms. "Just stop moving for one minute."

She freezes, and I think I've gone too far, but she presses her face into my neck. "I'm sorry. I didn't know. We didn't say anything. I left, and you let me go without saying anything."

I cup her cheek in my hand. "I'd known you for four days. You know what I am, how I live." I pause. "What I look like. How could I think you'd want me? I'm a broken man who, on rainy days, can barely move."

Her eyes are so green, I think of fields of dark grass, and I want to bring her somewhere, anywhere that's away from here.

She opens her mouth to speak, but I press my thumb against her lips. "I was scared to tell you because the last time I said it to a woman, she didn't say it back."

Batting my arm away, she says, "Then she was a fool." She crashes her mouth to mine, and I've never tasted anything so sweet, so intoxicating. Devyn's all passion, bottled-up lightning, and her energy, her spark, is slowly waking me up. My tongue tangles with hers, and I shove my hand under her top. The contact soothes me, but my blood boils. It's only been two days since I had her, but they've felt like years.

"Say it," I demand. "I need to hear you say it."

"I love you," she gasps, her breath fanning my face. "I love you."

I never let myself believe a woman could say those words to me after the accident. I never thought I'd meet a woman who could see the man I was trying to be underneath my injuries. Renata would look straight through me, and it shredded me.

"Thank Christ. Come on. Let's get out of here."

The truck's still waiting, double parked, its hazard lights flashing and pissing people off, and I toss her suitcase into the back. I haul her into my lap and don't notice Mack merging into the traffic toward a penthouse I haven't seen for two years.

Her pajama bottoms are thin, and her warm cleft cradles my cock through my jeans. I didn't give her time to put on her jacket.

"I'm sorry," I say, fluttering kisses all over her face. I don't know what I'm apologizing for. Forcing her to leave Beau's penthouse without a coat, or letting her come to Cedar Hill without me, or not telling her I love her when that's all I've wanted to say since the morning I watched her drive away.

"For what?" she asks, dragging her lips over my jaw and down my neck where she nibbles my skin with her teeth.

I choose one. "For not saying anything the morning you left."

She sits up and pushes away a piece of hair that fell over my forehead. I haven't bothered with a haircut in God knows how long. I haven't bothered with a lot of things.

"It's okay. There were things I needed to do before you did."

"Things like the accident?"

"No. Talia. My job. Figuring out what to do about Stevie. Some things I managed to take care of, some things I haven't."

"Then you shouldn't have said it to me if you weren't ready." I'm quick to jump to bitterness. I was so close only for it to get ripped away.

"You're saying you won't wait." She crawls off my lap and sits in the seat, pulling her cardigan closer around her.

"That's not what I said."

"That's what it sounded like."

I don't want to fight, and I gently link our fingers. "You were almost shot today."

She smiles, her eyes bright, and the streetlights shining through the window tint catch her face. "Occupational hazard."

"You like the danger," I say, surprised.

"I don't like it, not like some reporters who get off on the adrenaline high, but I won't quit because of it."

The car glides to the curb, and Mack parks in front of my building. He takes Devyn's suitcase out of the back, and the doorman, seeing that Devyn doesn't have a coat on, urges her inside. Mack hands me her suitcase with a quick, "Goodnight," his breath white in the cold.

The lobby's warm and looks the same as it did the day I moved out. Standing stiffly behind his desk, the concierge spots me, and startled, his eyes widen, but he only nods when we walk past him. I've kept housekeeping going, but I have no fucking clue what the state of the penthouse is. It could be completely empty for all I know, and I could have brought Devyn here only to have to check into a hotel. There's a very good chance there isn't a bed in the bedroom.

This elevator ride isn't the same as at Beau's, Devyn standing next to me, but not *next to me*. I said the wrong thing in the truck. It wasn't that she wasn't ready to say she loved me, it's that though I'm thankful she could, I wasn't ready to hear it. I expected her to take it back, wanted her to take it back, if only to prove myself right.

I'm only a beast moving from one prison to another because the reflection in the mirror is always the same.

The penthouse feels empty. As it should. I won't have food here, and I didn't think to ask to have the kitchen stocked. I was so focused on reaching Devyn and seeing for myself that she was okay that nothing else mattered.

She steps inside the foyer and takes off her flats. The artwork is still hanging on the walls, the little table that we used to drop our keys on is still by the elevator. The penthouse is dark except for the lights of Cedar Hill streaking against the walls. She walks across the vacuumed carpet and looks around as if trying to read the room, find me in these walls, but there's nothing left.

"This is where you lived with your wife," she says.

"It is."

"Where did she go?"

"I don't know."

She looks over her shoulder at me, but it's true. I don't know where Renata lives. Beau would know, but I never cared enough to ask.

"Did Beau feed you? Do you need anything? There's not much here."

"He ordered some food. I'm good, thanks. You seriously haven't been here since the accident?"

"I came back for some clothes. The rest should still be here."

She pads across the floor toward me. "What do you mean?"

"I don't know what she took when she left."

"Oh."

"I'll show you around. Make yourself comfortable."

She laughs, and it eases some of the tension. "That might be hard to do considering you won't be able to."

I tip my head. She's not wrong. I'll hate staying here, but I thought it was fair that she see the place, thought it best for her to see I've moved on from that time in my life.

Looking through the penthouse is like attending an open house. It could be a stranger's home, and I'm studying it objectively, tallying the pros and cons of the purchase. The fireplace hasn't been used for years. The kitchen hasn't been used in double that time because Renata didn't know how to cook. The bathroom is spotless, no dirty towels on the floor, no condensation on the mirror, no wet toothbrushes on the vanity.

The bed is still here, the comforter the one she chose when she redecorated last, and it matches the throw pillows on the chaise lounge tucked in the corner and the colors in the curtains.

"It's a beautiful place," she says, poking around the suite, skimming her fingers over a loveseat, peeking into the sitting room and the large walk-in closets.

"Where did you live?" I ask, standing awkwardly in the middle of the room. I don't belong here.

"Ooooh, on the other side of the city. A walk-up that kept me in good shape. I might have been doing well at the *Times*, but my salary didn't compete with the cost of living. Plus, I was helping Mom and Talia. There wasn't a lot of money to go around. Speaking of that, thanks for paying for Talia's rehab bill. You didn't have to."

"I wanted to. Something like that shouldn't cost money. She thanked me at Beau's, and you're welcome."

She stands uncertainly near the bed, like she wants to be intimate but she's afraid I'll stop her. I fucked up in the truck, but I had my reasons for saying what I did. I don't want her to get in over her head and regret it. She might come out of that without getting hurt, but I don't have much left of my heart. I need something to hang onto if she decides a future with me isn't what she wants.

"There's more if you want to see it. Upstairs." I shove my hands into the pockets of my jacket. I forgot to take it off, and

I'm starting to sweat. I need a painkiller, a drink, and a bed. The tension has me twisted in knots and I need to calm down and relax. It would be helpful if Devyn could give me a massage, but I don't want to ask if she's angry.

"No, thanks. I think I'll brush my teeth and go to bed. Do you want me to sleep here? With you, I mean?"

"I want you to do whatever you're comfortable with."

"I want to be with you." She crosses the room and wraps her arms around my shoulders, brushing her lips along my jaw. "I love you. I don't regret saying it, and I'm not going to take it back. You don't have to say it to me. The look on your face when you stormed into Beau's penthouse will be enough for a little while."

She leaves me standing alone in the bedroom, and though I know she's only going to get her suitcase to grab a toothbrush, the seconds are too much and I hold my breath until she's with me again.

———

Devyn slides between the sheets naked, and I feel like a dumbass for putting on a pair of pajama bottoms. I didn't want her to think I expected sex, but if she's offering, I won't turn it down.

She curls her body around mine and nuzzles my cheek with her lips, her hand roaming my chest and down farther until she's gripping my cock.

"We don't have to," I say chivalrously, but I want to be deep inside her more than anything.

"Maybe we don't have to," she says, tugging the waistband of my pants down just enough for her to crawl on top of me and slide my cock inside her, "but I want to."

I clench my teeth as she adjusts, my cock surging. "You could've let me get undressed."

She sits up, taking every millimeter her body will accept. Her hips are generous, her waist narrow, and her breasts are high and firm. She's a goddess sitting on top of me, her hair spun gold swirling around her shoulders. Bracing her hands against my chest, she lifts up until the tip of my dick almost slips out of her. "Do you want me to stop?"

Grasping her hips, my fingertips sinking into her soft skin, I push her back down, and she laughs. "No."

"Tell me if I'm hurting you," she says, moving up and down, so wet, and my cock glides in and out of her in a slow, steady rhythm.

I squeeze her delicate pink nipples, and her muscles clench around me. It's all I can do not to burst—I want her to come first.

She wiggles her fingers between us and finds her clit. Closing her eyes, she grinds against me. She's so beautiful. For now, she's mine, but I don't know how long it will last.

"Rick," she whimpers.

I nudge her hand away and rub her clit, wanting to be the one to make her come. I love feeling myself inside her, where we're joined.

"I'm coming," she whispers, but she didn't need to tell me. I can feel her all around me. Not only my cock, but her energy, her spirit. It twists around us. If she hadn't told me she loves me, I would have felt it, her emotions saturating the room. The orgasm surges through her, and her cum gushes around my cock.

I want to be on top to find mine while riding out hers, but I can't spare the precious seconds to ease into a position that wouldn't hurt my back. I grip her waist and encourage her to move, and she takes the hint, riding me in vicious strokes until I slam her down on my cock one last time and come, spurting hot inside her until I'm completely empty.

Gasping, she lies on top of me, her skin soaked with sweat.

I kiss her damp shoulder and brush at the hair that's sticking to her cheek.

"Tell me again you didn't want to do that," she mumbles.

"I didn't say it the first time. I was trying to be courteous."

"I'd rather you be courteous naked."

I chuckle. "I'll remember that for later."

She presses a hard kiss to my cheek and then goes to the bathroom, and I use a tissue on the nightstand to clean up.

Hopping on one foot and then the other, she wiggles her panties on and tugs a tank top over her head. She lies next to me, her head resting on her hand, one leg thrown over mine. She's on my left side, and I don't have to say anything. If she had done it on my right, my hip would have locked up and I would've needed to ask her to move. My injuries will always affect me, but until Devyn and I made love the first time, I hadn't thought of how limited I'd be in bed.

"Did I hurt you?" she asks, her fingers brushing over the sparse hair on my chest.

"I think that's supposed to be my line," I say wryly.

"You didn't."

I exhale. "Good. You didn't either."

She copies me, blowing out a breath, laughter lighting her eyes. "Good."

"Keep it up, and I'm going to think you're too good to be true." I sound like I'm joking, but I couldn't mean it more.

With her lips hovering over mine, she says, "If you love someone, you'll do anything for them. You know that. I haven't been married, or in a serious relationship for that matter, but that doesn't mean I don't understand it. Your wife should be here instead of me, I get that, but she's not here and that was her choice. Her loss is my gain, and I'm not going to feel second best knowing you tried for a baby in this bed."

I bite back a string of swear words. "I should never have told you that."

"Why? When you're married, it's what you do. Maybe if it would have worked, she wouldn't have left." She rubs her thumb over my cheek and nips at my lips with her teeth.

I slick my fingers down her spine and smile as she shivers. Devyn's so cool, so calm under pressure, and I never know how she's feeling unless she deliberately shows me. "Then I'm glad it didn't."

She searches my eyes in the city's lights glowing through the windows. "Do you mean that?"

"I can't compare you, Devyn, and I won't. What I had with her isn't the same, and the life I had with her I could never have with you even if I wanted to because you are two completely different women. Asking me if I prefer her over you is like me asking you if you would have preferred never to have met me at all. Maybe you would have met someone who isn't injured, who shares your love of journalism, who would fly all over the world with you writing the next award-winning piece."

"I would never share a by-line," she whispers, teasing, but I'm not in the mood to be teased.

"You know what I mean."

"I know what you mean," she says, snuggling into my chest. "Would you ever move back here?"

"To the penthouse?" Like the site, I've pushed away what I'm going to do with this place. I never thought about my clothes hanging in the closet, the artwork she didn't want, or the gifts she didn't bring with her. I let Renata clean it out because I didn't care what she took and what she left behind.

"No. To Cedar Hill."

"Beau wants me to. He says he's tired of working alone, and

he's pushing me to go out to the site and decide what to do with it." I sigh. "He'll keep me busy all day tomorrow. I bet he's setting up meetings right now to take advantage of me being here. But I like living in Old Harbor. I like the peacefulness of it, the water and the quiet. My doctor said if I moved somewhere warmer my joints wouldn't give me so much trouble, but I don't want to leave." I move my hand down to her ass and play with the edge of her panties.

"Okay. I like Old Harbor too, and I want you to know that Talia and I aren't moving out of Minnesota. Before I fell in love with you, I said something about getting away from Stevie, but I don't want to leave you."

"I think your sister would give you a tough time now," I say, but I'm relieved I don't have to ask her to stay. I never would. If she thought moving to someplace like New York was what she had to do, I would never ask her to sacrifice her safety for me. I need to start believing what she tells me. It's my job to keep her and Talia safe if she's going to stay here.

She lifts her head. "You're right. Before we left Beau's, I told her to be careful. I didn't know much about him before—when I lived here, I mean. I knew he was a partier, and I doubt that changed while we lived in Portland. I want her to live her life as much as she can on her own, make her own choices and feel in control, because when she was on Sweet, she had zero control over anything. I want her to have that back. I wanted to tell her to get to know him before sleeping with him, but I couldn't say that, not knowing I'd be here with you barely a week to the day since we met."

"I called him earlier this afternoon to complain about missing you," I say, scoffing, "and he told me you were here. I could tell he was already interested, and I told him about her addiction. I thought it was better he knew because you're right. He still plays hard, and I wanted him to understand what he was getting into if he started dating her. I hope you're not mad at me for it."

"No." She lightly brushes her lips over mine. "It makes me feel better about the way he was flirting with her today. Thank you."

I roll her onto her back, nudge her thighs apart, and pushing aside the material of her panties, find her slit. "Make love to me, Devyn," I say before crushing my mouth to hers and pushing my fingers inside her.

She tangles her fingers in my hair and arches her back. "I always have been."

CHAPTER FIFTEEN

Devyn

Talia doesn't look like something the cat dragged in, and I'm grateful Beau let her get some sleep. I don't know him, but Rick trusts him. That will have to be enough for now. I need to give Talia space to be herself, and if Beau can help instead of hinder, I could loosen my grip.

At nine, we meet in Rick's office, and true to what he assumed last night, Beau scheduled meetings for Rick back-to-back. I'll have plenty of time to talk to the crane operator and sort through more of the accident reports, interviews, and evidence. Rick's humoring me, but eventually he'll get aggravated and want to go back to Old Harbor. I need to find what I need to find soon or give up and admit the accident was only an accident.

"You need to stay here," Beau says, leaning against the window near the conference table, his eyes on Talia. The boxes we looked through yesterday are still here, and the piles of paper are where I left them, waiting for me to sort through them all again. I have no doubt that I will.

His eyes are hooded, broody, and he's different from the happy-go-lucky man we met yesterday.

"I can help," Talia insists, hands on her hips and a scowl on her face. She's dressed in black dress pants and a low-cut green blouse, and as she moves, I catch glimpses of her lacy black bra.

I'm sore from the way Rick went at me last night, and we didn't fall asleep until long past midnight. Something was on his mind, something more than the heavy conversation we'd already had, but he never asked me to not meet with the crane operator. He wanted to, though. Opened his mouth several times on the drive from his penthouse to the office building, and each time he'd look at me out of the corners of his eyes and press his lips into a firm line.

He doesn't like it, but he'll let me do what I want.

He's standing near his desk, sipping a cup of coffee. He looks good, wearing a black suit and a dark green and black tie. I complimented him on it, and he said he wanted to think about me, the green matching my eyes.

"Don't make me say it, Talia," Beau says, and she wilts and slides the jacket off her shoulders.

"Fine." She turns away and helps herself to coffee from the cart Beau's assistant wheeled in the moment we got here. Rick understands, but much to Beau's comic dismay, we're all drinking decaf.

I want to hear him say it. I want to know why Talia would back down so quickly. The smolder in Rick's eyes tells me he wishes he had the same power over me, but with his help, I put on the jacket I left at Beau's. He was thoughtful and brought it to the office for me.

"You can do some homework. I won't be gone long," I say.

She shoots me a withering look, but I don't have to remind

her how scared she was at the site. "Be careful," she says, her mug trembling in her hand.

"You don't have to worry about that."

Rick walks me to the elevator and punches the Down button with his thumb. "Mack won't let you out of his sight. Tony lives in an older residential section of the city. Lots of houses. It's not the same as being out in the open at the site. I don't think Stevie would take a shot at you on a neighborhood street."

I pat his cheek and brush my fingers over the scar. I like reminding him that I see it. He probably doesn't like it, but I want him to always know his injuries will never matter to me. "Are you trying to convince me or yourself?"

He grabs my wrist and squeezes. "Don't be funny. I don't like this, but you're determined to do what you want. It's an admirable trait, as I have it myself, but I just found you, Devyn. You can't let anything happen."

"I'll be careful. Talia's not strong enough yet to lose me."

"Neither am I," he says.

The doors slide open.

I step into the empty elevator, and no one gets in with me.

He blocks the doors, stopping them from gliding shut. "Mack's downstairs waiting. Stick with him. I mean it. He's an expert shot and he's not going to let anything happen to you."

"You make it sound like I want to get hurt."

"Things happen, and they come out of nowhere. I wouldn't be like this if it wasn't true. Stay safe."

I lift a hand in goodbye, and he lets the doors close. He's still standing there as inch by inch they block him out.

I try not to act like it, but it does worry me that Stevie Johansson knows that I'm in Cedar Hill and wants to do something about it. I was on to something, and if I hadn't believed it while digging around, I did after she threatened me. People don't do that kind of shit if they're innocent, but Rick's accident has nothing to do with her selling Sweet.

The driver's waiting, standing next to the same kind of black SUV both Beau and Rick seem to like. He opens the back door for me. "Miss Scott."

"Thanks."

He doesn't ask me for an address, only sits behind the wheel and merges into traffic. I wonder if he would drive me somewhere else if I asked, or if he'd call Rick and ask permission. It's different being around Rick in the city. His money is more evident. I didn't let him know it, but his penthouse impressed me, the size of it, the glamour. That he'd married a woman who belonged there . . . I prefer his lighthouse, the cozy space he made for himself.

He fits into both.

Maybe I could too.

Anthony Kelly, Tony to his friends, lives in an older part of the city where the houses are two stories, built with hardwood floors, and tall trees protect yards from the sun and rain. Where children play after dinner, and families sit on the porch and talk to their neighbors as the sun sets.

Mack eases the SUV to a stop alongside the curb, and he points across the street to a navy blue house with a large white porch. A rocking chair is in the corner, and a brown package is on the Welcome mat waiting to be brought inside.

"You'll wait?" I ask, confirming what Rick told me.

His face is smooth like a statue's. "Yes, ma'am."

"Thanks."

I could have driven my own car, but I can imagine the tantrum Rick would have thrown. It would have fit in on the street better. People with money can't hide that they have it, and it's the same for poor people too. I'm not either, and I think I would like living in a neighborhood like this.

I don't have my recorder or the little notebook I brought to the site yesterday. I don't want this to feel like an interrogation. Tony did nothing wrong, and he won't talk to me if he thinks I'm gathering evidence against him. I didn't call ahead, hoping he'd be home on a Thursday morning. If he's not, I'll have to try again, and if the second time doesn't work, I'll have to let it go. Rick won't let me try a third time, and I can't be stupid.

Pushing the doorbell and listening to it chime, I look over my shoulder. Mack's standing in front of the driver's side door with his feet spread and his hands clasped behind his back. His breath steams white in the cold.

The door opens, and an older gentleman peers at me through the storm door's screen. I thought he'd be younger.

"Can I help you?" he asks.

"Are you Tony Kelly?"

A guarded look crosses his lined face and his eyes narrow in suspicion behind gold-rimmed glasses. "I am."

"I'm Devyn Scott—"

"I know who you are. You were a reporter for the *Times*."

I blink. I'm not used to my fame, or rather, my notoriety. Stevie Johansson did a number on my reputation and still, years later, people remember she ran me out of the city. "I was hoping I could talk to you for a minute."

"About what?"

"The accident."

It's all I have to say, and he knows exactly what I'm referring to.

"I don't talk about that."

"I'm not here as a reporter. I . . ." I decide to tell him the truth. ". . . I'm in love with Rick Mercer and I just wanted to ask you a couple of questions. For my own knowledge."

Tony studies me, and after a moment, he nods and opens the door.

"Thanks."

He shuffles down the hallway toward a medium-sized kitchen, and I take off my ballet flats and follow him.

"You can hang your coat on the back of a chair. We're not too formal around here. Do you want a cup of coffee?"

"Please. Caffeine sounds great."

"Not a morning person?" he asks, pouring coffee out of a carafe that's half full into a plain black mug.

I hang my jacket on the back of a chair like he told me to and sit. "It's not that. My sister's in recovery. She was hooked on Sweet. We don't keep anything in the house that can be addictive in any way."

"Milk? Sugar?"

"Milk is fine, thank you."

He adds some to my coffee and carries it to me by the handle. With his own cup of coffee, he sits across from me. "That's tough. Is she doing better?"

"After three years in rehab, yeah."

He nods. "You can't get away from it here. I followed that story, and I think you were onto something. Maybe not with the Sweetheart of Cedar Hill, but you were on to something. I'm sorry that didn't work out for you, but you seem to have landed on your feet. Rick Mercer. He doesn't live here anymore."

"Neither do I. The *Portland Pioneer* assigned me to interview him, and I drove to Old Harbor from Portland. I didn't get the interview." I smile down at my coffee.

He chuckles. "You got something better."

"I did." I look up and tilt my head. "You were working the crane that day."

"Yep. I still pay for it every day." He taps his temple. "I have migraines now. Never used to."

"I'm sorry."

He raises a shoulder and wraps his hands around his mug.

"It's tough to complain when I walked away. The two iron-workers helping with the lift weren't so lucky. Rick wasn't so lucky."

"Can you explain what happened?"

"I can do better. I can show you." He stands up and tugs the hem of his sweatshirt lower over his stomach.

"I've seen the videos."

"I have something else. Come on."

I leave my coffee on the table and walk with him to a family room on the first floor at the rear of the house. Bookshelves line the walls and a large TV is mounted above a fireplace. In the corner, sitting on a glass table, is a huge replica of a crane.

Tony gestures for me to walk farther into the room. "I can show you what happened."

I stand next to the table, and he gently touches the boom. "It's beautiful, isn't it?" he asks.

"You won't believe this, but I was at the site yesterday and thought the exact same thing. There's something sadly beautiful about it all."

"Poetic, almost. I go out there sometimes and pray. Apologize to whoever's listening for my part in it. It doesn't help. OSHA cleared me, but I wish I could put it away."

"What would you have done differently?" I ask, the reporter in me coming out after all.

He grunts. "I've asked myself that a million times. More than a million, and every time I come up with the same answer. Nothing. I did absolutely nothing wrong."

"What *did* happen, Tony?" I ask, meeting his eyes.

"You know the crane needs to be balanced."

I nod. "Beau explained that to me. The truck weighed more than the framework, and the boom was balanced by counterweight."

"Yes. We put the weight here," he says, pointing behind the

boom. "That way, when the crane swivels, the weight is always where it needs to be." He pauses. "It rained the day before and it was windy."

"I saw the video. The tires were sinking."

"Sure they were, it's mud. Miss Scott—"

"Devyn."

"Devyn, I've worked on hundreds of construction sites. When I was a kid, if there was a building going up, my dad would bring me to watch. That's all I ever wanted to do. I have degrees in construction management and mechanical engineering, and I've been working sites since I could lift a hammer. The ground was stable."

"I was going to ask why you didn't use outriggers or bearing plates."

"We didn't need to. We didn't need the outriggers, or the bearing plates, even though the ground was mostly dirt." He points to what looks like legs coming out of the middle of the truck. "There was mud, but do you know how much it rained the day before the lift?"

I shake my head. I haven't looked into that part of it.

"Not even a quarter of an inch. Now you tell me if that's enough to make the earth move under our feet."

"The wheels sank. I saw it for myself in the video online."

"There was a puddle, yes, but I know that wasn't enough to make the truck tip over or I wouldn't have parked there."

I glance at the model. "Can you demonstrate how it happened?"

Tony adjusts the boom. "I don't have a replica of the framework, so you'll have to pretend it's hanging from the hook." He flicks at a little silver hook hanging from a thin string at the end of the boom.

"All right."

"The truck was positioned like so, parallel to the hotel's

lobby. We were building a tearoom on the fourth floor, and the framework was going to be part of a picture window. It wasn't heavy, not by my standards, anyway, but I don't want to shrug off how important the lift was. Rick planned it for days, and he had everything in place." He swivels the boom. "See, the weight is always in position."

"Yes, I see."

"Now, when I was positioning the boom so the framework would be situated where it needed to be, the truck was like this."

He adjusts the boom, and the counterweight is set to the side of the truck, right over the tires sinking in the mud.

"All of a sudden, the truck starts to shudder. I thought it was just a gust of wind, but the next thing I know, I'm slamming against the window and waking up in the hospital."

"What happened?"

"Hell if I know."

"You could have used the outriggers and bearing plates," I say, trying not to sound accusatory.

"I could have. I know that went into the report—that I had a lapse in judgment—but the ground was solid and I truly believed we didn't need them. The only thing I can think of is that the counterweight was too heavy, but that's impossible."

I perk up. That would make the most sense out of anything I've found since looking into this. "How do you determine that?"

"We go by the truck's manual. The tables specify down to the pound how much to use based on the weight of the load and the reach of the lift."

"And you had help," I ask to be sure.

"Oh, yeah. We use the truck's hydraulics system to place the weight. We can't do that ourselves."

"Do you have the manual?"

Tony put the crane back to the way it was before he acted out the accident. "No. They took it. If you've been digging through the paperwork from the investigation, you should have it."

"There was something, I think. I'm going back to Rick's office and I'll look for it. Beau said there were warning signals that should have gone off in the cab. Why did you ignore those?"

Shaking his head, he says, "There wasn't anything to ignore. I take the warnings seriously. It's what they're there for."

"Do you find that odd?"

"Yes and no. No because nothing was going wrong. Not until the second the truck tipped over, but there should have been a warning before that happened, even if it was too late to correct it. Devyn, I will swear until I'm buried in my grave that I didn't miscalculate that lift. I followed the counterweight table . . . my dashboard didn't say anything was happening. There wasn't enough rain the day before to do what they said it did. If you can figure out what happened, I'll be in your debt. I don't talk to anybody—I'm afraid someone's going to think I'm crazy."

"I'll do my best. I watched the clip online and something didn't feel right. Do you think someone could have tampered with the crane?"

"It's possible," Tony says slowly, as if considering it for the first time, "but I don't see how. And why would they want to? Why shut down Rick's project? What would be in it for them? It's not like he was building over endangered land and threatening to kill off the last of a species."

"I heard Declan Everett was angry Rick bought the land before he could."

Tony scoffs, and I follow him into the kitchen. "Land development can be cutthroat, sure, but they've been in competition for years. M&H has lost out on land to Everett. It's the way it goes. Rick was well liked in the city. Gave a lot of money to local charities. No one had a bad word to say about him, and people were disappointed when he left. It'd be difficult to find anyone who wanted to hurt him that way."

I want to believe that, but someone did something, and I intend to find out what.

"Can I have your phone number? I'll be in touch if I find out anything else." Beau already gave it to me, along with his address, but I'd rather use a number he gives me himself. Our connection will feel more sincere, and he'll be more apt to talk to me if I have more questions. He rattles off a number that I match to the one in my contacts app. "Thanks. I'm still not sure what I'm looking for. I'll ask Beau if someone can look at the warning system. Do you think they'll be able to find anything after all this time?"

"Equipment is usually left out in the open. It's built to tolerate that kind of exposure," Tony says, wrapping up our conversation and leading me to his front door. He wants me to leave, and I take the hint.

"Thanks for talking to me," I say, putting my coat and shoes on. I dressed in jeans and a sweater, not wanting to appear too professional just in case he didn't believe I was speaking to him for my own benefit.

"I watched you come up the sidewalk, and I knew I had to. It's been bothering me ever since I woke up in the hospital. I want you to figure it out for me as much as for Rick. I don't want to live the rest of my life thinking I killed two people and almost Rick too."

I pause near the door, my hand on the doorknob. "Do you know how Rick scarred his face?"

Tony shakes his head. "He knew the second things started

going wrong, and he tried to warn the workers on the fourth floor. He was too busy trying to get their attention to watch where he was going, and he tripped and hit his head on the edge of a toolbox. It stunned him, and when the boom fell, he couldn't roll out of the way. He always cared more about his crew than he ever cared about himself. He would have died a million times if it would've kept those two workers safe. Take care, Devyn."

"Thank you. You too."

Mack's waiting and holding the door open for me the second I step onto Tony's porch. I can't forget Stevie's after me, and wanting to keep my promise to Rick, I hurry to the SUV. While Mack drives to Rick's building, I use my notes app to write down all my impressions and what Tony said about the rain, mud, counterweight, and his warning dashboard in the cab.

I'm starving by the time I walk into Rick's office, and Talia's sitting with her laptop and a platter of sandwiches and plastic containers of soup at the conference table.

"This looks amazing," I say, taking my jacket off and sitting across from her at the table. "Where are Rick and Beau?"

"Meeting," she says, nibbling on a chip. "I've been getting some homework done. How did it go?"

I bite into a turkey and cheese sandwich, chew, and swallow. "Good. He's a nice old man." I explain what Tony told me about the counterweight, the rain, and the lack of warning in the cab. "Something isn't adding up," I say, opening a small bag of ranch chips. "How was your night last night?"

"You want to know if I had sex," she says, reaching for a container of chicken noodle soup.

Pouting in mock offense, I say, "That's not true. I can't be a hypocrite. You know I did. Rick and I didn't wait that long, either, before hopping into bed."

"Well, we didn't. We had more to eat and a little dessert, and then we talked for a bit. I told him about my time in rehab. He told me about working here without Rick. Not exactly chitchat, but we didn't get very deep, you know?"

I nod. They only met yesterday.

"Then I got ready for bed, and we said goodnight." She looks down at her laptop, taps a few keys, and closes it.

"That sounds . . . okay. Why do you sound sad?"

She jerks a shoulder. "It's stupid. I barely know him, and he shouldn't be able to hurt my feelings."

"What happened?"

"I heard him answer his phone, and I could tell it was a woman. She asked him if he wanted to go out, and he said that he couldn't, that he had to keep an eye on someone for a friend. He made me sound like a chore."

"I'm sorry." I push my sandwich away. "He's always been a partier."

"I know. That's the worst part about it. After I heard him say that, I did a search for him on my phone, and he's with a different woman every night. I was starting to have feelings for him, and, ugh!" she says, rubbing her cheeks. "It's not his fault he's a player, and it's not his fault I'm spinning daydreams. He lives here anyway, and I don't know if I'm well enough to move back to the city."

I think she's right about that, but I don't want her feeling any more insecure or apprehensive than she already is. Watching her sobriety, doing her best not to backslide, and taking care of herself is one thing, hiding and running because she's scared is another. "Did he say anything about it this morning?"

"I gave him the silent treatment, because I was hurt, you know? He thought I was mad you were going to question Tony Kelly without me, and he spent the whole ride telling me how you'd get more answers out of him by yourself, blah, blah, blah. It didn't occur to him that I heard him last night."

"Maybe it's better to leave well enough alone," I say tentatively. "We'll be going back to Portland soon, and Old Harbor is a nice town. Maybe you'll meet someone there."

"Yeah, maybe," she says, but she doesn't sound convinced. "Tell me how your night went."

I slide my sandwich toward me again and take another bite. I'm too hungry not to eat. "It was strange being in the penthouse he lived in with his ex-wife. Tony told me how Rick scarred his face, and I wanted to slap her for leaving him when he needed her."

"They live a lot differently than we did in the city, don't they?" she asks, looking around the office.

"They're still unhappy," I say. "Even with all their money. We don't have much, but in Portland, every day was a gift, and we knew that. We'll find something in Old Harbor that will belong just to us, and we'll get through it one day at a time."

Sighing, she says, "I don't want to be in your way."

"You're my sister, and I love you. You're not in my way. If anything, I'm in yours. Rick can keep me safe for only so long. Stevie might never stop trying to hunt me down."

"Then I guess we're stuck with each other, huh?" She smiles weakly.

"Yeah, I guess we are. If you're done eating, help me go through these boxes again. Tony said he followed the table in the crane's manual when he added the counterweight. Maybe he was looking at the wrong column or something."

I've always been good with pushing unpleasant things aside. Talia needs me strong, and a lot of my strength comes from being able to avoid worrying about things I can't control. Stevie knows I'm here and there's nothing I can do about that now, but leaving Cedar Hill may not be enough this time. She's guilty, and she knows I know. She'll protect herself.

If anyone I care about gets hurt because of me, I'll have to live with it for the rest of my life, like Tony taking responsibility for the accident.

I force the thought from my mind. Like Talia, I can only live one day at a time.

CHAPTER SIXTEEN

Rick

I don't breathe easy until Mack texts and says he dropped Devyn off at the building, and I log into the security app and watch her walk through the lobby.

"You are really in love with her," Beau says, leaning back in his chair.

We're sitting in a large conference room waiting for the next meeting. I could be pissed he booked all my time today, but I shouldn't have expected less. It's the first time I've been in Cedar Hill in two years, and he's been understanding until now. He wouldn't be a good businessman if he didn't take advantage when he could.

"She's everything I need," I say honestly, thinking about making love to Devyn all night. It hadn't mattered that we were in the bedroom I'd shared with Renata. The room has been empty for a long time, and Renata's presence isn't there anymore. "After she's done poking around and we're back in Old Harbor, I'm going to ask her to marry me."

I expect a congratulations or a slap on the back, but Beau glowers at me.

A feeling of dread shivers over my skin. I wanted it to be that simple. I don't know why it can't be.

Angrily, he tells me why.

"*What?* You think you're going to hole up in Old Harbor and have sex twenty-four/seven while I work my ass off for you? No thanks. I've been patient, waiting you out, but we've got that goddamned site to deal with, and maybe one day I'd like to get married too. Did you ever think of that? You do what you can from Old Harbor—I'll give you that—but it's nothing like being here, where I've needed you. If the accident's stopping you from working for your own goddamned company, cut me loose and move on. I'm tired."

"Is this because of Talia?" Maybe I underestimated how taken he is with her.

"No, it's not about Talia. I don't have time, Rick. I don't have time to date or go on a fucking vacation. I haven't seen my parents in years. I'm pushing forty, and I want kids. You wanted kids, why can't I have kids?"

I rear back and swipe my fingers through my hair. "What are you talking about? You date all the time."

"No one who means anything. Relationships need time to grow, and the only relationships that I'm giving my attention to now are on your behalf."

I know where this is going, and I don't like it. "I don't know what you want me to do."

"I want you to move back to the city and share the work like we used to. We had a great balance, and I need that back."

He's not asking anything he shouldn't have asked me six months ago, a year ago. Longer than that. I can't argue with anything he said. We work best when we're in the same building. But I moved out to Old Harbor thinking it was for good. Beau hadn't. He never thought it was permanent.

I didn't tell him that. If I had, he would have quit a long time ago.

Fuck.

Shoving a handout across the table in frustration, I say, "Then do what you need to do. Cash in your vacation, go on a leave of absence, do whatever you think you've been missing out on while I've been in Old Harbor. I'll figure it out."

"I don't want to flat-out leave. I want your help."

I squirm in my chair as his eyes flash with emotions he's never had a difficult time showing me. I've bottled everything up for so long, Beau's honesty adds another layer of guilt to my already aching back.

Defensively, I say, "Things will never go back to how they used to be."

He stands in agitation and puts his hands on his hips. "Maybe I don't want things to go back to the way they were. You and Renata, me and whoever I happened to be with at the time, double dating every weekend. Jasmine called last night and asked me to go out, and I said no. First night in weeks I stayed home, and I liked it. I liked knowing Talia was with me, I liked knowing I'd wake up to her—"

"Did you—"

"No, we didn't. I just met her, and she's too fragile to fuck around with. I like that too. That she would need time. That's the kind of relationship I want. With her, maybe. She's got a lot going on, and with my shit, so do I. Maybe too much to deal with hers, but I'd like to try and see where it leads. Things have changed, and things are still changing. You have to stop hiding from it."

I don't know what that would mean for Devyn and me. She

shouldn't be in the city now but running from Stevie Johansson isn't the answer. If it wasn't keeping Talia safe, I doubt Devyn would do it indefinitely. She'd stand up for herself, no matter the consequences.

"Can you give me until the New Year? Take the holidays off, and we'll regroup after the First. Devyn isn't safe here, and if she says yes, we'll have to talk about where we're going to live and where she'll work. I'm willing to support her, but I know she won't let me. Give me a little more time."

"I'm only willing to do that because you're here, right now. If you would've asked me something like that over the phone, I would have said forget it. I'm happy you found her, I really am," he says, holding out his hand over the conference table, "but I want a life too."

I shake it as a few others trickle in for the next meeting, breaking the tension.

Fuck. I'll have to tell Devyn that Beau wants me in the city, and I don't know what she'll say. They moved so that Devyn could stay out of Stevie's crosshairs and to keep Talia away from Sweet. That lasted while Devyn was out of Cedar Hill, but Stevie took aim the second she drove past the city limits. I miss most of what's said, thinking only about holding Devyn and running through all the ways I could ask her to marry me and all the reasons why she would say no.

"Can you do me a favor?"

Devyn and Talia are sitting at the conference table in my office, lunch leftovers pushed aside. It's a need, a hunger, that I haven't felt in a long time, to go over, drag her out of her chair, and kiss her, pouring my entire heart and soul into it.

She asks the question so casually, not realizing I would do

whatever she asked, whenever she asked. A quick question thrown at me as I walk into my office while she sifts through the old paperwork from the investigation.

"Whatever you need," I say, my voice scratchy.

Beau followed me into the office, and he scoffs, his eyes on Talia who ignores him. Only a day into it, and there's already trouble in paradise.

Devyn smiles, knowing me and tagging me for a sappy slob. She heard it in my voice, and she meets my eyes, acknowledging my feelings.

"Can you go out to the site and look at the crane's warning system? I asked Tony why he ignored the warning signals, and he said there weren't any. I'm trying to find who questioned him in the hospital, but I'm not getting anywhere."

"Fred McAllister, the OSHA rep who filmed the clip that's online. He questioned everyone. I'll find a copy of it for you," Beau says, stepping behind Talia's chair and resting a hand on her shoulder. She tenses, and then relaxes.

Devyn catches the exchange. "Thanks, I appreciate it. Tony was very sure he didn't do anything wrong. He followed the crane's manual and added the weight the table indicated. He said he didn't use outriggers or bearing plates because it hadn't rained enough the day before to need them."

Beau frowns, and I try to think back, but that time is hazy. What I know is from watching the same video as everyone else.

"The mud was deep, Devyn," I say.

"He said the crane was parked in a puddle and that made the mud look deeper than it was. I wasn't there, obviously, but Talia and I watched clips from other viewpoints, and I think he might be right. The ground doesn't look as soggy in other areas of the site. In fact, the area where the boom hit you, had the ground been softer, you might not have been hurt as badly as you were. Anyway," she continues, wanting to avoid arguing as much as I do, "can you check out the wiring and see if anything was tampered with?"

I haven't been out there since the ambulance carted me away, leaving cleanup and everything else to Beau. I would do a lot for Devyn, but I really don't want to do this.

Beau skims his fingers along Talia's jaw and then steps away from her. "I'll go with you. Meetings are done for the day. Are we doing dinner?"

The four of us eating dinner together. I like the sound of it. "Devyn?"

She catches Talia's eye. "Sure. You can tell me some Cedar Hill gossip."

"Beau will have to do that. I don't know anything about what's been going on here. Why do you want to know?" I give in and lean over, nudge her cheek with a finger, and ask her to look at me. She does, and I press my lips to hers. She sighs against my mouth, her breath whispering over my face, and my cock stiffens. Reluctantly, I break the kiss, and I roll my shoulders and tell my dick to settle down. He'll get his turn soon enough. "Doing a little freelance work?"

"Something like that." She wrinkles her nose. "Do you know what to look for?"

Beau shakes his head. "Nope. We'll have to drag a crane engineer with us."

"Will that be a problem?"

"No. Stay here until we come back, okay?" I ask. Devyn grins, and I don't believe it for a minute. "Fine, but at least use Mack. I don't want you to get hurt. I mean it. He'll wait for you downstairs if you need to go anywhere."

"Thanks." She blows me a kiss.

Beau and I step out of my office, and if I wouldn't have gotten shit from him for the rest of my life for it, yes, I would have been the cheesy asshole who pretended to snatch it out of the air and put it in his pocket. Instead, I point at both of them and say, "Behave."

The last thing I hear before shutting the door is them laughing.

———

"Christ, you have it bad," Beau says, turning onto the street from the underground parking garage. "You weren't this obnoxious when you met Renata."

"I'm not obnoxious." I settle in the seat and stare out the window. My stomach has started to do this sick roll, and it will get worse with every passing block.

Beau gives me side-eye and grunts in disagreement, but I'm too busy breathing through my nose hoping to keep my coffee from coming up to argue with him. He calls an engineer who works at the company where we purchased the crane, and the guy says he can meet us at the site in fifteen minutes. I'm only doing this to humor Devyn, not that I would say it to her face. The crane had just gone through a maintenance check, and I went over the plan with my foreman and Tony several times prior to the actual lift. Everything had been in working order.

We sit in silence and Beau grits his teeth, navigating the busy streets.

It's heading toward quitting time, and traffic's bumper to bumper, people trying to go home as quickly as possible after a long day at work. Vehicles start to thin as we near the site, this part of Cedar Hill not as built up as other parts of the city.

My stomach churns and sweat runs down my back. At some point I still would have needed to come out here, but in doing this favor for Devyn, I'm facing the site a lot sooner than I wanted to, but it will be one more thing to make Beau happy. He's been harassing me to come out since my doctor's official announcement that I was healing well and could resume my normal activities.

After Stevie shot at Devyn, Beau sent someone to pick up the truck he left behind, and there's nothing on the street now except stray cars belonging to people who work in the office buildings near here. He parks behind a car that looks like Devyn's, and I swallow around a lump in my throat. She could have gotten killed out here, and it would have been my fault for not reining her in.

Knowing what's going through my head, Beau slaps my arm with the back of his hand in a gesture of solidarity. He gets out of the truck, but I lag behind, unwilling to follow him. My feet touch the solid ground, and my stomach settles slightly. The crisp air cools the sweat covering my skin, and I suck it in, grateful to clear the sick scent of nausea out of my nose.

We walk across the empty street.

A white pickup truck that has a large black crane stamped on the driver's side door coasts to a stop opposite where Beau parked.

I shove my shaking hands into my coat pockets as we join him.

"Finally showing the old girl a little love, huh?" he asks, opening the door of the extended cab. He takes out a white hardhat and a small toolbox that he drops on the road with a clatter. He adjusts the hardhat over his grey hair, pushes his glasses up his nose, and fights with the zipper of his jacket.

The sound of tools clanking in the metal box grates on my nerves. I hate toolboxes. Can't stand looking at them without fighting a panic attack. I look toward the site instead, but that sure as hell doesn't help.

"Something like that." Beau tugs a set of keys out of his pocket. "Better to do it now than when it's colder than hell."

"Supposed to have a mild winter. John Seville. Not sure

you got my name. Haven't been with Merritt Machines for very long. Transferred here from Cincy so the wife could watch her grandkids grow up after she retired."

"Good a place as any," Beau mumbles. He unlocks the padlock holding the thick chains together and pushes the fence door open, the hinges shrieking.

"Too much Sweet on the streets," Seville says. "Don't like it. Don't trust that woman as far as I can throw her, and I'm not as weak as I look—I carry my grandkids around all the time."

"What woman?" Beau asks, amused.

Listening to their exchange, I trudge behind them onto the site. I can't think of anything I want to do less than this.

"The Sweetheart of Cedar Hill. She's got a slippery feel about her, that's all I know."

"You sound like my fiancée," I say, earning me a dirty look from Beau.

"You ask her when I wasn't looking?" he asks.

"Projecting."

"For fuck's sake."

"Your fiancée's got a good head on her shoulders. All right, what are we looking at here?" Seville asks, rattling his toolbox.

We crunch over the frozen dirt and walk toward the crane that's still lying on its side.

"The crane operator said the warning system didn't alert him when the truck was about to tip over," Beau says.

"Yeah?" Seville rubs his forehead. "That'd be something. Load numbers remained stable?"

"That's what he said. Anthony Kelly had years on the job. Was one of my best men," I say, smoothing my hand over a cracked tire.

"This might need more than a quick look-over. Might need to haul it back and pull it apart."

"If you can do what you can here, we'd appreciate it. We

don't expect you to find anything. Just a freak thing, you know?" Beau says.

"Yeah, sure. Malfunctions can happen. Hate it when it causes something like this, though. Can you keep yourselves busy for a few? I gotta get up in there, and it will be a hot minute. That's slang. My grandson taught me that."

"We'll go piss along a wall," Beau says, sliding his hands into the pockets of his jacket.

"Don't hit your shoes," Seville mutters, but his attention is already on the toolbox at his feet.

"What did Devyn think about being out here?" I ask.

We walk over the site, and the wind whips against my face, adding to the chill. I'm already cold, reliving the accident, tripping over my own feet as I tried to get the attention of the iron-workers four floors above me. It's a dreaded loop over and over, my head slamming against a toolbox left out in the open, and nothing but black after that.

"Before or after someone started shooting at her?"

I scowl. "Before."

"She seemed sad, but Christ, anyone would be, looking at this. What are we going to do with it, Rick?"

Uneasy, I lift a shoulder. "I don't want to finish it."

"Because of the two men who were killed that day, or because you still have an emotional attachment to Renata?"

I drift away from him, but he follows me into the building.

Renata and I had lingered after the groundbreaking ceremony, kissing and fantasizing about our vow renewal. The construction started a few weeks later. The first blocks of the foundation were poured, and we dug our initials into the cement. I walk across what would have been the lobby and through part of the west wing. I know the exact place I'm looking for, and I kneel and brush away snow and sawdust. It's still there, our initials in the middle of a large heart.

I had it all, and the accident took it away.

"Are you going to talk to her while you're here?" he asks.

"Why? There's nothing to say."

"I would believe that, except you're here, tearing up over a past you're not going to get back. She's gone, and you say you love Devyn. Which is it?"

"Do you think it was meant to happen? The blizzard and her getting stuck at the lighthouse? What would've happened if she'd listened when I told her to leave, or the snow wouldn't have lasted, or—"

"It was meant to happen exactly the way it did. You two lived in the same city for years, maybe all your lives, and never once, *never once*, did you bump into each other. She's a reporter, and she was working for the biggest newspaper in Cedar Hill. She never covered one of our projects, was never sent to interview you here. You never met her at a fundraiser, a concert, the zoo, the lighting of the Christmas tree in the Square. Tell me how that's possible. She knocked on your door in Old Harbor, and you had no idea who she was. You met her when you were open to meeting someone. When you needed her. You tell me it wasn't meant to be."

His words almost knock me on my ass. "I didn't realize you were such a romantic."

"It's not romance. It's more than that, it's . . . you look into her eyes and there's nothing left but her. I bet you know the moment you looked into Devyn's eyes and knew exactly what I'm talking about. Talia and Devyn, they have the same eyes, and from the second she and Devyn stepped into my office, I can't think of anything else. She's mad at me, and I don't know what I did."

I hold out a hand, and Beau hefts me to my feet. Getting on the ground is always a gamble. I brush off my pants. "If she was hit as hard as you were, it's tough to process. Maybe she's struggling with it. If she spends the night with you again, talk to her. You're what? Fourteen, fifteen years older than she is? It might be a little much to wrap her head around."

"Do you think she's too young for me? I've been worried about that."

"No, but Devyn's had to baby her for the past few years and you don't want to step in as her father. You need to keep her as an equal. That means talking to her and asking her what's wrong."

He nods and looks around. There's not much left except a random plastic crate that shouldn't be here. He digs through it and yanks out a hammer. "Do something with that," he says, gesturing toward the initials dredged into the concrete. "Take care of it, and when we get back to the office, ask Devyn to marry you."

Beau slaps the head of the hammer into my palm and walks away, his hands shoved into his jacket pockets, his head bowed.

I lower to my knees, picturing the afternoon. Renata hadn't given me any clue that her feelings for me were disappearing.

The ring on the hospital blanket sparkles, like the fading sun catching the dusting of snow.

I focus all my grief and pain, into my arm, and my back is a spasming mess by the time I'm done. Groaning, I slowly and awkwardly stand without Beau's help. I'm going to have to skip the hot sex tonight and ask Devyn to rub me down. I've neglected my body for too long, paying more attention to my heart.

I toss the hammer back into the box and limp through the lobby. Beau's staring over the site, the boom and framework still lying in the dirt.

"Ask her what's wrong," I say, stepping to his side.

"I don't want her to leave, but we've only known each other for a couple of days. Is it too much?"

"I don't know. I assumed Devyn would go back to Old Harbor with me, but they still have a house in Portland. I was thinking Devyn would move into the lighthouse and I'd build Talia an apartment over my office, but you want me here. I can't ignore that, but unless Stevie leaves her alone, it's not safe for Devyn to be in the city."

"You haven't talked to her." It's not a question.

"No."

I'm too afraid of what she'll say.

A shrill whistle shrieks across the site, and Seville waves at us.

"What are you going to tell Devyn when Seville says he didn't find anything?" Beau asks as we walk to meet him.

"I don't know how much more digging she can do to prove her theory, and it doesn't sound like Tony had anything to tell her. It was an accident, that's all. They might drive back to Portland tomorrow." I glance at him. "Go with them and take a break."

He scoffs. "That would be a bit presumptuous."

"Not if Talia wanted you to."

"She's barely let me touch her all day."

"But she did. You stood behind her earlier, and I saw her face. She wanted you to."

Seville cuts off our conversation. "Hey, who told you to check out the warning panel?" he asks, chewing on a toothpick.

"A reporter looking into the accident. She was the one who spoke to the crane operator, and he told her the warning signals didn't go off. She's always making something out of nothing. Why?" I try to pass off Devyn's suspicions as a silly woman thing and I feel like an asshole, but she knows I'm only doing this because she wants me to, not because I think anything will come of it.

Beau frowns, and I know he'll give me hell for it later.

"This your fiancée?" Seville asks.

"Yeah."

"Then put a ring on it, and make it a big one, because she deserves it. That's more slang my grandson taught me. Be-yon-cé," he says, drawing out the singer's name.

Beau perks up. "You found something?"

"Sure did."

I trade a look with Beau. His eyes are flashing, but I can't let myself get excited just yet. Seville said he might need to bring the truck back to the office for a proper look.

He shoves a loose panel into Beau's hands. Wires are poking up everywhere.

"You take the whole dashboard apart?" Beau asks, studying the piece.

"Yeah. This bastard's been sitting here for two years. You're lucky vandals haven't scrapped it for parts. Hell, you're lucky it's still here at all. Take a look. See these two wires?"

He points to a red wire and a white wire.

"Yeah," I say.

"The red one is for the audio warning. When the balance is off, the system's supposed to beep. Depending on how bad, it can be a quiet little blip telling you to adjust, or it'll scream like a fricken police siren. Ignore that, and you're gonna be hurtin'. The white one's for the lights. The dash will start blinking, though it's not as attention-grabbing as the alarms, 'cause most of the time the operator's looking up in the sky. See here, the tape on the wires?"

Beau tilts the panel, frowning. "The crane's system had work done?"

"It went through a maintenance check before the lift," I say.

Seville grunts. "Nice coincidence."

Apprehension slithers over my skin. "What do you mean?"

"I mean, I pulled the tape off, like this," he says, peeling the adhesive strip away from the red plastic coating and revealing the copper wiring. They're cut clean and don't connect. "Someone cut the wires and covered it with tape. Your fiancée's on to something. You might want to ask yourself who would want to cause problems on your project."

"She was here yesterday, and someone shot at her," I say, my voice low, though as far as I know we're all alone and have been since we got here.

Seville's eyes widen. "Wish you woulda told me that before I drove out."

"Can you keep this with you? I'm afraid if we have it, it won't be safe. Don't tell anyone you met with us," I say.

"You don't have any idea who'd want to do this?" he asks, putting the tape back the way it was.

"No. I didn't think I had any enemies, but it seems I was wrong. I'll let Devyn keep digging. She's close."

"Let me know when you need it. Someone's gonna get a lot of jail time for this. People were killed on this site. I wasn't here when it happened, but we've all seen the videos."

"I'll be the first person to press as many charges as I can."

Beau and I shake Seville's hand, help him store his toolbox and the piece of the dashboard in his truck, and watch him drive away, his taillights glowing in the dusk.

"Well I'll be a son of a bitch," Beau murmurs, standing in the middle of the quiet street. "How do you think she knew?"

I will never doubt anything Devyn says to me ever again. "The same way she knew Stevie Johansson's distributing Sweet out of her warehouse. She just knew."

"You cannot let her out of your sight. The closer she gets, the more pissed off someone's going to be."

I take my phone out of my pocket and connect to her

number. It rings six times, and then the line goes to voicemail. "Devyn, call me as soon as you get this."

"Mack's with her if she went anywhere," Beau says, trotting to his SUV. "He'll be enough."

I don't answer him. I'm too busy redialing Devyn's number.

All it does is ring.

CHAPTER SEVENTEEN

Devyn

I dig the beat-up crane's manual out of the box and hand it to Talia.

"This looks really unprofessional," she says with distaste, flipping through it, a grimace on her pretty face. The front cover's torn off, and the pages are splattered with mud.

"All he needed was a table in the middle. The weight's even highlighted. That's all he cared about."

"Is it the correct amount?" she asks, studying the chart.

"We'd have to do that math. There's a sheet somewhere that has the calculations on it," I say, digging through the piles of interviews. "Beau said something about the framework being two tons."

"And the truck weighs more than the load," Talia says.

"Right."

"And they use counterweight to balance the boom."

"Right," I say again.

"But why do they need counterweight if the truck weighs more than the framework? I don't understand this at all," she says, tossing the manual to me. It skids across the table's surface.

"They use counterweight to ease wear and tear on the truck, and it stabilizes the boom. A fifty-ton truck that's hauling a two-ton load for a lift sixty-two feet into the air, at that angle, is going to need 12,400 pounds of counterweight. I did the math and got a headache for my trouble."

"Where did you get sixty-two feet?" she asks, and I think back to where I found the figure. Sifting through the paper would be a lost cause. It all looks the same to me now.

"They were raising the framework to the fourth story. Each story is around fourteen to fifteen feet high. The boom had more than enough reach—a fifty-ton truck has a boom reach of forty-eight meters and sixty-two feet is a little over eighteen meters."

Talia lifts her hands, palms upward. "Then the lift should have been fine."

"That's the problem. It wasn't fine." I flip through the manual again. The cover and table of contents are missing. Very unprofessional.

"How do you think Beau and Rick are making out?" Talia asks, poking through more paperwork.

"I hope they're not making out at all," I say, teasing, wanting to perk up her spirits.

It doesn't quite do the trick, but she smiles, at least. "You know what I mean."

"Yeah, I did. They won't find anything. Mechanics fail all the time. It was probably just a glitch, or Tony stretched the truth. He ignored a warning and didn't want to tell me. It was a while ago now and maybe he doesn't remember clearly. If they don't find anything, we'll talk after dinner about what we're going to do next. We need to stay in Portland until at least Christmas break so you can finish your classes. I didn't talk to Barney about that part of it, but I have until February, then he wants me in the office full-time. Until then, I can commute and work out of Portland."

Talia twists a diamond stud in her earlobe. "Won't you miss Rick? I can stay in Portland alone."

Shaking my head, I say, "I don't want you to do that. We need that time anyway to put in our notice with the property management and pack our things. Rick said he has room for us. I don't know what he meant by that, exactly, but I trust him. We can drive home tomorrow." I'm disappointed there's nothing more to stay for, but maybe a little distance would be good for Rick too. We jumped into it so fast, a cooling off period would be good for both of us.

Talia doesn't look any happier than I do, but a relationship can't be built in a day, and if Beau wants to see her, he'll find a way.

I reach for the manual again. The yellow highlighter catches my eye against the white and black. Sitting up, I ask, "What did I just say the counterweight should have been?"

Talia searches through the paper in front of her and slides a sheet out of the pile. "12,400 pounds."

That's not what the highlighted square in the table says. Quickly, I flip to the front of the manual, and there on the page after where the table of contents should have been, it says in fine print, *Merritt Machines, eighty-ton crane, model FJ1504.*

I dig through my purse and pull out the notebook I brought to the site.

"What is it?" Talia asks.

I compare the two truck models, and I push the manual at

her. "Tony used the wrong manual. The highlighted number is wrong. If he used what's highlighted, he doubled what he actually needed, and the counterweight was way too heavy for the truck and the load. We need to talk to him again. Come on."

"I get to go with you this time?"

She should stay here, but Rick and Beau aren't back from the site yet and because of the late hour, the building's nearly empty.

"I don't want to leave you here by yourself."

"Cool!" She hops up and grabs her jacket, and I do the same, my heart pounding. I tuck the manual in my purse and check my phone. No word from Rick—they must still be waiting for the engineer to examine the warning system.

Mack's parked near the curb, sitting in the driver's seat of a huge black SUV with earbuds in his ears. He notices us trotting down the steps toward the car, and he jumps out and opens the back door for us. We climb in. "Can you drive us to Tony Kelly's house again? Do you remember the address?" I ask, leaning over the front seat.

"Yes, ma'am."

"Thank you."

We don't get to Tony's neighborhood as quickly as we did this morning, and it's dark by the time Mack eases to a stop in front of his house. He parks in the same place along the curb and leaves the engine running. Tony's already decorated for Christmas, and lights I didn't see in the sunlight hang from his roof twinkling merrily.

"We'll be right back," I tell him. "I only have a couple of questions."

Mack nods, slides out from behind the wheel, and opens the back door. A car slows as it passes us, and just for a second, I tense.

Talia and I get out, and we carefully cross the street.

Looking over my shoulder at Mack, I ring the bell.

Tony answers the door, dressed in the same clothes he was wearing this morning. "Did you forget something?" he asks through the screen door, and the scent of a beef roast floats out to us.

"No, but I have a couple more questions to ask, if it's not too much trouble."

He glances at Talia.

"This is my sister, Talia. She's been helping me sort through the accident's paperwork."

Reluctantly, he opens the door, but he doesn't let us go farther than the foyer. "What can I help you with? My wife's cooking dinner, and this whole thing upsets her. I'd prefer if we didn't talk about this in front of her."

"That's fine. I just need to know if this is the manual you used when you put the crane together." I pull out the booklet that's missing the front cover and table of contents.

He ruffles through the pages. "It sure is. Neil marked the counterweight for me. It's right here," he says and points to the highlighted number.

"Neil?" I ask, trying to keep my voice from giving away my excitement.

"Neil Simpson, the foreman at the time. He worked real close with Rick on that project."

"He gave you the manual?" I ask to be sure.

Tony narrows his eyes. "Yes. I've worked with Rick and Neil for years, and Rick always made sure communication was open on the site. I trusted them both, no questions asked. Why?"

"This manual is for a bigger truck. The counterweight highlighted would have been too heavy for the lift. You're sure this is the manual that you used, the counterweight that you used?"

"Son of a B," he murmurs, skimming his finger down a page in the back of the booklet and stopping at the model of the truck written in fine italicized print at the bottom. "I never double-checked. Why would Neil give me the wrong manual? Tell me the wrong counterweight?"

"That's what we need to find out. Do you have contact information for him?"

"Neil's in rehab for Sweet addiction. I can find the address for you. Hold on a second," he says, passing the manual back to me. I put it back in my purse.

Tony shuffles toward the kitchen.

"Why would the foreman want to sabotage the lift?" Talia whispers.

"The only reason I can think of is that he was bribed, maybe blackmailed. That doesn't tell me who was after Rick and Beau, though."

"Here's the address," Tony says, holding out a piece of scrap paper. "It's a little facility on the east side of the city. After the accident, Neil stopped talking to people, like a lot of us did. I know where he is because my wife and his were friends. We went out a lot when times were good."

"Thank you. I don't know what Neil's motives were, but I think you can put your part in this aside. The accident wasn't your fault."

"I appreciate that, but I should've double- and triple-checked. I trusted him and people paid for that trust."

I grip his arm. "He was a co-worker and your friend. You had no reason not to trust him. It's not my place to say you should have double-checked—you'll have to come to terms with that on your own. Thank you for this," I say, lifting the paper that has the rehab center's address on it. "I'll be in touch."

"Be careful, Devyn."

"I will."

Though Mack is waiting for us in the cold, Talia stops on the porch and asks, "Why would Neil Simpson let himself be blackmailed or bribed? He was friends with Rick and Beau too, wasn't he? Couldn't he have gone to them for help?"

I sigh, my breath coming out in a white puff. I hate this. I really, really hate this. "What would you have done for Sweet, Talia?"

Her sad green eyes meet mine and they sparkle in the twinkle lights hanging over us. "Anything."

"I think Neil was the same. We just have to find out who knew and used it against him. I don't know what the rehab's visiting hours are and I don't know if he'll see us, but we have to try. Come on."

I give Mack the address to the rehab center, and Talia curls in on herself. I let her be. I wish she wasn't fighting with Beau right now. She could use the extra support. I squeeze her hand.

The rehab center is a sprawling, single-story building located on a grassy block near a quiet residential neighborhood. The parking lot's cement is cracked, and weeds, withered from the cold, fight to live, much like, I imagine, many of the clients here. The front lobby doors face the road, and Mack parks on the side of the building.

"You don't have to come if you don't want to," I say to Talia. Her face is white in the parking lot's weak security lights drifting into the truck through the windshield. "If Neil's willing to talk to me, it won't take long to find out what I want to know."

She cowers against the door. "I can't go in there. I can't see what I've been trying to get away from."

"I understand. Stay here with Mack. I'll be back in a few minutes. I don't need help," I tell him, meeting his eyes in the rearview mirror. Over his objections, I scoot out and shut the door, the noise echoing through the quiet evening.

The lobby's already decorated for Christmas, though we still have weeks until Thanksgiving. A receptionist is sitting behind a high counter, and I paste a smile on my face.

"Good evening," she says. "Can I help you?"

"Yes, thank you. I was hoping to speak with Neil Simpson if he's accepting visitors right now."

The receptionist, too, is in the holiday spirit, and earrings shaped like tree ornaments dangle from her ears. "Let me find out for you." Swiveling in her chair and facing her back to me, she mumbles into a walkie-talkie. After a moment, she turns around. "May I have your name please?"

"Devyn Scott." There's no point in lying. Either Neil will know who I am and refuse to see me because he'll know what I'm here for, or he won't know and talk to me out of curiosity.

"He said he'll see you, but visiting hours end in half an hour. He's in the TV room. Lorraine can show you the way."

A young woman dressed in light blue scrubs gestures for me to follow her down the dark green carpeted hallway, and I follow her, sweating in my jacket. The scent of beef permeating the air is not as appetizing as what Tony's going to eat for dinner tonight, and my stomach lurches queasily in the sticky heat.

I walk with Lorraine to a room that's similar to the one where I would visit Talia when she'd let me see her. We weren't close while she was in rehab, and many times I tried to visit but she turned me away. After she came home, she explained she was embarrassed and didn't want me to see her like that.

"He's there in the corner," she says, nodding to a man not much older than Rick, slumped in a chair at a small wooden table. A TV mounted to the wall is playing *Wheel of Fortune*, but Neil isn't watching it, isn't trying to guess the phrase. A few other tables are occupied, and a girl who could have been Talia is sitting on a couch reading a Bible.

I take my coat off on the way to Neil's table, hang it on the back of the chair that's across from him, and drop my purse on the floor. It's so hot in here, and I push the sleeves of my sweater up. "Thank you for seeing me, Mr. Simpson."

He meets my eyes, and they reflect as much exhaustion and hopelessness as Talia's do when she's having a bad day. "Not much to lose," he says, his hand limp in mine, barely turning the touch into a handshake.

"Why do you say that?"

"You're the reporter, and I know what you're here for."

"Then why don't you tell me?" I ask, wanting to hear it in his own words. What I took for him being worn down is really just bitterness that he needs to be here at all.

"You don't give up, do you? Stevie ran you out of town, but you still came back for more. She let you off easy and you shoulda learned from that."

I lean back in my chair and twist my fingers on the tabletop. That's not what I expected. "This isn't about Stevie Johansson."

He leans forward, eating up the space I put between us. "You're shitting me. You can't be that fucking stupid. What do you think you're here for?"

"I'm looking into the accident at Rick Mercer's site two years ago. I heard that you knowingly gave the wrong information to Tony Kelly and that it made the crane tip over. That's what I'm here about," I whisper furiously, all my interviewing etiquette going out the window in my need to nail this asshole to the wall for what he did.

"You don't fucking get it, do you?" he whispers just as harshly to me, his face turning red.

"I guess I don't."

"Why do you think I'm here? I was hooked on Sweet, and I still am. A nurse smuggles it in to me, and I pay her big bucks to keep her mouth shut."

"*What?* You're taking up a valuable space in a facility that could be helping someone who really wants it. What the actual fuck?" I'm so angry that he disappears, and all I can see is red.

"Protection," he says simply. "They can't hurt me in here."

"Who's they?" I ask, though by now I should have known.

"Everett and Stevie. You're a fucking idiot. When I was working for Mercer, I was so hooked, it was all I could think about. It was on my mind twenty-four hours a day, seven days a week. I drooled for it. Couldn't sleep, I wanted it so fucking bad. Stevie knew who my dealer was and told Everett I'm addicted. He offered me a deal. Sweet, as much as I wanted, if I could stop the hotel from going up. That's it. That's all I had to do. We worked on that hotel for weeks until I came up with a plan. Throw Tony Kelly under the bus, sure. Why the hell not? And it worked. Too good. I never meant to kill anyone. I never meant to hurt Mercer. Everett, though, he was happier than a pig in shit with how all that went down. The score he asked Stevie to give me was so big, I was out of it for weeks. My wife left me, my kids don't talk to me anymore. I lost my house. I was high and homeless."

He stops and sucks in a breath, and his hands tremble on the table. They're shaking as badly as mine are.

"If you're best buddies, then why are you in here hiding?"

"I told Everett I wanted out, but he said I was too useful. That one day Mercer would start the project up again, and he was going to use me to stop it from happening. So I hid. Checked myself in here."

I scoff. "This won't last much longer."

"It's bought me some time."

"You really gave Tony the wrong manual and made him set

up the crane with the wrong counterweight." I want to hear him say it.

"You bet, and it worked better than I ever dreamed. I disabled the warning system in the cab myself. Easy. Tony's too trusting, like you are. You shouldn't have come back to the city, Miss Scott."

"This is exactly what I came here for," I say, standing and shoving my arms through my coat's sleeves. "Maybe prison will sober you up."

Neil laughs, and it twists his mouth into an ugly grimace. "You're trapped, just like I am."

I pick my purse up off the floor. "You're wrong."

"Am I? Tessa told me the notorious, the fucking *great*, Devyn Scott was here to see me, and who do you think I called? Have any guesses, *sweet*heart?"

Slowly, I back away from his leering grin. He could be lying, but I don't think he is. Staying on Stevie's good side is more important than keeping himself hidden. I turn and rush out of the sitting room. I head for the front doors, but I skid to a stop. It's the door I'd most likely use, and they'll be watching for me to come out. I reach for my phone, but I change my mind. If Talia knows I'm trapped inside, she'll want to help me.

That will only draw attention to her and Mack, and I can't have Talia anywhere near this mess.

No, Neil's right. I fucked up. I should never have talked to him alone.

I find a side door marked for staff and hurry through it, hoping Stevie hasn't had enough time to find me, but I'm naïve as well as stupid. She never does her own dirty work. She wouldn't be the one to pick me up, and it's not. Two of her thugs dressed in suits, their guns bulging under their coats, block me between them.

Trying to run would be useless.

One traps my arms behind my back so forcefully he threatens to rip them out of their sockets. The other jams a syringe into the side of my neck.

The last thing that flutters through my mind is Rick's face, and the last thing on my lips is a prayer that Talia will be okay without me.

CHAPTER EIGHTEEN

Rick

We look for Talia and Devyn, but they aren't in the office. I'm not panicking yet, and Beau helps, saying, "Devyn would never put Talia in a dangerous situation. They're probably talking to Tony Kelly again and getting a lead on someone else to talk to. Let's give them a little longer, and while we're waiting, I want to talk to the OSHA guy. Fucker. He knew there was something wrong with that crane."

I walk to the table and scan the piles of paperwork still scattered over the surface. I don't know what's still here and what, if anything, Devyn took with her. "You want to look up Fred McAllister now? Tonight?"

Beau shows his teeth in an angry grin. "Why not? Why should Devyn get to have all the fun?"

"Because I'm hungry, and I want to wait for them to get back so we can go eat."

"Devyn isn't answering her phone. We could be waiting for hours yet."

She wouldn't need that long to pry answers out of anyone, but there's no guessing when she'll call it quits for the night. "Text Talia then, and see where they are."

Beau shoves his hands into his jacket pockets. "Can't. We didn't swap numbers."

"For fuck's sake." I take my phone out of my pocket and call Mack. "Where are you? Did Devyn and Talia talk to Tony Kelly again tonight?"

"Yes, they did, and right now we're at a rehabilitation center in the east part of the city. Miss Scott went inside to talk to someone, and her sister is in the car waiting with me."

"Who is it?" I hear Talia ask.

"Mr. Mercer," Mack tells her, the phone away from his mouth.

"Okay. The second Devyn's finished, bring them back to the office. We're heading over to talk to someone ourselves. We'll meet up here."

"Got it," Mack says, and hangs up.

"They're at a rehab clinic. That's why Devyn's not answering her phone—she's talking to one of the clients. Talia's in the truck. She's probably not up to facing something like that yet. If we have to wait, we might as well talk to that son of a bitch. He knew. He knew and cleared it so no one else would go looking, and I want to know who he's working for."

He grins. "That's my man."

I scowl. "Don't do that."

"What? Hey, Devyn thinks I'm smarmy. Do you think I'm smarmy?"

Shaking my head, I open my contacts app. Only McAllister's work address is connected to his number. "We need his home address. I'll find it when we're in the car."

Beau drives, and I pull up McAllister's residential address from the online White Pages. I didn't have to bother. His wife answers the door and tells us he's still at the office. "He's working what overtime he can for the holiday gifts. We go broke every year spoiling the grandkids," she says, smiling.

"Thank you, have a nice evening," I say, backing away, unwilling to trap myself in a conversation I don't want to have.

Beau follows me to the truck, and we turn around and head for the local OSHA field office. Neither of us are strangers to the government building, and we park in the visitor's lot. Several of the windows are lit up—McAllister isn't the only one grabbing overtime before the Christmas rush. If I have it my way, he'll be locked up this holiday season, eating turkey off a plastic tray.

It's after business hours, and the doors won't budge. Beau pulls an ID card out of his wallet and taps it against the security pad. The light turns from red to green, and the lock clicks open.

"Why do *you* have a keycard?" I scowl.

"Some of us work," he says.

"You're a smart ass."

"You're lucky I am," he says, grinning.

He's not wrong, and it annoys me. Wanting to get in the last word, I yank the door open and say, "Sometimes you *are* smarmy."

"Hey, that wasn't necessary."

"No, but it was fun."

The OSHA office is located on the fifth floor, and the elevator creaks as it carries us up. It feels pretty shaky for the kind of building this is. On the other hand, if all the OSHA reps are as crooked as McAllister, it wouldn't be that ironic if someone fell to their death because the elevator wasn't up to code.

His office is located toward the back, and we walk past a receptionist's desk and several potted plants. He doesn't have a light on, but McAllister's sitting at his desk, looking over paperwork by the glow of his computer monitor. He glances through his open door at us, and the color drains from his face. "Fuck."

Beau grins. "Indeed."

"We have a few questions for you, McAllister," I say, helping myself to a chair in front of his desk. I kick the other one out for Beau, and he sits on it backward, resting his arms on the back and casually propping his chin on his hands.

"We had a crane engineer tear the dashboard apart," I say, and that's all I need to say to make McAllister start panicking. Fear shoots through his eyes, and beads of sweat form along his temples. "I don't think we need to tell you what he found."

McAllister finds courage from somewhere, and he says, "I cleared Anthony Kelly. Ground instability and the wind caused the crane to tip over. If you found anything wrong with the warning system, that happened before that particular lift and I'm not responsible for it."

Beau clicks his tongue. "See, we didn't say it was the warning system. We said he took the dashboard apart. We could have been talking about anything, but you go straight to the warning system. You knew it had been disabled. Who disabled it?"

"Neil Simpson." McAllister's voice comes out in a whine.

"Why would he do that?" I'm seriously confused. Simpson had been a good foreman. We worked well together, and I trusted him. We brought several projects to completion, sometimes well ahead of schedule. After the accident, I lost track of what happened to him, like so many others. Healing mentally and physically has been my number one priority since I was released from the hospital, and I've made damned little headway.

"He made a deal with Declan Everett."

Beau shoots me a look: *See, I told you so.*

"What kind of deal?"

"Simpson's addicted to Sweet. Everett said he'd give Simpson as much as he wanted if he could stop your project."

I close my eyes and sigh. "Fuck. And of course he had an unlimited supply thanks to his fiancée."

Beau growls. "How do you know all this? Are you on Everett's payroll too? Is that why you cleared Kelly? Is that why OSHA wrote off the accident? A serious investigation would have led to this. Instead, two years later, a reporter didn't like the way the crane tipped over and starts digging . . . Who's Devyn talking to tonight?" he asks me sharply.

"Mack didn't give me a name," I say uneasily, and I take my phone out of my pocket. I bring up Mack's number and press Connect. "Mack. Who's Devyn talking to at the rehab facility?"

"I don't know. She only gave me the address. Maybe Miss Scott does. Hold on. I'll pass the phone to her."

"Rick?" Talia asks.

"Yeah." I move my phone away from my ear and press Speaker, letting Beau and McAllister hear what Talia has to say. "Who's Devyn talking to tonight? Who's in rehab?"

"A man named Neil Simpson. He gave Tony Kelly the wrong manual and told him the wrong amount of counterweight to balance the boom. That's why the crane tipped over."

I glance at McAllister. He's not looking very good. "You knew this, yes?"

Miserably, he nods.

"Is Devyn still talking to him?"

"Yeah, but she's been in there for a long time. Almost an hour."

I don't like the sound of that. "I'm going to hang up and call the front desk—"

"No. I'll do it. Keep her on the phone," Beau says, already

bringing an internet browser up on his cell. "Talia, what's the name of the rehab facility?"

"Cedar Hill Restorative," McAllister says in a strangled voice before Talia can answer.

"Yeah, that's right," she says.

Beau clears his throat. "Hang on for a second, love."

He searches for the number online and taps on it to connect the call. Holding the phone out for the rest of us, he sets it on Speaker, and we listen to the line ring. A polite voice answers the phone, "Cedar Hill Restorative Center, how may I help you?"

"This is Beau Hendrickson, and I'm looking for Devyn Scott. She was there speaking with a client of yours, Neil Simpson."

"Yes, I remember," she says, her voice sounding tinny but clear. "Visiting hours ended half an hour ago, but I didn't see her leave."

"You're sure she's not still there?" Beau asks, his voice steady.

My hand starts to shake, and I set my phone on McAllister's desk so I don't drop it.

"No. Mr. Simpson is scheduled for group therapy after visiting hours. No one is allowed to be here then."

"Thank you," Beau says and hangs up.

He meets my eyes and reaches for my phone. He turns off the speaker and mumbles, "Talia. Tell Mack to drive you to my penthouse. Now."

"What happened to Devyn?" Talia cries, and she shrieks such an ear-piercing wail that the phone doesn't need to be on speaker for me to hear. "I'm not leaving her!"

"Rick's going to find her, I promise. I'm going to meet you at the penthouse and stay with you until Rick's got her. We're talking to someone who knows where she is. Do this, please, love. Don't look for her. She's not there."

Her voice is so garbled with tears that I can't understand what she says.

"Thank you. Hang up now and go. Mack will stay with you until I get there."

Talia disconnects without saying goodbye, and Beau tosses my phone back to me.

He steps away from McAllister's desk, then toward me, unsure.

"Go. She needs you."

"Do you need help?" he asks, and I can see on his face how much it cost him.

"No. I have someone right here who will be a big help. Won't you, McAllister? Where do Everett and Stevie do their business? Where would they have taken Devyn?"

Beau doesn't stay to listen to the answer.

"I don't know," McAllister moans.

"The fuck you don't. Tell me where they took her!" I stand up from my chair so fast it skids backward. I swear to God, if he doesn't tell me what I need to know, I'll kill him, just like he helped kill my men.

"They used to do all their business from Stevie's warehouse on 120th and Pike. She kept some candy there, but what she really did was distribute Sweet."

"Jesus Christ." Devyn was telling me the truth. "Get up."

"But they don't use that place anymore. She built a new warehouse off the Ventura exit on Highway 65, south of here. She and Everett have been using that as a home base since your girlfriend was snooping around the first time." He blinks at me through smudged glasses.

"Get the fuck up. You're coming with me." I yank him by his shirt's collar and drag him out of his office.

At the last second, he flails for a jacket hanging on a coat rack near the door, and I let him grab it. He won't be of any use to me if he's too frozen to talk.

His truck is parked in the staff parking lot, a huge grey extended cab that has an extra-long box. If he's trying to make up for something, I feel sorry for his wife.

Agitated, he fumbles the keys and drops them on the ground.

"Hurry up," I bark.

McAllister unlocks the doors with the fob, and I climb into the passenger seat.

He drives through the city and glances worriedly at me out of the corners of his eyes. I want to call the cops, but I have no proof, and if Stevie and Everett hear us coming, they'll disappear and I won't find out what I need to know.

I rub my forehead—a headache has started to pound through my skull. "Why would you do that?"

The lights fade the farther we drive. Stevie was smart to set up a new storage facility on the outskirts of the city. 120th Avenue and Pike is too crowded and busy for her to have any privacy.

"Not all of us are fucking rich, Mercer," McAllister says, speeding past an older couple out for a Sunday drive on the wrong damned day of the week. "OSHA pays shit. Working for the government is a joke. Everett gave me a decent offer, and I took it."

"I hope you enjoyed it. No amount of money is worth someone's life."

"It wasn't supposed to go down the way it did."

"Tell that to the families who lost men that day."

I keep trying to convince myself that Everett won't hurt Devyn and that Stevie will only scare her again, but it's a lie my heart won't believe.

The warehouse is huge, a glowing ball of security lights in an otherwise empty field.

McAllister parks, and we're one of a handful of cars in the parking lot along with commercial vans decorated with Stevie's Sweetshop logo—a piece of hard candy wrapped in pink cellophane.

He slams out of the truck, and I follow. "We're just going to walk right in?"

"Do you think she has piles of Sweet out in the open? Do you think they're going to tell you anything? They ran Devyn Scott out of the city—for knowing the truth. And they did the same to you. Where have you been for the past two years? They always get what they want, Mercer. Don't you understand that by now?"

The front doors aren't locked, and we walk past an empty receptionist's desk.

The son of a bitch knows exactly where to go, and I follow him down a carpeted hallway to a meeting room where Stevie and Everett are standing at the window, looking out over the highway. They could literally see us coming from miles away. A huge model of a hotel sits in the corner, and I don't have to study it to know it's what Everett would have built had he been able to buy the land Beau and I purchased. The fact I wouldn't sell after the accident must have eaten him up inside.

"Rick, what a pleasure! What can we do for you?" Everett asks, reaching his hand out as if we're good friends, or at the very least, civil business associates.

I'm not falling for anymore bullshit. "Where is she?"

Stevie blinks her large grey eyes, a smug smile on her mouth. "Who? I have no idea what you're talking about." She resembles a cat, high on cream, and she acts like one too, lithe and lethal.

I push the panic away. It's been hours now since Devyn

went to talk to Neil Simpson. "You damn well know who I'm talking about. Where's Devyn?"

Stevie shrugs. "I don't know. Are you having trouble keeping track of your own girlfriend? It sounds like a personal problem. McAllister, what are you doing here?" Her upper lip curls in a grimace of disgust.

"Mercer made me come."

"You always were a spineless twit," Everett sneers.

"Apparently a lot of my team were," I mutter.

Everett laughs. "Well, what can I say? There are things stronger than loyalty. Things like money . . . or the addiction to Sweet." He nuzzles Stevie's cheek with his lips and pulls her close to his chest. "Love." He throws me a look. "But you wouldn't know about that, would you? Your wife left you, Devyn took off. You've got nothing."

"I want to know what you did to her." I try to keep my cool because Christ, if they don't tell me where they're keeping her, I'll never find her.

Everett shrugs and shuffles to the model hotel. "You know I've always been in your shadow? From the second you staked your claim in Cedar Hill, I never stood a chance. Always a day late and a dollar short. I could have done something with that land," he says, skimming his finger along the model's roof, where a blue plastic swimming pool is lit up with tiny yellow bulbs. "I thought after you got hurt and ran out of the city with your tail tucked between your legs you would give it up, but no. You had to be a prick and let it sit there. Just fucking *sit there.*"

"You sabotaged my project and you murdered people, because of jealousy."

"I wanted what you had," he agrees calmly. Stevie steps across the room and wraps her arms around him. Wearing high-heeled boots, she matches his height, and she rests her chin on his shoulder. "And now I do, thanks to Stevie. I have the love of my life, I have professional success, and it's you who has nothing. Look at you, you can't even move without pain. We didn't do anything to Devyn. She didn't want you. Neil Simpson told her what a worthless piece of shit you are, and she took off. Forget about her. Sell me the goddamned land and let me build something the city can be proud of. Something you can't because you're just as spineless as your team."

Suddenly, I know exactly where Devyn is.

The hotel. It's always been about the property.

I jerk McAllister's keys out of his grip. "I need to borrow your truck."

"You can't leave me here!" he howls, shooting fearful glances at Stevie and Everett. I don't know what they're going to do to him for bringing me out here, but whatever they do will be exactly what he deserves.

"Watch me," I say and head toward the conference room door.

Stevie and Everett don't stop me, sure all their secrets will stay hidden. We may not have much evidence, but we have more than what we did before Devyn decided to get involved: witnesses. Tony Kelly will talk, and so will Neil Simpson if we press him hard enough. McAllister will squeal like the pig he is, and John Seville has the warning system and can testify it's been tampered with. Plus, if what Talia says is true and Simpson gave Tony Kelly the wrong manual and he balanced the boom with more weight than what was needed, the counterweight should still be attached to the crane—all we have to do is look.

Right now, I can't think of anything else except finding Devyn. If Stevie gave her Sweet and she's addicted, I'll stay by her side until she's through rehab. I'll do whatever I need to do after what she's done for me.

My cell rings, and I dig it out of my pocket. Beau's number glows in the cab of the borrowed truck.

"Yeah?" I answer.

"Did you find her? Talia's going out of her mind."

"Not yet, but you can tell her that I know where she is. Everett and Stevie brought her out to the site and I'm driving there now. Get security on Simpson and Kelly. Seville, too. They're going to start covering their tracks. They let me go too easily not to have a plan."

"Be careful, Rick. The site's not safe. It could be a trap, and Devyn could be the bait."

"Copy that. I'll get a hold of you when I find her. If she's hurt, I'll have to call an ambulance. I can't—" My breath hitches— "I can't pick her up." There's no way my back can handle that.

"Keep us posted. I'll talk to Talia and make some calls."

Beau disconnects, and I tuck my phone back into my pocket.

The site's security lights have flickered on, and the soft white light drifts down over the abandoned equipment. When I came out of the first surgery that repaired my leg, I didn't know what had happened. I didn't know about Tony's brain bleed. I didn't know two of my workers had lost their lives. I didn't know that when I would look at the site years later, the abandoned equipment would so eerily resemble my own life.

I park McAllister's truck on the street. Swearing under my breath, I remember I don't have a key for the padlock. I dig through the truck, desperately looking for something that I can use, and find a toolbox. I grab the biggest pair of wire cutters I can find, but I waste several minutes I don't have cutting through the fence.

When I'm on the other side, I toss the wire cutters on the ground and take off at a hobbling run. They could have hidden her anywhere. I stagger down the west wing, past the spot where Beau told me to say goodbye to Renata once and for all. The crate full of tools is still there, and I rush past it, searching the site for any sign of Devyn or for something that isn't right. Everett would have an easy time getting his hands on explosives. He's blasted his share of buildings, demolishing the old to make way for the new. He wouldn't have needed any effort at all to boobytrap this place, to time a detonation at the exact moment he knows I'm in the middle of the structure.

I can't let that stop me.

Devyn isn't down this wing.

I want to call out to her, but I'm already out in the open, and if those assholes gagged her, she won't be able to respond anyway.

The frigid air cuts through my wool jacket, and the suit I wore to the office today wasn't made to keep someone warm in below-freezing temperatures.

I trot down the other wing, but she's not here. The foundation is empty except for the steel supports that hold up the second floor. Bits of plastic and fluffs of snow swirl around the concrete, and the security lights create dangerous shadows anyone could hide in. Turning, I'm about to search a different part of the site—the crane or the framework that's still where we left it after the truck tipped over—but I stop. There's a whisper, a feeling, something in the cold air. Later, when I look at her while we're eating dinner or I'm sitting next to her on the couch in front of a fire, I'll say it was love, but now, I pause, listening, and I don't call it love. I call it a premonition, intuition, a hunch. She's here.

I don't see her, or her jacket, or her purse. I don't have anything to go on except a voice that tells me I can't leave.

The only place she could be from here is up, but there isn't a ladder.

A portable outhouse lies on its side, forgotten by the sanitation company, and the contents have frozen in the cold. Graffiti covers the beige plastic, and the door is locked from the inside. That will be something I'll need to check into, because God only knows what's in there, but not right now. There's a dumpster a couple hundred feet away, and I roll it over to the outhouse, creating a crude staircase as a way to reach the second floor.

That still isn't going to be enough, and quickly, I look around, searching the site for something that can boost me the extra two feet I need. Near the truck, there are two wooden pallets covered in snow, and I drag them over. I stack them on top of the dumpster's rusted metal lid, hoping everything will hold just long enough.

Gripping the dumpster for balance, the cold biting into my skin, I step up onto the outhouse. My dress shoe slips against the smooth plastic and I slam my knee. I swear, my breath coming out of my mouth in a white stream. I try again, and from there I climb onto the garbage container and crawl onto the pallets. Carefully, I stand up. My muscles are already straining, and I grip the floor of the second story. As I haul myself up, my back aches and my shoulders burn.

Panting, I lie flat and catch my breath. Something like that shouldn't take so much out of me. I'll never feel my age, never get to fully enjoy the rest of my life, all because Declan Everett was jealous of my success.

Dragging in a cold and shuddering breath, I force myself to roll onto my knees, and I stand woozily to my feet, a searing pain traveling from my shoulder into my neck. Glimpses of working on this floor flash through my mind, laughing with my men, pounding a hammer, just like when I destroyed the initials below me. Nothing satisfied me more than a hard day's work.

That's not true anymore. Since meeting Devyn, nothing makes me happier than waking up to her.

The floor is clear, and for hundreds of feet, support beams create a grid. The wind is sharper up here, blowing my hair into my eyes, and desperately, I begin to search. There isn't anywhere to hide her, not like on the ground where they could have thrown her into the dumpster or locked her in the portable outhouse. I don't see anything, but something tells me she's here.

I search the entire floor and push back tears of frustration and hopelessness. If I don't find her soon, I'll have to call for help. I don't know what kind of condition she's in. Hell, I don't even know for sure she's on the site, except for a feeling deep in my bones. Everett couldn't get this project out of his mind for one fucking second. Obsessed, he'd add more misery to this place.

Stopping near the south side, I scan the construction site, searching for any sign of her. A mitten, a shoe. *Anything.* The boom lies like a broken arm in the dirt, snow shimmering like crushed diamonds, and it's jarring against the ugliness of what happened that day.

She isn't here.

My gut was wrong.

Clouds drift away from the moon, and out of the corners of my eyes, I catch her blonde hair glinting in the light.

"Devyn! Christ."

She's hidden behind a wide support beam, her arms tied behind her. She's not wearing a jacket, and her lips have turned blue in the cold.

I pat her cheek. "Devyn, come on, baby. Open your eyes."

She doesn't respond, and her head lolls, her chin resting against her chest. She's out, and I don't know if they hit her, if it's from a Sweet overdose, or if they drugged her with something else. My hands are shaking, and I pull out McAllister's keys and use one to hack through the zip tie holding her wrists together. I try not to cut her, but it's difficult to see in the dark. After a strong yank, it comes apart, and she slumps over. Quickly, I take my jacket off, drag her into my lap, and cover her the best I can. She needs my body heat, and I tuck her head under my chin.

With my arms wrapped around her, I dial 911 and tell them where we are. I hang up on the dispatcher who's determined to ask me meaningless questions and call Beau.

"I found her. She's at the site. I don't know what's wrong with her—she won't wake up." My words are jumbled, my teeth chattering from cold and fear.

"Fuck," he growls. "Did you call an ambulance?"

"Yeah," I say, and I swallow back shame that I can't carry her to the truck and drive her to the ER myself. "She's on the second floor and I need their help. I can't get down with her in my arms." *I'm not man enough.* I push the thought away. This isn't about me. Not right now.

"The second floor? Why in the hell would they do that?"

"So I couldn't find her before she died of hypothermia? They hoped I'd hurt myself looking for her? She's so cold, Beau. They left her here without a coat."

"Listen," he says urgently, and I focus on his voice instead of the guilt gnawing at me, "she hasn't been out there long, do you hear me? It hasn't been that long since she and Talia were at the rehab center. She's going to be okay. You found her."

"Tell me what's going on!" Talia demands in the background, her voice full of tears.

"Rick found her," he says, turning away from the phone. "We'll meet them at the hospital."

Talia whimpers and fabric rustles, and it sounds like Beau wrapped his arm around her.

He stays on the line with me until sirens wail in the distance.

I forget about him when the EMTs skid to a stop behind McAllister's truck. They break the fence door off its hinges in their urgent effort to find a way inside, and two medics carry a gurney between them. I'm in too much pain to drag her to the edge, and I call out, letting them know where we are. A tiny woman with her hair pulled back into a ponytail climbs up the same way I did and hoists a black medical bag onto the second floor. She presses two fingers to Devyn's neck to check her pulse, counting the seconds using a watch around her wrist.

She says that Devyn's stable, and two others climb up, help lift her across the second floor, and lower her onto the ground. They help me too, one assessing me when I'm shakily standing near the dumpster, beads of sweat rolling down my face from exertion. "Do you need medical attention, sir?" he asks, watching me lean against a support beam, heaving, sick with pain, fear, and blame.

I shake my head. "Help her first."

He shoots me a look, but there's no time to argue.

Sitting in the back of the ambulance, I hold Devyn's hand the entire way to the hospital, and I don't let her go until they wheel her away.

CHAPTER NINETEEN

Devyn

Sweet.

I ease into consciousness, and it's the first thing that flutters through my mind.

I'm hooked on Sweet.

There is absolutely nothing else in my head, and I scramble to sit up, clawing at my throat, tearing at my hair, attacking the IV that's attached to my wrist, so sure I'm already being treated for drug addiction.

Strong arms wrap around me and push me back onto the mattress, my cheek rubbing against the starched white of a pillowcase.

"It wasn't Sweet," the voice says, but I don't believe it and I scratch, kick, anything to get free. Tears leak out of my eyes, my heart pounds in a frantic, desperate rhythm, and I clench my jaw against an anguished scream.

"It wasn't Sweet it wasn't Sweet it wasn't Sweet," the voice

chants, lips against my ear, breath hot against my skin. "Devyn, listen to me, baby. It wasn't Sweet."

I stop fighting, and my scream dissolves into tears.

Rick.

"It wasn't Sweet," he whispers, his grip never loosening. "Everett and Stevie knocked you out with a sedative. You've been in the hospital sleeping it off. *Trust me.*"

I do. I do with my whole heart, and I stop fighting, my tears of fear turning into tears of relief.

"I've got you," he promises, holding me and brushing kisses over my cheek. "I've got you."

I lose track of how long we lie like that, his body curled around mine, until he groans.

"I have to get up. I'm sorry," he says, and he lets me go, sitting up with a stifled moan.

Rolling over, I force my eyes open.

Rick's sitting on the edge of the bed, dressed in jeans and one of the casual button-down shirts I love, his sleeves rolled to the elbows. He wipes the tears off my cheeks. "Hey."

I let out a watery laugh. "Hey. Is Talia all right?"

"Yeah. She's been here with me waiting, but the hospital makes her skittish and she's been spending most of her time with Beau. What happened, Devyn?"

"I need to sit up too," I say.

"Easy. They've been flushing it out of you for two days. What do you remember?" With a hand to my back, he helps me sit up, and unable to stay even an inch away from him, I rest my cheek against his chest.

He wraps his arms around me and presses his lips to the top of my head.

I've been out of it for two days. There are so many questions I want to ask that have nothing to do with his accident, but I can't skip over what happened because of my need for reassurances.

"Not much. I talked to Neil, and he admitted he gave Tony Kelly the wrong manual and highlighted the incorrect counterweight needed for the lift. He said he's addicted to Sweet, and Declan Everett knew it and used it. I said I was going to make him pay for what he did to you, and he said that while a nurse showed me where to meet him, he called Stevie. I knew I was trapped."

"You should have called Mack," he says. "He's trained for that kind of thing."

"All I could think about was keeping Talia safe. I went out a side door, and that's where they got me. I don't remember anything else." I lean away and meet his eyes. "We figured it out, didn't we? We have what we need to send Declan Everett and Stevie Johansson to prison."

Rick sighs. "Not exactly. Simpson killed himself, Devyn. He overdosed on Sweet in his room, and a nurse found him when he didn't show up for group therapy. He left a note explaining his part in what happened and Everett was brought in for questioning, but he lawyered up and denied the whole thing. They had to let him go. When Beau and I went out to the site and met with the crane engineer, he found the warning system had been tampered with. He turned it over to the police."

I rub at my eyes, and the tape holding my IV in place tugs at my skin. "How did you find me? *Where* did you find me?"

"Beau and I went to the OSHA offices and talked to Fred McAllister. He knew about the whole thing, and I made him drive me out to Stevie's warehouse. Not the one on Pike—she built a new one on Highway 65. She and Everett were holed up there, and all he could talk about was the fucking site and how he'd had plans for the property. That's how I knew where they left you."

I brush my fingers through his whiskers. He hasn't shaved in days. "They let you go. Just like that?"

"I thought about that for a long time. Everett knew it was our word against his, and he and Stevie let McAllister go too. There's not enough to charge Everett, but McAllister's definitely going to prison. We might have to be happy with that."

I shake my head. I'll never be happy with that. "And there's nothing on Stevie—again."

"No."

"Then that's it." I sag in disappointment.

Rick adjusts the bed into a reclining position and nudges me back against the pillows. "What do you mean, that's it? You did it. You proved it wasn't an accident. You went with your gut and it paid off. I never would have done what you did. I never would have believed it was anything more than my impatience and stupidity. Men lost their lives because Everett had a grudge against me. Even if we can't connect him, we know he did it. That should mean something."

"It does. I just wanted more."

"How about this for more?" he asks, holding my hand.

I suck in a breath. I didn't think he would ask me so soon. I thought we'd live together for a while. Find a routine in Old Harbor, maybe figure out how to split our time between there and Cedar Hill because now that he knows what happened wasn't his fault, he'll stop hiding and run M&H with Beau again.

"I talked to Newsom. We can't make anything against Everett stick, but you still busted that accident wide open. He's going to give you your reporting job back. As soon as you feel ready to go back to work."

Startled, my eyes widen in surprise. "What? What about Stevie?"

"In Simpson's suicide note, he said she and Everett gave him Sweet and used his addiction to keep him in line. Everyone knows they're engaged, and she's keeping her head down. She can't afford to be connected to Sweet, and she won't bother you anymore. You're safe to move back to the city."

"But—" But I don't want to move back to the city. I don't want to work for the *Times*. I want him to ask me what I thought he was going to ask me. I squeeze my eyes shut, and stars burst behind my eyelids. He's putting a wall up between us. I can feel the grit of the cement under my fingertips where it's going to harden, and once again, he'll be alone and I won't be able to touch him.

He grunts as he gets off the bed. "You should call Talia. She's going to want to see you."

"I lost my purse. I don't have my phone."

Rick takes his cell out of the front pocket of his jeans, but he won't meet my eyes. "The cops found it in an alley near the construction site. The manual was still inside, and they kept it as evidence. A police detective is going to go over everything, and maybe he'll be able to find something that connects Everett better than we have. The son of a bitch is guilty, but we've done all we can." He huffs a laugh. "It's probably the only time I'll be able to rub it in Beau's face that the site is exactly the way we need it to be for a little while longer."

He dials a number for me, and it must have been Beau's because he says, "Devyn's awake. She wants to talk to Talia." Giving me the phone, he kisses my forehead.

"Where are you going?" I ask.

He steps away from the bed.

Steps away from me.

"I have to go home."

"Rick . . ."

His back is stiff as he limps out of the room.

With my heart sinking, I realize his definition of home doesn't include me.

CHAPTER TWENTY

Rick

"What are you doing?"

Beau's voice cuts through the dark living room. I'm living dangerously and sitting on the floor in the corner sipping Glenlivet, hiding and waiting for Devyn to leave for Portland. She'll pack up her things and move back to the city, work at the *Times,* and be the journalist I know she can be.

I didn't tell her goodbye.

I didn't have the heart.

"What's it look like?"

He sits in the chair closest to me and rests his elbows on his knees. "Are you hurting?"

Beau means my back, my hip, my arm, my leg, and those things *do* hurt. When I climbed onto the second floor, I strained my shoulder, and now my whole body is paying for it.

I raise my glass, the liquor slightly relaxing me. Always careful not to rely on short-term relief, I cut myself off after a couple of fingers every time. "Not anymore."

"Did you end it with her then?"

"Not in so many words."

Devyn's smart. She got it. She hasn't tried to call or text since I walked out of her hospital room, and that was three days ago. From what Beau's told me, she's been staying at his penthouse while she gives her statement to the police and goes over her side of things until they're satisfied. A friend at the *Times* told me she went up and had a meeting with Newsom. Probably ironed out her position and her salary.

I'm happy for her.

"Rick, I love you like a brother, so excuse me when I ask, *what the fuck are you doing?*"

I empty my glass. "I can't live here."

"Rick—"

"I had to come back after Stevie took her shots at Devyn, but I never thought it would be for good. This doesn't have anything to do with my accident—it has to do with my mental health. Maybe the memories don't help, maybe knowing Renata still lives here doesn't help, maybe this fucking penthouse doesn't help, but I'm not strong enough to move back to Cedar Hill. I can't. You want me to work more, and I get that. You've been carrying the load for a long time, and I can't ask you to do more. I've been thinking about how I can have both, and I want to open a branch in Old Harbor." I hold out my hand, and Beau hauls me to my feet. I limp toward the kitchen, each step feeling like a mile, and push through the door. At the sink, I rinse out my glass. Any more booze and I'll get shitfaced, and I can't, not with the painkiller I finally took.

If Devyn was here, I could have asked her to rub me down, but she's not, and I'm damned lucky I didn't get dependent on her. She's just as dangerous as the whiskey and the drugs.

Her fucking green eyes see everything, and she'd call me out. She'd call me a coward, but surprisingly, Beau doesn't.

"Is there room for growth up there?" he asks, leaning against the counter, his arms and ankles crossed, considering.

I nod, grateful I did a little research so I'd have something to shove at him if he asked. "There is. Lots of lakeside property up for grabs. Old Harbor's population is declining. They have Sweet on the streets too, and can't avoid the problems it causes. I can help build it up and pay them back for giving me a place to recover."

"What about Devyn?"

"What about her?"

"You're in love with her, that's what."

I fill my glass with water. "She can do better than an old fool who can barely move. She'll meet someone at the paper, and they can run around writing articles while they make the world a better place. She's proven she's got what it takes. She'll hit it big."

Beau scoffs. "Come on. You don't believe that any more than I do."

"What?" This conversation is starting to annoy me. "I was barely strong enough to climb up to the second floor and I almost didn't find her. Do you know how easy that would've been for me before the accident? Now, five days later, I *still* feel like I got hit by a truck. I should have looked into the accident myself. You told me to pull my head out of my ass, and I didn't listen. She could have died because she was brave enough to do what I was too spineless and stupid to do. She can do better. You know it's true."

He stares at me, and I use every single ounce of willpower I have not to fling my glass against the wall.

"Okay. You're right. You'd rather sit in your lighthouse and hide for the rest of your life. Sure. Tell yourself you'll open another branch of the company if that will make you feel better. Go for it. You have my blessing. I'll keep on here, finish the hotel after OSHA clears the accident—*again*. Maybe *I'll* have my wedding reception in the ballroom."

My lips turn into what could have passed for a half-assed smile. "You and Talia, huh? Good for you."

"There's a lot going on there, and it would have been a whole lot easier if Devyn would've sent Stevie to prison with McAllister, but yeah, we're gonna try and see if it works. You telling me not to be her dad, it hit home, and I have to remind myself of that every time I want to pick her up like a little girl. It's good advice, but Christ do I have to check myself whenever she looks at me."

"You want to protect her. There's no harm in it."

"You wanted to protect Devyn too," he says, pushing away from the counter.

"Yeah, I did. And I failed."

He shrugs. "When are you going back to Old Harbor?"

"Tomorrow. I'll get going on the new office. It wasn't bullshit. You were right about some things. I wasn't pulling my weight, and I'll start." I hold out my hand. He pauses before he shakes it, but he turns it into a hug, slapping me on the back.

"I'm going to miss you."

I step back, ashamed. I forgot that's what Beau had really been bitching about. He missed our friendship. I do too, but I have to look out for my peace of mind, and moving back to the city would destroy what little I've managed to hang on to.

I can't be here. Especially knowing I could bump into Devyn.

"You should talk to her, Rick. You shouldn't leave without saying goodbye. It's not right. Don't be a prick."

"Yeah, okay," I say, but I have no intention of telling Devyn anything. She's smart, and she knew what I was saying when I walked out of her hospital room. Maybe I am being a prick, but I have been since the accident, so why should falling in love change that?

CHAPTER TWENTY-ONE

Devyn

"You really don't mind that I want to stay here?" Talia asks, looking at me with concern out of the corners of her eyes.

It's been seven days since Rick found me at the site, five days since he walked out on me, and four days since the hospital discharged me after treating me for dehydration and a mild case of hypothermia. Whenever I look at Talia, I feel so guilty for the terror that zipped through me when I woke up thinking Stevie had followed through on her threat and hooked me on Sweet.

Talia lived through it, and she feels every second of her recovery.

I'm not as strong as she is.

We're walking through one of the city's parks—one, actually, that's close to our old apartment. After she left rehab, we used to spend a lot of time here, talking, getting to know each other again. Bill hadn't fired me yet, and things were shaky but good.

Looking back, he did me a favor. I needed a sign to move Talia out of the city, and that was it in spades. She's thrived in Portland—we both have—the smaller town giving us room to relax and slow down. I don't believe two years is long enough, but I've tried so hard to be a sisterly support and not her mother that if this is what she wants, I won't try and stop her.

"I don't mind," I tell her honestly, shoving my hands into the pockets of my new jacket. A jacket that Beau bought for me. Though everything was still in my purse when the police found it, to be on the safe side, I canceled my credit cards and told my bank that I needed a new debit card. My cell phone was still inside my purse too, and I traded it in and changed my phone number.

The first call I made was to Barney. I explained what happened and promised him the exclusive just as soon as I could find the time to sit down and write it. Beau's been letting me rest, but he wants to be alone with Talia and I don't see any reason to hang around. After our walk, I'm driving back to Portland. I'll give our notice to our property management and start packing up the house. I'll have to commute to Old Harbor until I can relocate, but I won't need to do it every day. There are a few things I'm going to have to do in person, but with the way things happened, I can start a lot earlier than I thought.

I didn't plan on Rick dumping me, but here we are.

"Are you still moving to Old Harbor?" she asks.

"Yeah. Barney gave me a job, and I'm going to respect that. Besides, Old Harbor is big enough I won't have to worry about seeing Rick. He keeps to himself at the lighthouse, and I'll find a small apartment out of his way." I try to smile.

She still sounds miserable when she says, "I'm sorry. I feel like I'm abandoning you. Why don't you move back here?

When we were at the hospital, I overheard Rick talking to someone at the *Times*. Why didn't you tell me Bill wanted to give you your job back? If you worked here, I could still see you all the time."

We pass a coffee kiosk near the edge of a food truck area, and I order us two decaf coffees with lots of cream. It smells delicious, and we both sip, enjoying the rich roast. I swallow and answer. "Stevie ruined the city for me, and maybe I'm petty, but I don't want to give the *Times* another chance. It felt so good to say it right to Bill's face. Neil Simpson said Stevie and Declan gave him Sweet, and I thought I finally had what I needed, but she's untouchable. On the off chance they can charge Declan with something, maybe they'll have a reason to look into her too, but I doubt it. If I decide to keep going, I'll do it with Barney. I promised I'd help him clean up Old Harbor. Besides," I say, nudging her with my elbow, "you're going to be busy with Beau. The way he looks at you is sickening, and I'm glad I'm getting out of your way. I just hope you keep on with school. Stevie took a lot away from us. Don't let her take any more."

"He was unhappy after he talked to Rick. He wants Rick to stay here. I wish the four of us could live in the same city."

"Maybe one day Rick will move back. He's still dealing with a lot of things, and he wasn't ready to jump into a relationship with me."

I've tried to be practical about it. I've tried to explain away his dumping me with logic, and sometimes, when I'm lying in bed awake in the middle of the night, I can. I never should have let Walt talk me into driving to Old Harbor in the first place, and the second Rick said he wouldn't talk to me, I should have left instead of standing outside crying. I'd just felt so helpless I didn't know what else to do.

He said he wasn't still in love with his ex-wife, but soon, if she hasn't already, she'll hear that he wasn't to blame for anything that happened, and maybe they'll get back together. They can have the family they were trying for before the accident.

I just want him to be happy.

That's all.

"Maybe I should move to Old Harbor with you, and I'll see Beau long distance."

"If that's what you want," I say gently, not wanting to influence her decision. "You need to do what will make you happy. Cedar Hill has a lot of negative emotions attached to it for both of us, but maybe Beau can turn that around for you. There's no chance of that for me, and I'll be happier in Old Harbor, even if Rick and I aren't together anymore. Come on, let's go back to Beau's. I need to get on the road. Choices can be made and unmade. If you and Beau decide it's not going to work, or you change your mind for a different reason, just call. I'm always here for you, you know that."

She stops me in the middle of the trail and hugs me, resting her head on my shoulder. "I love you, Devyn, and I never want to let you down. When Mack and I were waiting for you and you didn't come out of that rehab center, I was so scared. Beau helps, but you're my family." She pauses. "I wish I could do something for Mom while I'm in the city."

I want to scream at her to stay as far away from Mom as possible, but how can I tell her that when I've wished for the same thing? Does she have a place to stay? Does she have food? I know she doesn't, and I'm terrified because I can't help her.

"Sometimes, Talia, the best thing we can do is watch out for ourselves. You're risking a lot staying here for Beau. You know that or you wouldn't feel so nervous about it. Beau's penthouse is as far away from Mom as you could possibly be in Cedar

Hill. Use that, stay on the right side of the tracks, and don't court trouble. Let Beau court you instead and be thankful for small blessings. You managed to get off Sweet. She never will. Remember that."

She nods and grips me again before letting me go.

Silently, we walk back to the car, and at Beau's, I tell them goodbye.

"Be good to her," I say, giving him a hug. "I'll start packing and send some of her things. Clothes, books, whatever else she needs, let me know."

"I'll take care of her, I promise." He leans away and holds my hand. "I'm sorry that you and Rick didn't work out. If there's any good that came out of it, it's that you proved nothing was his fault. He needed that. He needed that truth smoothed over his soul, and I think once it's managed to soak in, he'll come for you."

I jerk a shoulder and slightly shake my head. "I don't want his gratitude. I'm a journalist—I'll never stop fighting to report the truth. I would have done it for anyone."

Beau meets my gaze, his brown eyes warm and steady. He'll be good for Talia. "I truly believe that, Devyn. I truly do. Text us when you're home. The roads are slippery."

"I will."

I hug Talia again. It will be strange going back to Portland without her. We've been attached at the hip since she left rehab. "Call anytime."

"I will." She swallows and hides her face against Beau's chest.

I leave them like that, holding each other, and step into the elevator.

As much as I'll miss Beau and Talia, it's a relief when the city fades in my rearview mirror, but as Portland grows nearer

and nearer, my heart grows emptier and emptier until there's
nothing left but the trace of Rick's touch the day he couldn't be
bothered to say goodbye.

CHAPTER TWENTY-TWO

Rick

The lighthouse that once was a refuge is now a prison, and I lock myself up in solitary confinement, talking to no one. Beau and Talia invite me for Thanksgiving, and I say no, knowing there's a good chance Devyn will be there. My parents, who I rarely speak to, invite me to their Florida beach house for the holidays, and I'm almost tempted to go and get out of the cold, but my mother hates confrontation and conflict and I'm too surly to keep my attitude reined in to visit them.

The three weeks between Thanksgiving and Christmas are a poor time to do business, but I do it anyway and purchase an office park located in downtown Old Harbor. I don't want Beau to accuse me of lying, and I probably made the realtor's whole year by buying the huge, neglected building. The space needs a complete overhaul, but it will be a decent first step in investing in the city since all of the suites will be put up for rent when the renovations are completed.

At one point, I was walking with the realtor down the sidewalk near the parking lot, and I thought I saw Devyn's blonde hair fluttering in the cold wind, but the woman went into the building where the *Harbor Herald* has its offices and I knew it wasn't Devyn. She wouldn't bother working at a small newspaper like that when she could write for the *Times*.

I read the article she wrote about the accident, and I was so proud of her. Picked up by the Associated Press, it was printed everywhere, and everyone wants to interview me and ask about what happened and if I'd be pursuing legal action. I tell them to contact Beau and our company's PR department. He has more patience than I do and I can't talk about Devyn. I miss her too much.

My body's still recovering from climbing up to the second floor to look for Devyn, though my massage therapist, who I usually agree with, told me I can't get better physically if I'm sick mentally. "I'm not sick mentally," I said, irritated as he rubbed me down.

"Heartbroken."

"I'm not heartbroken."

"Yes, you are. The first time you came to see me, it was over your ex-wife. Now it's a different woman. Find balance, Rick. Your body's tired of the stress."

I didn't talk to him for the rest of our session.

I know what he wanted to ask. She loves me and I love her, so what's the problem?

The problem, I think, as I step over branches and rocks looking over land I want to buy along Harbor Lake's coast, is that she deserves better. It's why Renata divorced me. She knew she deserved better, and she left to find it. It's debatable she found it with Bill Newsom, but if that's what she thinks, then who am I to argue with her? I can save Devyn from facing the same choice down the road. Should she stay, should she go.

I sit on a log and press my hands to my eyes. Christ, I miss her.

What is she doing right now while the sun sinks into the horizon? Getting dressed to go on a date? Sitting at her desk at the *Times* typing out a story, some guy hanging over her shoulder, breathing in the scent of roses the way I used to do?

Is she making love with a man who can hold her, who can push her against a wall while driving inside her?

I couldn't do that. I can barely handle missionary without having to adjust my body just right. She was always asking me, "Am I hurting you? Are you okay?" So fucking romantic, yeah? So fucking romantic to stare at my scar.

Fuck.

I'll buy this land and leave it how it is. Fuck it. All these trees torn down, a luxury resort blocking the view. What's the point?

If Devyn was here, she could tell me what to do. A small resort, tasteful. Not some gaudy thing that would ruin the landscape. I sound like a little kid. Since when have I ever needed anyone's help to do my fucking job?

I walk back to the truck, tiredly, carefully, limping now, snow and sticks crunching under my work boots. I dressed in a suit for the meetings Beau forced me to go to, and the material, the fit of the jacket, the gleam of my wingtips, they all felt so foreign. When had I lost the business side of the man I am? When had I stopped caring?

The streets are packed with people leaving work and going home. Stevie's Sweetshop is full of customers, and that's another regret I have now that all this is over. Devyn never found what she was looking for. I don't mean me. We fell into a relationship we shouldn't have, but she should have had the evidence she needed to take Stevie Johansson down.

Simpson's suicide note wasn't enough to warrant even a

hint of an investigation. Once again, she slipped through Devyn's fingers, and there's no way that I can see to expose her. Her affiliation with Everett could have been enough if there had been just one piece of evidence, but there's nothing. Nothing but her standing by Everett's side, declaring injustice.

The road to the lighthouse is plowed, salted and sanded, creating a brown slush my tires spray as I wind my way up. I reach the top and I want to slam on my brakes, but I steady myself, gripping the steering wheel.

She picked a helluva time to visit.

I park next to Devyn's car. She's walking along the lighthouse and disappears from my sight, maybe to stand and look over the water the way I've started doing for hours, searching for some kind of answer, some kind of miracle that could keep her in my life.

I want to shake her, crush her to me and kiss her. Drop down on my knees and beg her to forgive me and come back, though I'm the one who left.

I want to ask her to marry me, but I won't. I can't listen to her say no.

Walking around the lighthouse, I slow. She's there, wearing a dark green coat and jeans that are tucked into black boots that stop at her knees.

She turns when she hears me crunch through the snow, and my breath slams out of my lungs. Christ, I missed her so fucking much.

"What are you doing here?" I ask gruffly, the ache in my bones and muscles wearing me down, my patience next to nothing.

She steps toward me but leaves plenty of space between us. "I wanted to see how you were."

"You drove all this way to see how I am? You could have called."

"I tried. All I get is voicemail."

"Sorry. I've been busy."

Her green eyes glow against her coat and the bright color sets off her pale skin. She reaches out her hand but lets it drop. "What happened, Rick? Did I do something? If I did, I'm sorry. Are you angry that I looked into the accident? Do you blame me because we didn't have enough to arrest Declan? You were in my hospital room holding me, and then all of a sudden we were done. I don't understand."

Her pleas break my heart. Why can't she see it's me, not her? That it's my own shortcomings I'm dealing with and that it has nothing to do with her?

She swallows. "Is it your ex-wife? If it is, you can tell me. Ever since we met, all I've wanted is for you to be happy. If that's not with me, I can handle it. I just want to know." Tears fill her eyes. "You wanted babies with her."

"It's not Renata, Devyn. Okay? It's not her. You're always pushing, always poking around, sticking your nose into other people's business, and you never think about your own. Never think that maybe it's you. Why do you think I never said it? Ever wonder why I never said I love you? Because I don't. I didn't want you then, and I don't want you now. Go back to Cedar Hill. Go back to your fancy job at the *Times* and leave me alone."

She stumbles back, her eyes never leaving mine. "You're right," she says, as if she's just realizing how true my words are. "You never said it, but you showed me. You showed me when we made love. You showed me when you sent me that interview. You showed me the day you flew to Cedar Hill when Stevie shot at me. You showed me when Stevie and Declan kidnapped me and you found me, and you showed me at the hospital when I woke up. I can still feel your arms wrapped around me, holding me so close, telling me that I hadn't been hooked on Sweet. Even the kiss on my forehead before you left, before you *ran away,* showed me. I could go on and on with the ways you've shown me you love me. You're showing me now—I can see it in your eyes. I don't know why you're doing this, but I'll leave you alone. I don't need to be told twice." She laughs a little and nudges the snow with the toe of her boot. "You know that's a big fat lie. I need to be told more than once, but hey, this *is* twice, right? I can work with that." Her voice cracks, and I can't do anything.

I can't do anything but wish she would wrap her arms around me and thaw me out. I am so cold. So fucking cold.

She walks away, tears dripping down her cheeks.

Just before she rounds the lighthouse, she says, "If you change your mind, you know where to find me."

I listen for her car, but the engine is too quiet for me to hear it over the wind and the water.

I trudge to the edge of the cliff, Harbor Lake crashing angrily against the rocks below.

That's the problem, isn't it? I know exactly where to find her, and it's not anywhere I want to be. She shouldn't have to choose between me or the job she wanted most in the world, just like I shouldn't have to choose between living in Cedar Hill with her or staying here and trying to put my life back together in the only way I've come to know how.

I stand outside until the sky is pitch black and my back can't take it anymore.

CHAPTER TWENTY-THREE

Devyn

I do what Rick asks and I don't bother him again.

Beau offered to fly me to Cedar Hill when I visited for Thanksgiving, but I said I'd drive, needing my car and my freedom after the holiday weekend. On my way out of town that Sunday afternoon, I searched for Mom on the streets near Camden Way and along Arrowhead Alley.

While I dug for scraps against Stevie, I got to know the harsher side of Cedar Hill well. I made connections with snitches, druggies, sex workers, homeless shelter directors, and the elderly priest who prays for his small congregation at an old Catholic church. Because of Talia, I never approached anyone with judgment—I treated everyone with respect. I walked the cold streets, garbage blowing in the wind, people huddled around fires flickering in old oil barrels, and they would greet me with tired eyes and faint smiles on their cracked lips.

I'm one of them, fighting the same war, and they let me join their ranks.

I stopped at a big-box store and bought as many jackets, scarves, mittens, and hats as I could. With the job Barney gave me and Rick paying Talia's rehab bill, money is, for once, the least of my worries, and I paid that kindness forward.

As I searched for Mom, I gave away the jackets and mittens, wrapped scarves around women and children. I pressed money into trembling hands, and I prayed with Father Will over soup I helped him serve in the basement of his church.

No matter where I am, I will always do what I can knowing that until Stevie Johansson is behind bars, it's not enough.

It will never be enough.

I searched the streets until midnight, but I didn't find my mom. Several people promised me they'd look out for her, and it's the best I could do. I gave Father Will an envelope with her name on it. She'll spend the money on Sweet, but maybe, if he catches her on a good day, she'll buy a little food, too.

The thought of Talia on the streets looking for her sends shivers down my spine. I don't want her to go back there—the temptation is too great. Sweet is on every corner, the toll etched into every face.

The drive back to Portland was long and lonely. I wish Rick would have been with me, walking with me while I searched for Mom, steadying me with his presence, and later, holding my hand on the drive home. I don't know why he won't talk to me. I don't know what made him change his mind about us. All I can think is that I'm too much trouble, shook up his tidy world, and he didn't want to bother with me anymore.

It's okay. I know I'm a handful. It's better for him to do it now, before I fell too much more in love.

It hurts, but we weren't together for that long, a week at most, and it wasn't enough to gamble my whole life. I hope Talia and Beau do better than Rick and me. It was so fast between them, and something that bursts so bright doesn't have much of a chance of not flickering out.

Without Talia and her chatter and the clicking of her keyboard while she did her homework, the house is quiet. The living room is full of boxes, and I brought a lot of her things when I visited. I was surprised to see she moved into one of Beau's guest rooms, but I didn't ask what their living situation was like. If Beau's respecting her space, maybe they have more of a chance than I thought.

Time goes by quickly, snow falling several inches a day, and everyone's full of Christmas spirit.

Twice a week, I stay overnight in Old Harbor, but since the day Rick told me he doesn't love me, I haven't spoken with him.

I officially move to Old Harbor the week before Christmas and I hire a moving company to help with the heavy furniture and all my boxes filled with books. The apartment the real estate agent helped me find is only four blocks away from the newspaper's offices, and I'll be able to walk to work most days. It's bigger than the walkup I had in Cedar Hill, and I'm paying a little more per month for a month-to-month lease agreement. I still have hope that one day Rick will change his mind about us, but he has enough money to buy out any lease agreement I sign. Sometimes, I forget he's rich.

The movers set up Talia's furniture in the second bedroom in case she wants to visit or needs time away from Beau. I miss her, and I keep her door closed.

Barney asked me what my plans were for Christmas, and I told him since I wasn't going anywhere, he should take the time off. It will be the first holiday in years he'll get to spend with his family, and I was happy to give him that. After the first of the year, he wants to buckle down and see how we can get Stevie and her Sweet off the streets.

I don't have any news on Declan Everett except they didn't

have enough to hold him, and he and Stevie are planning a summer wedding.

They let Fred McAllister go the night he drove Rick to Stevie's warehouse on Highway 65, knowing he'd get fired and do time for falsifying reports. With Tony Kelly innocent, Neil Simpson dead, and Fred McAllister in prison, the police detective handling the case came to the same conclusions we did. Though Neil's suicide note pointed at Declan, nothing came of it, and he tied up the investigation with a not-so-neat bow at the end.

There hadn't been paper trails, Beau explained. Simpson was paid in Sweet.

Another reason, maybe, Declan was able to walk.

No one trusts a druggie.

I thought I'd be lonely spending Christmas without Talia, a dim light on my desk at the newspaper office my only company. I don't need to be here, but I like roaming around the bullpen, answering calls from people saying they've seen aliens and Santa Claus. The bullpen's not as large or as energetic as the one at the *Times*—quite a few reporters and columnists short of the *Times'* staff—but I like the people I work with. The *Herald's* ratings and ad dollars skyrocketed when I gave Barney the exclusive to Rick's accident. The AP picked it up too, and several job offers came out of it. I turned them all down, much to Barney's surprise since he knows Rick and I didn't work out. Even if he and I aren't together, Barney took a chance hiring me, and I'm thankful for it.

On Christmas Day evening, Talia calls me as I'm locking up the office. Because of the holiday, the streets are empty and the stores are all closed. It's already dark, and the sidewalks are lit up with Christmas lights and giant candy canes made out of garland that are attached to the streetlights. The temperature is mild, the stars glint in a cloudless sky, and somewhere, someone is playing "Silent Night."

"Merry Christmas," she says, her voice soft.

"Hey, honey," I say, holding my phone between my shoulder and cheek. "How are you?"

"Good. Miss you."

"I miss you too. What are you and Beau doing?" I walk down the sidewalk toward the apartment where I plan to run a hot bath, drink a mug of spiked hot chocolate, and go to bed early.

"We're home. It's been a quiet day. I asked him to put up a tree yesterday, and he grumped about it all day. He said he never bothered before. Can you believe that? I don't know why you didn't drive in."

"Ah, I don't need to be a third wheel on every holiday. Did . . . Rick go into the city?"

"No, and Beau's disappointed. It's hard for him to understand why Rick doesn't want to live in Cedar Hill anymore, especially since you proved the accident wasn't his fault."

"Maybe it wasn't enough to give him closure. He told me he's over his ex-wife, but maybe he's not and doesn't want to admit it. There could be several reasons, but if he won't say, then we won't know. There's a lot of buzz around here that he's going to start investing in Old Harbor. People are excited." I slip on a patch of ice, and I reach out and grab a traffic light to steady myself.

"How long are you going to wait for him, Devyn?"

"I don't know what you mean. I'm not waiting."

"Yeah, you are."

"I'm not, really. I know how he feels, that's all. I don't want to live in Cedar Hill, either. Old Harbor is good enough. I have everything I want, and I like being near the water. Barney's a great boss, and he said he's going to start prepping me to be the next editor-in-chief. He wants to retire in a few years. The university reached out and asked if I could teach a Journalism 101 class, and I might go back to school, too, and get my master's degree. You're close enough that I can see you whenever I want. I'm happy, Tal."

"How long will that last without Rick?" she asks. With her time in rehab, the experience has given her a wisdom beyond her years, and as my sister, she can see right through me.

"I'll meet someone else," I say lightly, opening the building's back door and trotting up the short flight of carpeted stairs to my apartment.

"No, you won't."

Juggling my purse, keys, and phone, I unlock my door and let myself in. I didn't feel like decorating for Christmas, and I only put out a couple of candy apple scented candles. Lately, I haven't been turning on my lights, preferring to putter around in the dark. It fits my mood.

I take off my jacket—I'm still wearing the one Beau bought for me—and hopping on one foot then the other, pull off my boots. "Meh. You're probably right, but what does it matter? I don't need a man to be happy. I was fine before I met him. Tell me about you. Were you able to finish up your classes online? Are you enrolling at a school in Cedar Hill for spring semester?"

I was worried she'd drop her classes completely or go back to the university she was attending when she got hooked on Sweet. I don't want her going to a campus that's tainted with bad memories.

Her voice drops, and she sounds so sad and confused. "No, I'm going to take spring semester off and figure things out. Devyn, I just don't know."

"Oh, honey. You barely know him. How do you expect to have a relationship with someone you've known for only two months? You can't. I didn't want to tell you what to do, especially since I fucked up my relationship with Rick, but maybe you're just asking Beau for too much."

She sighs, and I hear shuffling and then a door close. "See, that's the thing. I'm not asking. I'm staying in his guest room, I know you saw that so there's no point trying to hide it. He says he doesn't want me to think he expects sex. That's sweet, really, but I was a drug addict, not a sex addict, and I want to do it!"

I pause in the middle of my dark living room. "Wait. You mean you and Beau haven't slept together yet?"

"No! He looks at me like I'm dessert, but he kisses me goodnight and goes to his room alone. I feel like . . . I don't know how I feel. He wants me, but he won't take me."

"Oh," I sigh, sinking on the couch. "Oh, that's so romantic. You're a lucky girl."

"I don't feel lucky," she says darkly.

I laugh. "Well, you are. If you two would have fallen into bed the second I left, then your complaints would be a lot different from the ones you have now. You'd think he was using you or playing with you. He cares about you. That's big."

"Yeah?" she asks hopefully.

"Yeah. I have so much respect for him—he's a keeper. Give it time. I wish you wouldn't stop going to school, but I can see why you would. Just promise me that you'll enroll somewhere in the fall. You'll be a great psychologist."

"Thanks. Beau's looking for me, so I should go."

"Okay. Goodnight, and thanks for calling. Merry Christmas."

"Merry Christmas."

I hang up and toss my phone on the coffee table. She sounded homesick, and I can relate. I miss her too, but that doesn't have anything to do with home. I lost my home the minute Mom tried Sweet at a dinner party and decided nothing else mattered except the next taste. It gives me an idea to write a series on how normal middle-class people like Neil Simpson and my mom can become addicted and how it can drop them so low they're killing people and hooking on the streets for the next hit.

While my bath is running, I scribble my ideas down to run by Barney. Maybe I'll be poking Stevie again, but if I don't do it, who will?

Up to my chin in bubbles, my hot chocolate sitting on the toilet's lid, I let a few tears trickle down my cheeks. Talia's right. I'll never meet anyone else. At least, I'll never meet anyone I'll love as much as I love Rick. He slipped under my skin with his pain and into my heart with his bravery.

I sigh and wipe my face leaving a smear of rose-scented bubbles behind. I'm not the first woman to get dumped, and I *do* have a good life. I'm excited for everything moving to Old Harbor is going to give me. With or without Rick, relocating was a good choice, and I have no regrets.

After a long soak, I dry off, and in my pajamas, I sit in front of the window. I can't see much except a sliver of moon that isn't hidden by the taller buildings around me. When Rick looks up into the sky, does he think of me? He said he doesn't love me, but that's not true. He's decided he can't be with me for a reason he won't say, and I'm going to drift away. I'll always love him, but I need more than a hope and a wish that one day we'll be together.

Oh, who am I kidding? I close my eyes, rest my head against the back of the couch, and relive the last time we made love. The way his whiskers scratched against my cheek, the way he slid into me so slowly, so careful not to hurt me.

I'll wait forever.

It would be just like Rick's stubbornness to make me.

CHAPTER TWENTY-FOUR

Rick

"Rick, man, whatever you're doing, you have to stop. Your muscles feel like steel, and in your case, that is not a good thing."

"Rub it in," I mutter, lying on Liam's massage table for the third time this week.

Only a handful of days into the new year, and it's already kicking my ass.

"I can only do what I can do," he says, going to work on a particularly nasty knot in my lower back. "What *are* you doing? Shoveling snow? DIY maintenance? You need to stop it and hire that shit out. You're going to hurt yourself, and even I won't be able to fix you."

"I haven't been doing anything."

"That's not what your back's telling me."

I like Liam's office space, which is good because I spend a lot of time here. The music, the scent, the landscapes hanging on the walls, they're soothing. When the building downtown is refurbished, I'm going to ask him if he wants to move or open another office. If he wants to expand, I'll invest. He's already saved me more times than I'll ever admit since I left Devyn without an explanation. I owe him.

He pauses. "Is this about Devyn?"

"Can you please not go into your heart, soul, mind, and body crap?" I hate it when he brings her up. Hate that maybe, if Devyn and I were together, I would feel better. That maybe I'd stop having nightmares, stop waking up in the middle of the night drenched in sweat. Last night I woke up stiff and in so much pain from a fucked-up nightmare that she was marrying someone else, that I fell out of bed, landed on my bad hip, and I had to drag myself to the kitchen for a drink and a handful of ibuprofen. I almost called an ambulance, but I couldn't get Devyn's cold and lifeless body out of my head, and I made it through until morning alone.

"You know it's true or you wouldn't sound so pissed off. Why don't you tell me what's going on? From the beginning."

I stare at the wall, my lips pressed together.

"I blocked off two hours for you, dude," he says when I don't speak. "You're not getting out of here any time soon."

"I miss her." The words sound like twisted metal.

"She dump you? Tell you she never wants to see you again? Is that why you're telling me and not her?"

He kneads another painful spot along my lower back, and wincing, I say, "No. I broke up with her." I haven't told Liam much about anything, only that I'd fallen in love with a woman named Devyn and we weren't together anymore. He needed a reason why my body continued to be in this fucked-up state, and I had to give him something. A love affair gone wrong was just enough to shut him up, but not enough for me to stop dealing with the consequences.

"If you love her, then why aren't you with her?"

"She's a big-time reporter and works in Cedar Hill. I can't live there. You keep talking about mind, heart, and soul, and yes, I can't live there because of what it would do to my mental health. I cut her loose. I didn't want her to have to choose between me and her job. It sounds dumb, but she'll set the world on fire. She really will."

"Why is Cedar Hill so evil?" Liam asks, digging his thumbs into my muscles in such a way that I want to scream.

"All of it," I say around grunts of pain. "The traffic, the noise. I was hurt there. Do you think I need to be reminded of it every fucking day? That accident ruined my life. I don't want anything to do with that fucking place."

"Are you seeing someone? Talking this out? You went through a hell of a traumatic experience. You could be suffering from PTSD—it might help smooth things out." He dribbles more oil on my skin.

"You're it." I hadn't considered talking to a therapist. Devyn told me she and Talia banked hundreds of hours in therapy dealing with Talia's Sweet addiction. The closest I've come is talking to my doctor about pain management and how important it is to make an appointment with him to hash things out instead of taking matters, and pills, into my own hands. "Any advice?" I ask to humor him. Or maybe I'm so desperate I'll listen to any kernel of wisdom I can find.

Liam goes to work on my shoulders. I can still feel a sickening pain from rescuing Devyn that night, and I've been avoiding seeing my doctor in Cedar Hill. I don't want another surgery to repair something I might have (definitely) torn. "Seems to me you're going to be miserable no matter what you do, so you might as well pick the option that will leave you the least miserable."

"Fuck. Thanks a lot."

He laughs. "What? You don't think it's true? You don't

want to live in Cedar Hill, I get it. I'm not cut out for big city living either. I like it here, same as you. But you're not happy here. What would make you happy here?"

"Devyn." Her name is sweet and fast on my lips.

"Okay. So it seems like you have three choices—"

"Three?" That sounds like a lot from where I'm lying.

"Sure. You can go back to Cedar Hill. There has to be more than only Devyn that would help you tolerate it. You had friends there, probably still do. You don't have to live in the city, in your fancy, claustrophobic penthouse. Build a house in the suburbs with a huge yard. Pick a neighborhood with good schools and knock her up. But if you really can't live in Cedar Hill anymore, like mentally, it would ruin you, ask her to move here. If she loves you as much as you love her, she would, you know, because that's how love works. You'd still be miserable because she did what you didn't want her to do—choose you over her job—but not as much as you are now. Or three, do nothing. Let her set the world on fire, while you stay here in Old Harbor and turn into an icy old man. She'll meet someone else, and you can have all the nightmares you want."

He's got me pinned to the table or I'd turn my head and glare. "Who said anything about nightmares?"

"The big bruise on your hip, dipshit. You fell out of bed, don't deny it. I'm a massage therapist for crap's sake. I've seen it all."

"What would you do?"

"Seriously?" he asks, jabbing at the muscles in my shoulder.

Yep. I'm going to need it checked out. I've given it two months, and it's not healing.

"Yeah."

"I'd talk to her. There's a good chance she's just as miserable as you are, and moving here could be what she wants, too. But you know underneath it all, that's not the point, right? The point is your mental health gave you an excuse to push her away instead of sitting down and talking to her. You can't live in denial. I tell you that every time you come in. Avoiding your fears produces a toxic environment in your body. It creates stress, and stress puts you on constant alert. You can never rest. You're not sleeping. I already know that. You need to change, or you're going to cause some serious damage. You work in construction, right? You don't build on a shaky foundation, and dude, you are so shaky, how do you ever hope to build a future on how you feel?"

I let him rub me down, and my body loosens. Not as much as I need it to, and not as much as I know it can, but by the time my two hours are up, my muscles aren't as tight. When one pain recedes, another has room to take its place, and I miss Devyn so much I can barely speak.

He always lets me lie and rest for a few minutes, my muscles absorbing the rubdown, and I prop myself up on my arms, a towel covering my ass.

"What's your biggest fear?" he asks, leaning against the sink, his arms crossed and his biceps bulging.

It's not so comfortable to talk when he's not doing his job, and I stare at the table, that little space between my forearms. "That she won't love me while I'm like this."

Liam chuckles. "Dude, she met you while you're like this. She's not your ex-wife. Your ex didn't know how to handle who you were going to be after the accident. That's her weakness. It's not yours, and it's not Devyn's. You're making her pay for what your ex did to you. That's cool, but if you're gonna make her do that, then at least tell her the score. I'm no shrink, but I think any one of them would say you weren't ready to meet her. You weren't ready, and you should man up and tell her that. Tell her the truth so she can move on. None of this job stuff, or Cedar Hill versus Old Harbor. Tell her that you have a lot more healing to do, and you wish her the best."

He shuffles to the door.

I can't look at him. I can't see through the stupid tears he put into my eyes.

He wants to say more, but in the end he leaves the room in silence, and I lie there, my forehead resting on my arms as I cry.

———

I'm stubborn, hard-headed, and obstinate—all colorful (and true) adjectives Liam uses to describe me—and I do a lot of thinking in the next few days. Instead of growling at him while he works the knots out of my back, I ask him to meet me for coffee and we talk over lattes and chocolate chip croissants.

He asks me how Devyn and I met, and I talk him through our time in the lighthouse during the blizzard. I tell him about the interview she never published and her digging into the accident even though I told her to leave it alone. I explain how I rescued her from the second floor, and he raises his eyebrows when I admit I hurt myself doing it.

We meet every afternoon for a week, and with every conversation I have with him, I fall in love with her all over again.

It took me long enough to realize it, but it's not where I am that will calm me down and make me happy. It's that I'll be with her, wherever that happens to be. In my penthouse, in the suburbs, here in Old Harbor at the lighthouse, or in a house we build together on the land I purchased. It doesn't matter.

She said she loves me, and she wouldn't lie.

"Thank you," I say, gripping his hand outside the little coffee shop. Liam turned from massage therapist and psychologist into a friend.

"Remember—mind, body, heart, and soul. They're all connected. You can't find physical health if your mental health is out of whack. Fix your heart, Rick, and your body will follow."

A week ago, I wouldn't have believed it, but I do now.

"It won't be easy. She may not forgive me."

"With everything you've told me about her, that doesn't sound like something she'd do. She was brave for proving there was more to your accident than how it looked. She didn't know what she was getting into, and that takes courage. All those things you've been running from—you need them. After she's settled in, I want to meet her. Happy New Year, man. You deserve it."

"Yeah. Thanks. Same to you too."

He leaves me leaning against the brick wall of the café, wanting to stay and hide, but knowing I need to go and face my fears.

I build hotels, malls, and office parks. I refurbish buildings and restore old houses that have historical and sentimental value.

I'm good at fixing things.

Time to put those skills to use and fix something that will really matter: the relationships I've broken while I tried to run from something that will never go away.

What the accident turned me into.

———

I don't want the time with Liam to go to waste, and I drive into Cedar Hill. I want to take my feelings and study them. How do I feel driving closer to the city that ripped my life apart? I expected to sweat, shake, and want to turn back, but the only thing I know is that as the miles fade in my rearview mirror, I'm closer to Devyn.

The day Beau called and told me someone shot at her while they were walking around the site, I couldn't think about anything except getting to her and seeing for myself that she was okay.

That should have been my first clue. That as long as she was with me, I could handle the city.

I didn't tell Liam, but I'm sure he knew I didn't abandon Devyn at the hospital because of the city and how it makes me feel when I'm there. It was my weakness as a man who could barely search his own goddamned site for her. That terrible truth will come out, and either she'll understand and forgive me, or she'll look at me the way Renata did the day she walked out on me in my own hospital room.

The high-rises and skyscrapers feel like steel and glass prisons, but I can't think that way if Devyn wants to stay here and keep her job at the *Times*. I'll have to find the beauty that's still in the city. I've known only the ugliness for too long.

I walk into the *Times'* lobby a little after lunch, and I'm out of place wearing my work boots, jeans, button-down shirt, and wool coat. I haven't shaved or cut my hair. I look like the beast reporters called me the day I was discharged from the hospital and I limped out the front doors. Maybe I did it on purpose. This is who I am, and I will never change. Maybe I want Devyn to see it.

Liam would give me a stink eye. Through all this, only Beau and Devyn *have seen* the real me. I don't have to force her to see anything. She sees enough all on her own.

Newsom's office door is shut, and I rap once before I open it and walk in.

Renata's sitting in his lap and he has his arms around her. They're kissing, and startled by the interruption, they break apart. She jumps off his leg and wipes her mouth, her cheeks flushed. "Rick. What are you doing here?"

She looks good wearing dress pants and a black and cream sweater. She's always been beautiful, and she still has that sparkle I fell for all those years ago.

"Mercer! Good to see you!" Newsom booms, rounding his desk and holding out his hand. "Helluva thing with that fucking accident." He glances at Renata. "Devyn sure uncovered a pile of shit, didn't she? She's the best goddamned reporter I ever had. Does this mean you're going to clean up and rebuild?"

He's talking about the site, but he could also be talking about my life. Yeah, I need to clean up and rebuild.

"It will be up to Beau, but for now, that's the plan."

"Good, good. Let me pour you a drink. What are you doing in the city? Moving back now that the truth is out in the open?"

"What do you mean?" I say, taking the glass of whiskey from him.

Renata stands near Newsom's desk, watching us.

"Everyone knows what really happened and you don't have to take the blame for it any longer. It wasn't your fault those two men were killed. You moved to Old Harbor to hide from the rumors, didn't you? You were blackballed in our circles, Mercer. You knew it. Renata knew it. You had nowhere else to go."

Like I cared about any of that shit.

I turn my sharp gaze to Renata. "Is that why you left me? It didn't have anything to do with the way I look, did it? You left because the accident was my fault, and you didn't want to be near it."

"I—"

"All you wanted was to be on top. Why didn't I see that?"

Disgusted and disappointed, I stare into the amber liquid. I don't want it, and for once since the accident, I don't need it.

"That's not it, Rick," she says, stepping forward.

"Then what was it? I was in the hospital for months. I had no idea what was being said about me or about the accident, but you did. What were they saying about *you*, Renata? That you were just as guilty if you stayed with me? While I was in the hospital, did the invitations dry up? Did your friends tell you to divorce me to keep your reputation clean?"

She lifts her chin. "You might have forgotten that I tried to talk to you. I stayed with you for days, sleeping on that cot, and all you would do is glare at the wall. What did you expect me to do?"

"Let me process what happened, for fuck's sake. Give me time to mourn those men. Give me time to grieve what I lost."

"Oh, and what exactly did you lose?" she asks, crossing her arms over her chest.

"My health. You know that. That's why you didn't stay—you didn't want to be chained to a guilty cripple. Christ, how would that have looked?" I knock back the drink, and the alcohol slides smoothly down my throat.

Newsom watches us from his place near the bar, studying my ex-wife.

"No, that's not why. You know why I left? Because of this, right here." She points to me. "Your attitude, your bitterness. You didn't talk to me for weeks after the accident, and I saw you turn right in front of me. You're cold and unfeeling. Blame whoever you want—Declan Everett or Neil Simpson—but at least take responsibility for the fact you shut down and you shut me out. A weight lifted off me the day I walked out of your room. I didn't have to deal with your anger or your hate."

I blow out a breath. "I didn't hate you. Why would you think that?"

"Because it felt like you did, and it still feels like you do. You can't look at me without glaring, and you can't step one foot in this city without rage coming off you like a wildfire. This isn't about me, not anymore. Maybe it used to be—I know how I looked leaving you the way I did—but the accident was two years ago and you haven't changed. You're still the same angry man who walked out of that hospital, and I'm glad I left you."

I nod, tilt my glass, and watch the last drop of whiskey run along the clear bottom. I *am* still bitter, and I need to let it go. For my own mental health and my own happiness. "You're right. Knowing the accident wasn't my fault will help, and finishing the project and putting it behind me will help too, but I'm sorry, Renata. The accident changed me. I'm not the same man I used to be."

"No, you're not, and I hope you can find a woman who will love the man you turned into. And I don't just mean your injuries, I mean your attitude and how rough you've become. I can't handle it. I don't want to live with constant conflict." She pauses. "Bill and I are getting married. I hope you can be happy for me." She steps across Newsom's office and wraps her arms around his waist.

I need two hands to count the number of times he's been married and divorced, but maybe Renata will straighten him out. It's not for me to say, not with my own love life in shambles.

I hold out my hand, and he tentatively shakes it, watching for any sign I'm going to beat the shit out of him, but I don't care enough about my ex-wife and what she's doing to waste the energy.

"Did you know Renata was here? Is that why you stopped by?" Newsom asks, wanting to push me out the door.

I set my glass on the edge of his desk. "No. I came to see Devyn. I need to talk to her."

He frowns and pours another inch of whiskey into his glass. "She's not here."

Raking my fingers through my hair, I ask with frustration, "What do you mean? She's on an assignment? Went to lunch?"

"No, I mean, *she's not here*. I told her she could have her desk back, but she didn't want it. Gave me hell for it too, and told me I was a spineless asshole. She put me in a tight spot, and she knew that. I can't have my reporters pointing fingers without evidence. I was on her side, but I had no choice. This isn't my paper."

"She didn't want it?" My skin spikes hot, and a cold sweat covers my body. Where did she go? Did Everett do something to her? Did Stevie finally get her way? I force myself to breathe. If something happened to Devyn, Beau would have told me. To be okay, Talia needs her sister to be okay too. "Then where has she been for the past two months?"

Renata quirks her lips. "Maybe she wanted to get away from you."

If I wouldn't have spent the past week talking to Liam about her and what happened between us, I would have believed that. But not now.

She loves me, and I know with every ache and pain I feel every second that I'm awake, she's waiting for me to figure out my shit.

I lied to her and said things I didn't mean. She called me out on them and said I'd know where to find her, but I thought she meant here, at the *Times*. I don't know where she could be.

Forcing a smile, I say, "That's not who she is. You had your reasons for leaving me, and I won't think badly of you for doing what you thought you needed to do. But Devyn has more tenacity, more stubbornness, and more integrity in her little finger than you do in your entire body. You gave up, and you can pin that on me. I'll even take the responsibility you want to shove on me to feel better about yourself. She's not like you, and maybe the man the accident turned me into needs a woman like that. A woman who won't give up. I'll find her. I wish you two the best."

I'm already reaching for my phone when I step out of Newsom's office, slamming the door shut. I call Beau and jab at the elevator's Down button, waiting impatiently for him to answer.

"Rick. What's up?"

"Where's Devyn?"

He chuckles. "Good afternoon to you too. How about Happy New Year? Belated Merry Christmas, seeing as how you didn't bother to call. How's Talia? She's fine. Cedar Hill's good. We rode in a carriage through the park on New Year's Eve and looked at the lights. That was a first for me. Do you feel like coming into the city? Talia and I would love to see you and Devyn and start off the New Year together. It isn't too late."

Beau always knew how to put me in my place. "I would if I could find her."

A door opens in the background, then closes. Voices on his end quiet.

I step into the elevator and hope we don't lose connection.

"Wait. Are you serious? You don't know where she is? Talia told me you kicked her off your property. Well done."

I'm not getting anywhere with him. He enjoys needling me whenever he can—especially when it's justified like it is now. "Let me talk to Talia."

"No can do. She's at home, and I'm working. Someone has to, considering you promised you'd start putting in some time, and so far, all I've gotten are bills of sale for property around Old Harbor, though the pictures of the shore are beautiful. I want to see a rendering of the resort you're thinking of no later than the end of the month. I want to break ground the second it thaws."

"I don't care about any of that. I need to know where Devyn is." I step into the lobby and dodge around people in my hurry to go . . . where?

He sighs. "Rick, she's in Old Harbor."

I stop dead in my tracks, and someone slams into me from behind. I turn around and frown.

"Sorry," a young woman says and hurries away, flinching at my annoyed expression.

"Old Harbor?" I repeat.

"She was in the middle of *moving there* when she drove up and asked you why you broke up with her. Talia talked to her that night and I had to hear every gory detail. I have never been ashamed of anything you've done until then. What happens between you and Devyn isn't any of my business and I've kept my mouth shut, but the way you've treated her . . . Rick, I'm speechless."

"She's been in Old Harbor all this time," I murmur. "The blonde hair, the woman going into the *Herald*'s office. That was her."

"It probably was, but I thought you knew and were being a dick about it."

Feeling a headache coming on, I rub my forehead and say, "I had no idea."

"So I was only half wrong," he says, contempt twisting his words.

The day I lied and told her I didn't love her, the day I told her to go back to Cedar Hill and her fancy job here at the *Times,* she had already found a job at the *Herald* and was planning to move to Old Harbor. She'd been rearranging her life for me, and I didn't do anything except tell her to fuck off.

"How can I make it up to her?"

People rush through the large lobby, but I can't see anything except the tears on her cheeks as she ran away from me, her boots pushing through the snow, her hair flying behind her as she raced to her car.

"I don't know, Rick. That's between you and her. But you owe me an apology, and you owe Talia an apology for hurting Devyn. We all want to see you move past this accident, and we've stood by you. Devyn put herself on the line to clear your name. No one thought it was needed except her. I don't know what you've got going on inside that head of yours, but it needs to stop before you ruin every relationship that means something to you. I assume you're at the *Times* looking for her. Go back to Old Harbor, and get down on your knees and beg. It would mean a lot to me and Talia if you would visit. There's still time to bring in the New Year with a party, write some New Year's resolutions, and plan what we want this year to be like. We've been friends for a long time. I don't want that to change."

"I'm sorry." I force the words out, and I'm lucky he hears them over the chatter humming around me.

"Save it and say it to Devyn first. She deserves it more than I do. Buy her a ring and thank your lucky stars if she lets you put it on her finger. I need to go. I'm in meetings today, and we've been talking about the hotel. I'm going to finish it."

He says it like he expects me to argue, but there's no reason for me to. "Good."

"I gotta go. Take care." He hangs up.

Devyn's been in Old Harbor all along.

I don't want to drive the five hours back, and I call the airport and ask them to have the plane ready. An hour later, I'm in the air, and we're touching down in Old Harbor as the sun begins to sink into the horizon.

I skip the ring—there's no point in buying one if she's going to throw me out on my ass—and I text Beau and ask for her address. I haven't put Talia's phone number in my contacts, but I should. If she's going to be my sister-in-law, I should be able to get a hold of her if I need to, because I think of this on the flight to Old Harbor: If Devyn changed her mind about loving me, the least I can do is wait for her. I can be just as tenacious and just as stubborn. I never would have been successful in this business if I bailed at every little roadblock.

If she says she needs time, doesn't trust me anymore, or needs to think if being with me is what she wants after all, then I owe it to her to stick by her and wait.

If it's courting her with movies, dinners, and long, ah, short, walks through the park, then that's what I'll do. If she needs proof, I'll give her proof.

I fucked up.

I'll fix it.

Beau texts me her address. Her apartment isn't far from the *Herald*'s offices, and I beat on the door, but she doesn't answer. She's not avoiding me, she just isn't here.

It's half past six, and I hope she's at the newspaper. Carefully, I walk down the sidewalk to the building four blocks away. I skim the directory that's mounted on the wall between two elevators and find the newspaper's floor.

The lobby's empty, and I walk past the receptionist's desk. Cupping my hands around my eyes, I peer through the glass wall into the bullpen.

She's sitting in the back corner with her computer monitor glowing. It's the only light in the entire space, and she's resting her head on her arms, her shoulders shaking.

She's crying.

CHAPTER TWENTY-FIVE

Devyn

I spend a lot of time at the newspaper, giving Barney a much-needed break. At first I thought I'd be stepping on toes, but after my investigative work and the article about Rick's accident, I've been welcomed with open arms and nothing I say or do is taken the wrong way. There's a positive vibe here I didn't feel at the *Times*, and people actually seem happy when I offer story ideas, suggest edits, or gently remind them about deadlines.

I might have made faster progress with my career at the *Times*, but the friends I'm making at the *Herald* are more important to me. I can still get ahead, still make a name for myself reporting on news people have the right to hear, but without the ruthless attitudes some of my peers couldn't seem to let go of no matter how friendly, helpful, or noncompetitive I was.

It made it easy to fill in during the holidays when I didn't have family to visit. Talia and Beau invited me for New Year's

Eve, but they're still exploring their relationship, and I didn't want to be in their way. She understood, and now that the excitement of the New Year has faded into a boring normalcy, I'll drive into the city soon to see her.

Father Will emailed me and said my mother turned up and he'd given her the money I left for her.

Barney liked the idea of a series featuring middle-class, minding-their-own-business types of people who have gotten hooked on Sweet, and I wrote about my experience with my mom first. I've interviewed several people since he gave me the okay to run with it, and it breaks my heart that here, too, in Old Harbor, Sweet has brought so much pain to the small city's population.

I haven't heard anything from Rick, but I didn't expect to. Whenever I talk to Talia, she doesn't have any news either, which means he's not talking to Beau. I wish he'd talk to me. He's been alone since the accident, and he doesn't have to be.

Since he told me to go to hell, we've been broken up for a lot longer than we'd been together, and I'd laugh if it wasn't so sad. I was worried about Talia and Beau getting serious too quickly, but it seems I should have been more worried about myself. I jumped in with both feet like I usually do, not waiting one second to see what was at the bottom, and I got hurt.

Nothing new there. Move along, nothing to see.

I've been spending the evenings at the office instead of my apartment, a habit I should break. I don't need to be here past five, but sitting with the desks helps me feel not so alone, even if they're empty.

I miss Rick, and as the days go by, I'm beginning to think that we really are done, no matter how much time I'm willing to give him.

Two weeks after New Year's Day, I'm sitting at my desk, trying to work on an article, and I can't type another word. My eyes are too blurry with tears, and instead of pushing them back, I rest my head on my arms and let myself cry. I don't give in very often because there's no reason to cry. Rick and I didn't work out, simple as that, and I wouldn't have told Talia I liked living in Old Harbor if it wasn't true.

Someone opens the door to the bullpen, and I sit up and wipe the tears off my cheeks. The door should have been locked, but Old Harbor isn't like Cedar Hill, and I don't feel like there's danger waiting around every corner.

I should have known better.

Rick meets my eyes from across the room. He's dressed in his usual jeans and button-down shirt, with a dressier wool jacket than the leather one I'm used to him wearing. His hair is longer, and a beard hides half his scar.

He looks tired, but I don't get up to go to him.

I stare, and he says what is a completely normal, and clueless thing for him to say.

"What are you doing here?"

CHAPTER TWENTY-SIX

Rick

She dries her eyes with a tissue she pulls out of a box on her desk and lifts her chin. "I wish you'd stop asking me that. Since the night you let me into your lighthouse, I've been where I'm supposed to be."

I don't have a good argument against that, and I shove my hands in the pockets of my jacket and step toward her. She's beautiful, the glow from her monitor catching the dark circles under her eyes, the red skin around her nose where she keeps rubbing.

"I'm sorry, Devyn." I don't know what else I can say. Well, I have a shit-ton of things I have to tell her, but whether she'll listen, believe it, and forgive me . . . I'll be a lucky son of a bitch if she does.

She shrugs and balls up the tissue in her hand. "It's fine. Whatever. You could have been a little nicer about it, but I'll get over it."

My heart sinks. Maybe she's already over it, but I plow

ahead. "Why are you here, in Old Harbor? I talked to Newsom. He said he offered you your old job back."

"I didn't want it. After the blizzard, I drove into town and met with Barney that morning. He signed me on, and I found a realtor who helped me find my apartment. Talia was going to go to the university, but she met Beau and changed her mind. I'd been planning this since the day we said goodbye. I told you that you were worried about the wrong things. I guess you still are."

"You knew you wanted this since the blizzard?"

She huffs a laugh and rips the tissue apart. "I fell in love with you, but I've made bad choices before. It's fine, Rick. You didn't have to come here to apologize or try to talk your way out of what an asshole you are, but I'm not going to leave because we didn't work out. I like it here. Cedar Hill doesn't have good memories for me either, you know."

I take another step closer. "If I explain, will you listen?"

"That depends on what you have to say. If this is another talk to make sure I understand we're done, that's not necessary. You said you didn't love me, and you couldn't have gotten any clearer than that. I got it. I think you're lying to yourself, but that's not my fight. If you've got something else, then maybe. But it will have to be fast, and it will have to be good, and it will have to be honest, because I'm tired of listening to bullshit. I love you, and I've always been truthful about that, but it doesn't give you the right to treat me the way you have been."

I nod. "That's fair—"

She opens her mouth to say more, but I speak over her.

"—and it's more than I deserve. I know that. If we can go somewhere and talk, I'll try to explain where I'm coming from, and if it's not enough for you, then I'll accept it. No questions asked."

It's difficult to say that to her, to say that I'll let her go when it's my fault she'll want to. Before the accident, I'd always been self-assured to the point of arrogant, but getting injured and Renata leaving me smashed my confidence and self-esteem into nothing.

"Answer this for me first," she says, rolling her chair away from her desk and standing.

"If I can."

"Do you love me?"

I open my mouth, but I pause. There's so much I could say to answer her question. So many promises, so many dreams I want to make come true for her.

She meets my eyes, her green irises glittering and tear tracks still shining on her cheeks.

The words tumble out. "More than anything."

"For just a second there, I thought you were going to say no." She tosses the tissue into a trash can already full of them, and I look away, ashamed.

I've done so much damage, and I should know that some-times damage can't be fixed, can never be repaired. Modern medicine probably saved my life, but even the most skilled doctors I had working on me couldn't put my body back together again. Not the way it was. I'll always live with pain.

Her jacket is hanging off the back of her chair, and I help her put it on, my hands lingering on her shoulders. "Beau asked me when I knew. Said I probably had the exact second seared into my brain. He wasn't wrong."

She looks up at me, lines of fatigue fighting with a small hint of a smile on her mouth. "What did you say?"

"The afternoon I came into the kitchen and you were sitting at my table with soup cooking on the stove. I knew I wanted you, knew I needed more of that. I barely knew you, but in that split second, you turned into my whole life. I was so scared because you didn't belong to me, Devyn. So scared that what I am would run you off. Terrified, because that feeling had come out of nowhere and I knew you didn't feel the same."

"How did you know? You were so busy telling yourself you deserved to be alone that you wouldn't have seen it if I had. You *didn't* see it. The day I helped you with your back, when we were lying there and I woke up cuddled against you, I knew something was happening. But you wouldn't have believed me even if I had told you—you would have taken it as pity. I've never pitied you, Rick. I've pitied a lot of people in my life, but I've never pitied you."

Rubbing my thumb over her sticky cheek, I say, "I wouldn't have believed it. I didn't believe it while you were looking into the accident, and I didn't believe it when I brought you to my penthouse after Stevie shot at you. I didn't believe it when I was waiting for you to wake up in the hospital. I didn't believe it because I didn't feel like I was good enough to have it. I'm trying to change because I believe it now."

Squeezing my hand, she says, "What made you change your mind?"

"There were a lot of little things that added up to a couple of big things. Let me tell you when we get there."

"Where are we going? The lighthouse? My apartment is down the street. We can talk there."

"Do you trust me?"

"Yeah." She skims her fingertips down my chest. "Yeah, I do."

"Then I have something to show you."

She locks up the office, and we stand close to each other in the elevator as it carries us down to the building's main entrance. I haven't lost her, but there's still a chance that she won't like what I have to say. She won't like it, or she won't believe it, or she'll think it's a pile of shit—which, of course, it is.

The concrete glitters with black ice, and we walk slowly

down the sidewalk. She's wearing high-heeled boots, but I'm sure the snail's pace is more for my benefit than hers. Devyn never forgot how broken I am. I turned that into a flaw, when looking out for my health and well-being should have been the thing I loved most about her.

We stop near the rental I picked up at the airport.

"New truck?" she asks.

"My truck's in Cedar Hill." I unlock the door and help her into the passenger's seat.

"Oh," she says, dropping her purse by her feet. "When you said you talked to Bill, I thought you meant on the phone."

"No. I drove to Cedar Hill to look for you at the *Times*. Bill told me you weren't there, and I was in a hurry and flew back."

I shut the door, and the sound echoes down the empty street.

As I drive up the coast to the land I bought, we don't pass anyone, and I'm grateful people are home for the night. I want to be alone with her, but I also want Devyn to have a clear view and understanding of what I'm going to ask.

The area is raw and undeveloped, and I have to park on the shoulder of the highway. There's a kind of a makeshift path to the edge that looks over Harbor Lake, and I help Devyn over the debris lying on the ground.

The air is scented with pine, snow, and cold.

Squirrels rattle the bare branches, and moonlight struggles through the drifting clouds.

We hear the water pounding against the rocks before we reach the edge, and when we walk out of the trees, we can see the lighthouse shining its light across the water, a hopeful beacon to anyone else who can see it. It had been my haven, my place to hide, but with Devyn by my side, I don't have to hide anymore.

"I never thanked you for what you did," I say, flicking a glance in her direction.

Staring across the water, she says, "Beau did, and it's okay. You didn't want me to, and I can understand if you're still mad, but Rick, that's who I am. It's what drove me to be a reporter in the first place. I don't do it to cause trouble. I do it because the truth should always come out. No one knew Fred McAllister was a lying scumbag. Why would anyone think that? Why would anyone think Neil Simpson was hooked on Sweet? I had no idea I would find something like that . . . I'm only glad that I did. I hope it can help you feel better about things."

"It does, and I'm not angry. I went to see Bill to ask him where you were, and Renata was there, in his office. They're getting married. She said the accident turned me into a different person, a person she didn't want to be with. She said if I'd been able to let the bitterness go, we would still be together."

"Are you okay with that?" Devyn asks. It's the same question she always asks because she thinks if the accident wouldn't have happened, Renata and I would still be married, maybe even have a couple of kids, but it did and I can't change it.

"Yeah, I am." I shrug. "She's right. The accident *did* turn me into a different person. I'm not the same man who went to work that morning, and that's been part of my problem all along. I was scared you couldn't love me like this. I did a lot of thinking after I told you to leave me alone, lots of talking to someone who knows better than me, and he made me realize that you have nothing to compare me to. You didn't know me back then and you don't know how I've changed. You love me now, how I am, and I found that impossible to believe."

Her shoulders sag. "Rick—"

"I found it impossible because I've let you down in so many ways." I blow out a breath. "I hurt myself looking for you. I've been putting off an appointment, but I did something to my shoulder when I climbed up to the second floor. I almost didn't find you after Everett and Stevie dumped you at the site, and I've been struggling with that, not being enough to keep you safe. I can't make love to you the way I want. I'll never have you against a wall, outside under a tree, maybe not even on the couch. You're always asking me if I'm okay, and I hate it. *I* should be the one asking *you* that." I pause. "There will be days when I won't be able to get down on the floor to play with our children. You say you love me, but sometimes I don't think you understand just what you've fallen in love with. I'm a beast, Devyn, and I always will be."

She tucks her hands into the pockets of her jacket. The Cedar Hill police never did find her other one. Carefully, she steps over the sticks and rocks, stands by my side, and looks over the water. "Then I guess this is confession time, huh?"

"What do you mean? There's nothing you can say that will make me change how I feel about you."

"Maybe not, but if we're getting things out in the open, then I should do my share of it now." She takes a deep breath and says, "I won't be able to let it go, you know that right?"

Without her having to tell me, I know she's talking about Stevie and Sweet. In a roundabout way, we can thank Stevie and Devyn's stubbornness for us meeting. Without Newsom firing her, she never would have moved to Portland and never would have been assigned to interview me. I think Beau had it right. We didn't meet in Cedar Hill because it wasn't our time.

"I know." I take a chance and touch her, moving some of her hair away from her face.

Leaning into me, she says, "But what you don't understand is, it won't be safe. She'll fight back. You know now, from what Declan did to your project, that she's guilty. I can't let that go, and that's something you're going to have to decide if you can live with. I'm going to find trouble somewhere, every time. So, when you talk about me loving who you are, you have to do the same. If you love me, you have to love all of me. The part of me that found out your project was sabotaged, and the part of me that will, one day, bring Stevie and her drugstores down. You need to walk if you can't handle that, Rick. I mean it."

"If you think I'm going to let you go out on your own after just telling you that I love you, then you're just as bad off as I am. I would never let you do that without me. I love you, and that means all of you. Talia, too. If she's ever in trouble, that's for me to deal with, do you understand me?" I turn and grip her shoulders, searching her face, her skin sparkling in the moonlight.

Tears fill her eyes, and they glitter like crystal. "Thank you."

"You don't have to thank me for loving you. I should be thanking you for giving me the chance to explain. Leaving you alone at the hospital . . . I was a bastard. I knew how devastating that was, and I should never have done it. I'll spend the rest of my life trying to make it up to you. Beau said I owe a lot of people an apology, and I do. I owe him more than an apology. I owe him time. He's been carrying the company since I got hurt, and I need to start pulling my weight. Especially since Talia's there. He should be able to spend time with her."

"What does that mean for you? Are we moving back to Cedar Hill?" she asks.

"No. That's why I brought you out here. I bought this land, and I wanted to ask you what you thought. What if we built a house here?"

She turns in a circle. We're surrounded by trees on all sides except one. "I heard you were going to build a lake resort."

"I was going to, but what if we lived here instead? I could design a beautiful house for us, Devyn, with extra bedrooms. We didn't talk about kids, and we're getting older, but maybe one or two? It's a lot to ask, especially after everything we just talked about, but it would mean a lot to me if you said you'd have my babies."

She bites her lip. "There are things I want to do first. If we have children at home who need me, I can't be out doing the things I need to do."

"I know, and I'm okay with that. I can wait." I pause. "What do you think?"

"Are you asking me to marry you?" she asks, wiping her eyes. "I'm really hoping you're asking me to marry you."

I try to joke, but all I want to do is cry with relief. "Yeah, but I can't get down on my knees. I might not be able to get back up."

Laughing, she turns and snuggles in my arms, and I hug her close, pressing my lips to the top of her head and inhaling the delicate scent of roses. I almost lost her because I was scared. I almost lost her because I believed the nasty things I said about myself.

"I think you should keep your promise to Beau and build the resort. If we need to split our time between here and Cedar Hill, that's okay, but I want to live in the lighthouse."

"You really like it there?" I ask, surprised.

"Yeah, I do. But there's more to it than that. Look," she says, pointing across the water to where the light gleams strong and sure.

"I see it."

"No, you don't. You see a place where you ran after the accident to hide from the people blaming you and to get away from Renata and her leaving you. Do you know what I see?"

"No," I say, knowing she's right about all those things.

"I see a place where you can come to rest, where you don't have to be anything other than who you are. I see a place where you will always be welcome no matter what happens. I see a place where we'll grow our love, our lives, and our children. Do you know what else I see when I look at the lighthouse, Rick?" She tilts her head to look at me.

"No." My throat is scratchy and rough with tears. She knows so much about me, and I'll always have her to tell me the truth. That I'm worth her love, and she'll tell me over and over again.

"I see the light. Whenever you lose your way, look for the light, and it will guide you back to me."

I hold her for a long time, our eyes on the white beam that warns weary travelers to stay away from the rocky shore.

Devyn's right . . . but it's not this light that will show me the way. That light lives in her pure heart, and it doesn't matter where we are. As long as we're together, I'll always know my way home.

Talia and Beau's story is now available!

You can find it on Kindle, in Kindle Unlimited, and Paperback.

https://www.amazon.com/Addicted-Her-VM-Rheault/dp/1956431101/

BLOG SIGNUP

If you loved Devyn and Rick's story, sign up for my blog! Stay up to date on future releases, sales, and extra content. As a thank you, you'll be able to download a free, full-length novel, *My Biggest Mistake,* a billionaire, ugly-duckling romance!

Sign up here! https://vmrheault.com/subscribe/

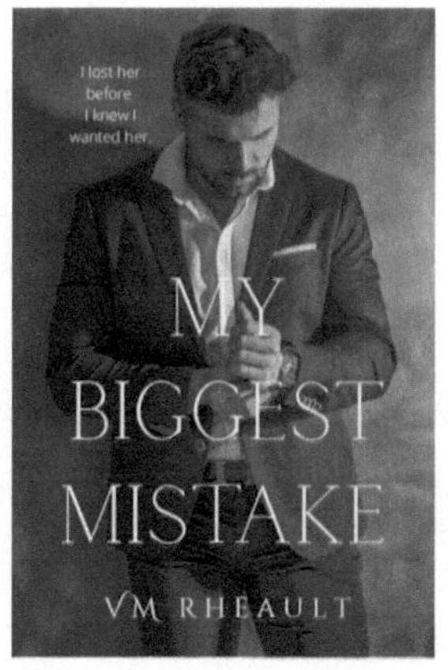

ABOUT THE AUTHOR

VM Rheault writes several subgenres of romance including billionaire, romantic suspense, and small town.

She lives in Minnesota with her two children and their newly adopted tuxedo cat, Pim. When she's not writing, she's working her day job, sleeping, or enjoying the four seasons with a hot cup of coffee in hand.

Find her at vmrheault.com.

ALSO BY VM RHEAULT

Captivated by Her (Cedar Hill Duet Book One)

Addicted to Her (Cedar Hill Duet Book Two)

———

Rescue Me

———

Give & Take (The Lost & Found Trilogy Book One)

Lost & Found (The Lost & Found Trilogy Book Two)

Safe & Sound (The Lost & Found Trilogy Book Three)

———

Faking Forever

———

Twisted Alibis (Ghost Town Trilogy Book One)

Twisted Lullabies (Ghost Town Trilogy Book Two)

Twisted Lies (Ghost Town Trilogy Book Three)

———

A Heartache for Christmas

———

Cruel Fate (King's Crossing Book One)

Cruel Hearts (King's Crossing Book Two)

Cruel Dreams (King's Crossing Book Three)

Shattered Fate (King's Crossing Book Four)

Shattered Hearts (King's Crossing Book Five)

Shattered Dreams (King's Crossing Book Six)

———

Loss and Damages

———

Wicked Games